The Ritual
of the
Four

CARLA TRUEHEART

World Castle Publishing, LLC
Pensacola, Florida

Copyright © Carla Trueheart 2015
Print ISBN: 9781629893471
eBook ISBN:9781629893488
First Edition World Castle Publishing, LLC, October 12, 2015
http://www.worldcastlepublishing.com

Licensing Notes

Cover: Karen Fuller
Editor: Lisa Petrocelli

Part I
Rockpoint

Chapter One

I am marked for death.

I'm not sure when it will happen. It could be one minute or one month, and when it happens, it won't be pretty. Not in the particular way they are going to kill me.

Right now, I'm hiding out in one of the few places a guy of sixteen can disappear from the eyes of the world — the top of a Ferris wheel. When I jumped on board, a couple of teenagers were getting a lift in the cart just behind me. A guy and a girl, laughing and snuggling. I'm sure they were hoping to get stuck on top, where I am now, so they could disappear from the world just like I'm trying to do. For once, I was the lucky one this time. I'm stuck up here, hidden, but with a pretty good view of the carnival below.

The autumn carnival in Fairchester, Massachusetts, is a pretty big deal. It's not like I know this town all that great, because I just got here a month ago, but I did hear from some guys at school that most of the town shows up at the carnival at one point or another. From up here, at the top of the world, I can see why people in Fairchester like their autumn carnival so much. The air is icy, the leaves brown and dying, but smack in the middle are all these neon flashing lights and laughing kids. Game booths with huge stuffed animals. Fat clowns with balloons. The scent of fried dough and cotton candy.

I came here alone but soon had the feeling I *wasn't* alone.

That's why I'm hiding out. It's calm now — they can't reach me up here if they did follow me to the carnival. And I'm pretty sure they found me, because I can smell the blood laced into the breeze. It comes along with them. It probably comes along with me, too. That's how they always find me, even when my mother and I change our names and move around the coast. America is not the great hiding place it seems.

The Ferris wheel shifts and vibrates, and I start my decline. My hand shakes on the bar. On the ground, shadowy figures move around, but I don't freak out because they could be anyone. Maybe some kid's parents watching the wheel. Maybe some girls making a decision whether to board or try something a little scarier. But the scent of blood grows stronger, and as soon as my cart lands on the bottom, I hop off onto the metal platform, then dash through the back gates. I don't stop until I'm hidden in a patch of black, between two old trailers.

A thick red hose rests on the ground before me, running toward the giant slide ride. Electricity hums in my ears as I pull out my cell and text my mother: *Come get me.* And then our code word: *"lightsaber."* (Quick backstory: *Star Wars* fan, but please don't tell anyone). I'm just about to find my way to the street when the smell of blood overpowers me, and my stomach pitches.

"Shaw Huntley," a familiar male voice says. "We always seem to find each other in the strangest places."

It takes me a minute to remember that Shaw Huntley is my real name. For the past few years, I've used every false name I could think of, from Johnny Ray to Brent Cappo to Frank Mulebottom (Mulebottom was not one of my better ideas). In Fairchester, I go by Lee Greznick.

Okay, so they found me. I already knew they had. My mother is on the way, and she'll have all our belongings packed and ready to go to the next town, wherever that should be. All I have to do is get out of this now. And to get out of this, all I have to do is remember that I have the same power they have.

The man who chased me down is middle-aged and dangerous, and though it's dark, I can just make out the long, silvery scars etched into his cheeks and forehead. Not pleasant to look at. Not pleasant to fight. He raises his pointer finger and makes a downward slicing motion. I feel the pain instantly on my forearm. I grab the skin and hold it together, not knowing how far down he cut me. It doesn't feel too deep. Just a warning slice.

"Don't make me do it," I tell him.

He doesn't respond, so I have no choice. In my mind, I imagine a gold dagger—*my* gold dagger—jeweled and sharp. I project it from me, using force and pressure, until I'm sure I hit. Through the blackness, I can just make out that he's slapped his palm to his cheek.

We go back and forth. One cut. A slice. Face and arms. Until the game gets tired and I know what's coming next. From behind him steps the long silhouette of my cousin, Alexander. We look alike, Alexander and I, tall and broad-shouldered, with messy blond hair. But the similarities end when it comes to our views on what was left behind in our family bloodline.

"Shaw," he says.

"Alexander," I return.

This is going to end in a bloodbath—it always does. They want me dead, they find me, and we slice each other up until I get away. Luckily, even though they've marked me for death, I always get away. So far. One of these times I won't, and like I said, it won't be pretty. By now, you get the idea of what we do, even if I still don't fully understand it myself. All I know is that they killed my father for this ability—the ability I have as well.

I'm short on time, so I'll be quick. Using the power of my mind and visualizing a specific gold dagger, I can stab, scratch, slice, or cut a person. It's another reason why my

9

mother and I travel so much. If I get angry enough the cutting sometimes comes out without my consent. Sometimes, I can slice someone I care about by mistake. It's like the werewolf who kills his best friend because he just didn't know what he was doing. The slicing takes on another form. And that's why it's best I don't get close to anyone. No girlfriends. No buddies. Just me and my mother, who admittedly, keeps a few boxes of Band-Aids around whenever she has to yell at me for something.

"Guess you like the air here in New England," Alexander says. "You come here a lot."

I make a mental note to get the hell out of New England.

"You can't keep running all the time," he says. "That must get exhausting after a while."

You think?

"You can give us what we're looking for," Alexander continues, "and this will all end for you right now."

"You're not getting the dagger," I say. The actual, physical dagger is one of my prized possessions, and I'm sure the thing is priceless.

"We need a few things," Alexander says. "I'm sure your father must have told you."

My father didn't tell me anything. Well, nothing except that I have this ability, and Alexander does, too. "You guys want the dagger," I say in my best fight voice. "And you're not getting it."

Alexander moves toward me. His eyes flash an eerie green. My mother always tells me I'm more powerful than he is, but in these moments, I question it. Without making a motion, Alexander tears the flesh in my neck. It's deep. A gush of blood soaks into the collar of my sweat jacket. Closing my eyes, I retaliate. Sometimes I wonder if they do this just to provoke me, see how powerful I truly am, how much my father taught me before they murdered him. Whatever. It works. Before I can make a judgment call on right or wrong, the jeweled dagger in my mind propels from me—and I imagine it soaring right into Alexander's chest.

He stumbles backward, and the scarred man catches him. Alexander breathes into the air, sharp and raspy, then palms his heart. As I start to flee, the scarred man drops Alexander right on the frosty grass and runs after me. I guess killing an enemy is worth more than saving a friend.

He's behind me, so I pull through the night, dashing around telephone poles and onto the sidewalk, trying to keep him from slicing me worse than I already am. It's my bad luck, or maybe my good luck, that a group of girls from school are hanging out on the sidewalk, by the entranceway to the carnival.

"Lee!" a girl calls out. I'm not sure what her name is, but she's got feathery brown hair and perfectly straight teeth. A nine or a ten, for sure. "Come over here with us!"

Obviously, she doesn't see that I'm bleeding to death.

"Can't!" I yell back. "Have to go!"

One of the girls she's with, a sporty redhead, spots the blood on my face or my neck. I'm not sure which place she sees it, but she's looking in my general direction with her mouth open. She also takes note that I'm running from someone and grabs hold of her friend's arm, pointing. From this, I gather that the scarred man is right behind me, fairly close. Quickly, I scan the street for my mother's car but know it might be another minute or two. She had to grab all our belongings from the hotel, the clothes I left on the floor, and the few things I can't bear to leave behind, then stuff it all into bags and fly over here.

Now I'm kind of confused about where to go because I need to hide, but I need to stay close to the street so my mother can reach me. The scarred man probably won't attack while I'm with a bunch of people, so I slip myself into the group of girls from school, just behind the girl with the feathery brown hair. She smiles at me but still looks concerned.

"Drugs?" she asks.

"What?"

"Are you buying drugs from him?" she says.

The group stares the scarred man down as he stops to face them. In the light, up close and personal, his hair is black and slicked back, and he's balding a touch, leaving a big *V* in the center of his forehead. Yeah, he looks like he could be a drug dealer. Or a mobster.

"Out," he says to me.

I'm too tall to hide behind these girls, but it's not really a hiding place I'm after right now.

"You hurt him," the girl with feathery brown hair says to the scarred man. She sticks her hands on her hips, ready to fight for me, and I don't even know her name.

In a second, he makes a swiping motion through the air and the girl falls. Her friends must assume he has a knife because they all gasp and shriek and run to her aid. When I look down, her cheek—her pretty cheek—is sliced in an X.

This is what I mean by uncontrollable anger. Before I can tell myself not to, my dagger forms in my mind and zooms through the air at the man. One on one, he's not quite as powerful as Alexander, so maybe I have a chance here. He's just as dangerous as Alexander, obviously ruthless, but not as powerful. It's almost as though, and I've suspected this before, Alexander gets his ability from our family bloodline, but this man had to somehow learn the ability.

The scarred man takes a step backward, clutching his shoulder. He stumbles right into the street, where an older black Jetta swerves to avoid striking him, just missing. The black Jetta screeches to a stop right in front of me. My mother is behind the wheel.

"*In!*" she says like I need to be told.

I really hate leaving the girls behind. Not like this. And I'm never even going to see them again, will never get the chance to apologize for what happened.

With a vague wave, I race around the car and launch myself into the passenger's seat. In a blur of streetlights, we're

12

speeding ahead, dodging oncoming traffic, swerving in and out of lanes. My mother, when it comes to protecting me, is a woman possessed.

****

At the hotel, my mother looks out the blinds for a full five minutes, then turns to me. I'm sitting on the edge of the bed, holding a rag to my neck.

"So you think you might have killed him?" she says.

I shrug. Alexander's fate is unknown for now. I even got the scarred man pretty good with a cut to the shoulder blade. But that's only going to make him angrier, I'm sure.

"Well, were you trying to kill or not?" she says, pacing just in front of the beds. "Was it a kill wound or just a warning?"

"Huh?"

"Honestly," she says and goes back to the window.

I'm not sure what she expects from me. From the beginning—my thirteenth birthday when my father told me—I didn't fully understand my ability. I didn't understand how to work it or how I got it. And maybe I play dumb with my mother because I'm pissed at her for not giving me answers when I ask for them. Or maybe I play dumb to keep myself from getting so mad that she ends up looking like she just danced through a knife parade.

"We can't stay in Massachusetts," I say. "Alexander mentioned something about us always being here in New England."

My mother taps the windowpane with her finger. She pushes back a sheet of shiny blond hair, then sighs. "I think New York next," she says. "I was avoiding that, but—"

"Why were you avoiding that?"

"Because I wanted to be close to home base," she replies. "The farther inland we go, the farther away we are from help."

Again, she's lost me. Nobody can help us. Nobody even knows what I can do. In family gatherings, it's just hugs and

13

Sunday night dinners. Sometimes we play a game. My mother's family thinks my father died of a heart attack. Every outsider thinks my father died of a heart attack. It's difficult to lie to the people who love you, but it's also crucial that nobody knows what I do and that we stay away from them as much as we can.

"You could just homeschool me," I say. "I'm almost done with high school anyhow."

"You have two more years," she says. "And I'd like to keep you in a normal lifestyle as much as I can."

"Yeah, that's working out well." I fall back on the bed and stare up at the ceiling. The gash in my neck stings and throbs, but the bleeding has stopped. I don't know if Alexander was going for the kill, but if he was, he messed it up royally.

"Okay," my mother says like she just snapped into a decision. "Tomorrow morning, we're going to upstate New York. It'll be different up there, quieter, but maybe that's what we need."

We've tried blending into the crowd before, in populated areas. We've also tried Vermont where it can be pretty desolate. But we've never been in quiet, upstate New York.

"You'll like it there," she says and tries to give me a cheery smile.

"It doesn't matter if I like it there or not," I say, tossing the bloody rag beside me. "We never stay long."

"No, we'll be there awhile," she assures. "They won't think to look there for a long time. They'll think we stayed close, maybe in Connecticut or Rhode Island. That's assuming Alexander makes it through tonight." Her eyes, normally a vivid blue, fade to gray as she gazes out the window. One thing she's always tried to avoid was her son becoming a murderer.

"How will we know?" I ask in a low voice. "If I...killed him tonight."

"Let me deal with that," she says. She moves away from

14

the window, whips the blinds closed, and opens her travel bag. "It doesn't matter because either way...." She stops talking, pulls out a hairbrush, and starts nervously brushing her hair.

I know what she's trying to say. If I killed Alexander, the scarred man who travels with him will come after me, hunt me down to finish the job as a solo project. Not only did I wound Alexander, I wounded the scarred man as well. And he's pissed. I could almost smell the rage flowing off him, mingled with the scent of blood. The guy is unpleasant from every angle.

"They always tell me to give them what they're looking for," I say to my mother. "What exactly are they looking for?"

She turns away from me, sticks her hairbrush back into her travel bag, and heads for the bathroom. "No idea," she says over her shoulder.

"No idea," I repeat, rolling my eyes.

"That's what I said." She opens the bathroom door. "Leave it alone, okay?"

"They want the dagger, right?" I ask. "But what else?"

She shakes her head. "Leave it alone, Shaw," she says again.

"I think I have a right to know what they're after," I say. "I have a right to know why they killed Dad and why they keep chasing me and trying to kill me."

"It's not your concern right now."

"It's *completely* my concern!"

She sighs. "I'll need your stuff packed up in the morning," she says, changing the subject like she always does.

"I never *un*pack." Why bother unpacking? We never stay in a place for too long, and even if we did stick around, it's not like I could make any friends or have a girlfriend, so what does it matter? "I'll never have a normal life," I tell her. "I mean, you can tell me a million times that you're trying to do that for me, but it's just not happening that way."

15

"I'm sorry," she says. "Let's just get settled in New York. That will be the last time for a while." She smiles. "I promise."

She closes the bathroom door, and I rub my forehead, thinking about what happened at the autumn carnival. If Alexander does survive my attack, that means they'll double their efforts to find me. I have something they want — the gold dagger plus whatever else — and they've marked me for death because of that. It doesn't matter if we hide in New York or we head off for the sunny west coast. They will find me.

They always do.

Chapter Two

So far, Rockpoint, New York is a quiet town, just like my mother told me. Usually, we find a hotel, settle in under false names, and give those false names to the school. My mother does this some sneaky way because when you register for school you need records, and I'm really not sure how she finagles all that, but she somehow manages to pull it off every time. This time, though, she's doing things a little differently.

For the first time in years, we've rented an apartment. She found a small complex just on the edge of town, not a high-rise, but a group of apartments in a square shape with a water fountain and benches set just in the middle. It's a nice place but called something unimaginative like Rockpoint Apartments. Maybe they should have called it Fountain Square Apartments—something that would make it stand out. Although I guess it's best that the place doesn't stand out. It's ordinary but comfortable, and that's probably why my mother chose it.

Our apartment is a two-bedroom, and to lease it for a year cost more than we really had. We're probably going to lose all that money anyhow. A year? In the same place? It's really unheard of. We are professional travelers, professional starter-overs, and professional movers. We don't even have furniture. That's why we always use hotels, or in this case, a furnished apartment.

"Chase?" my mother says from across the breakfast table.

17

I look up.

"Just testing it out," she says and ruffles my hair like I'm nine again.

"I've been through the name change thing a million times," I say and scoop up some scrambled eggs. "Chase Chandler. We could have done without the alliterative, though."

"See that?" she says. "You're learning some good stuff in school."

She goes on to tell me, while I eat, that she'll be unpacking during my first day in the new high school. Then, she surprises me by going on and on about how she'll try to find an under-the-table job as soon as she can. Again, not sure how she manages all this, but it's probably best that I don't know. My brain is filled up with enough unpleasantness as it is, and I'm sure what she's doing is illegal. In another lifetime, or in an alternate universe, maybe my mother and I live in a big house with my father, and we don't do things like lie about names and social security numbers and backgrounds. But in this universe, this is how it goes. This is life right now.

In my new bedroom, I look into the mirror by my bed. I assume this room belonged to a girl last time or was set up for a girl. The dresser is white and curvy, the mirror is oval and fancy, and the bedspread is rose-petal pink. I've already pulled that off. As I gaze at myself in the mirror, I wonder what kind of adjustments I should make. Every time I start a new school, it's a new chance to reinvent myself. Should I be the punk rocker? The book geek? The football star? The criminal? The preppie socialite? The sky is the limit. Who is Chase Chandler? Because he sure as hell isn't Shaw Huntley. Shaw Huntley is nothing but trouble. Shaw Huntley is marked for death.

Back in Vermont, my mother bought me a black leather jacket for the cold nights. Because I'm so tall—six foot two, last my mom checked—the leather jacket makes me look kind of intimidating. If I can mess up my hair even more than it's currently messed, that adds to the image. So that's what I decide on. I'm the outcast here in Rockpoint, New York. I'm Chase Chandler, the outcast. Don't bother me, because I'm messed up.

My mother rolls her eyes when I come out of my bedroom.

"So I'm guessing we don't tell anyone about the *Star Wars* marathons and the visits to the comic book store?"

"Hey," I tell her, zipping up my leather jacket. "*Star Wars* fans can be pretty badass."

She does the mom thing, checks my hair, and tries to smooth it, even though it's a cowlick festival up there and always all over the place, even without my extra help.

"Handsome," she says. "Just like your father."

At that I smile, but something inside sinks like a weight in water. It's been a few years, but the wound still feels brand new. I would love to tell Alexander and the scarred man, face to face, what I go through every morning, wishing my father was still sitting at the breakfast table and wishing he could explain more to me about the dark ability we both share. But they wouldn't care. If they cared, they wouldn't have killed him the way they did.

"You keep me away from them because you're afraid of what they did to Dad," I say to my mother. "You think they'll do that to me."

"They will."

"I know." My hands curl into fists. "But that doesn't mean we always have to run." It's occurred to me, once, twice, or a million times, that I could stand and fight back. That I could slice them up just as ruthlessly as they sliced up my father. I could leave them bleeding to death in a pool of blood. But when it comes down to it, I know my mother would hate for me to become that person.

"Shaw," she whispers.

"Chase," I remind her. "Chase Chandler and Mrs. Abbie Chandler."

"Yes," she says and grabs her keys. "I know...I remember our names. But what I wanted to tell you is...."

"That I shouldn't be thinking murderous thoughts about cutting up the guys who killed my father?"

"No," she says quickly. "You're entitled to that fantasy. I have it, too. But whatever happens here, whether we have a month or a year, I wanted you to know that you should just be a teenager for once, okay? Let go a little. Meet people and have fun. Let's make this time different."

"Trying to make it different doesn't mean it's going to end differently," I say, holding the door open for her. "The apartment, the furniture, the new names...it's still going to end the same way."

"You may be right," she replies as we step outside. "But that doesn't mean you can't give it a try."

****

I've done the register at the school office thing more times than I care to count. I'm sort of an expert and can usually answer questions before they're shot at me. Chase Chandler. Ninety-one Uptown Road, Rockpoint Apartments, Unit Nine. Rockpoint, New York. I don't want a reduced-priced lunch. I don't have any glaring health problems. I've got it all down already. In fact, I've already forgotten my last address.

The wrinkled lady in the school office seems impressed with my quick responses and just gives me a sheet of paper with my schedule and locker number. Rockpoint High is no different from any other school I've attended. It smells the same. It has the same fluorescent lighting, the same chatting students passing in the halls, and the same stone-faced teachers.

Nobody looks at me as I step into the hallway, just as the bell rings. I'm about ready to find my homeroom when the lady inside the office calls me back.

"Wait here a moment, Mr. Chandler," she says. Her hair is up in a white bun but it's falling down, making her look not only old but also a tad batty. "We have a welcoming committee coming for you."

"I really don't need —"

She points to a chair, sternly, so I drop down and wait for the damn welcoming committee. I'm Chase Chandler, the outcast bad boy, and the last thing I need is to be seen with a parade of peppy students from the welcoming committee. As I imagine a horrible scene of the school band blowing horns in my face and confetti floating through the air around me, I see a girl standing out in the hallway by one of the lockers. I said I can't have a girlfriend because of my situation, but that doesn't mean I don't look on occasion.

She's tall for a girl, about five nine or five ten, and has curly black hair. She might be Italian or Spanish, it's hard to tell, but she really is beautiful. Out of my league, obviously, but still worth the risk. I'm sixteen, but when it comes to asking girls out, I may as well be twelve. I have zero experience. It can go horribly wrong, or so I'm told. But my mother did tell me to meet people and have fun, and it seems weird that her advice coincides with me fixating on this girl.

"Hello?" a girl's voice says, somewhere from my left. A hand waves in front of my face.

"What?" I snap.

The girl waving her hand at me takes a step back, frightened. At least I know I've got the outcast "leave me alone" thing down.

"I'm here to show you around the school," the girl says, stepping farther away still. "My name is Melody, and I'm the welcoming committee."

"Just you?" I laugh. "Seriously?"

Melody doesn't laugh back. It's kind of funny, I think at least, that she alone is the welcoming committee at Rockpoint High School. She watches me until I stop laughing, then swishes her long brown braid behind her shoulder and gestures me to follow her out into the hallway.

"Welcome to Rockpoint High School," she says in an obviously rehearsed voice. "I'm Melody Tufts, and I'll be your tour guide. We'll be taking a journey through the school, where I'll show you the many points of interest and then get you acquainted with the schedules and activities. If you have any questions —"

"I have a question," I interrupt. "What's that girl's name?" I point to the girl with the curly black hair, still standing by her locker.

Melody rolls her eyes. "Ariana Gracia," she says. "And she's waiting for her boyfriend."

Do I detect a touch of bitterness? I've seen enough female rivalry to spot it pretty quickly. In every school, there's a girl who stands out and shines, reducing even the nicest girls to puddles of mad envy. Ariana Gracia seems to be the "it" girl at Rockpoint High.

"Follow me," Melody says.

As I pass by Ariana's locker, she catches my eye. We watch each other for a moment, in a slow motion, nonverbal introduction.

"Hi," she says to me finally.

"Hey," I say back.

"Ariana," she says.

"Chase." I leave it at that. Play it cool.

Melody keeps going, quickening her pace, until we're around the corner, moving down a long, locker-lined corridor.

"Don't think you're special," Melody says, losing her all-business tour guide manner of speaking. "She flirts with every guy."

"I thought you said she has a boyfriend."

"She does." Melody stops by two large wooden doors. "And when he catches her talking and flirting with any guy, he makes beef stew out of their brains." She pushes open one of the doors. "On that note, here's the cafeteria."

I laugh until I remember I'm supposed to be the outcast loner type who finds humor in nothing. Then, I just step through the cafeteria door with Melody until we're standing in front of a huge open room, where most of the long tables have chairs still placed upside-down on top. It smells like fried things and spaghetti sauce in here. Typical.

Melody whips out a sheet of paper. It has my name on it, and I see they've given her a copy of my schedule.

"Your lunch is *C-wave*," she says. "So you'll be going at—"

"You really don't need to do all this," I say. "My mother and I move around a lot, so I know how to find my way around a new school. It's not new to me, and I've done it plenty of times without a tour guide."

She pulls her phone out of the pocket of her jeans and slides her finger around the screen. "Listen," she says, not looking up at me. "I was up late playing Gemstone Smash last night, so I really need to get out of my first period Algebra test. Just play along, okay? I'll give you a shiny hall pass when we're done."

With that, she guides me out of the cafeteria and back down the hall. She shows me the gym, the auditorium, the pool, and finally, the outdoor break area. It's cold as we stand outside, but even as she shivers, she plays a game on her phone. I stand by one of the picnic tables, waiting for her to finish. Talk about cell phone addiction. And she's not even using the thing to text, she's using it to play games.

"Hey," I say finally. "Can I get to my first class now?"

She hands me her phone. "Angry Birds?"

"That's out," I say. "Long over."

But when I see she's got the *Star Wars* version, I can't help but sit down at the picnic table with her. I know she's just trying to dodge class, but hell, that's fine with me. So we sit for another twenty minutes or more, shivering and shaking in the late October air, playing Angry Birds. I'm pretty good at the game, but she beats my high score every time.

****

When my mother picks me up at the end of the day, the car radio is playing some upbeat eighties tune, her hair is pulled back in a purple clip, and she's tapping the steering wheel along with the beat. I'm not superstitious, but I don't really want to jinx this whole "Rockpoint is going to be different" wave I'm being carried on, so I don't open my mouth. I just let her carry on with her tapping as she takes in a few of the students, then pulls away from the school.

"So did you successfully pull off the tough guy act?" she asks.

"With a few people," I respond. "Most people."

I go on to tell her about my day, how it started with a tour of the school by the welcoming committee. I leave out that the welcoming committee was one lone girl who uses the job as a ruse to get out of classes so she can play games. Then I tell her about classes and break and lunch and gym. It's obvious she has some kind of good news, so I finish pretty quickly and sit back. It's not like we haven't talked about first days of school before.

"So I have a job," she says. "I rented a chair at some no-questions-asked place, and I'm going to put fliers out for services."

She's a licensed beautician, but that's under her real name, Jenna Huntley. When we travel, she usually has to rent out a chair or just cut hair from home under a false name. It has crossed my mind a few times that this is how Alexander and the scarred man find us. It's probably easy to locate all the new beauticians in town.

"That's probably not the best—"

"I'm doing it differently," she says, going along with the theme of late. "Instead of cutting and coloring, I'm going to focus on just manicures and pedicures."

"Touching strangers' feet," I say and make a face as we turn onto Uptown Road. "Great career."

Some of the wind goes out of her high sails as she pulls into the apartment complex. As usual, I look around for any signs of trouble. My eyes scan the area, then I take in the front door of our apartment, making sure it's secure. It would be too early for them to find us; usually, it takes at least a month. But after what happened, I know they're full-out pissed and ready to kill.

"Alexander survived," my mother says and parks the car.

"How do you know?"

"I have a contact back in New England," she says. "Someone I trust who looked into the situation for me. It was killing me to think that you might have...."

I want to tell her that Alexander deserved what he got, but I stop myself. It was self-defense. Of course anyone in my situation would fight back with the only weapon they possess.

Inside the apartment, I see that she has unpacked and organized. I'm not sure how she got it all done, because she had to go out and find a job, too, while I was at school. With the promise to come out for dinner, I head to my room for some alone time to absorb my day. I sit for a while on my bed, then walk over to the white dresser. Inside, she's unpacked my clothes and my personal things. I search around until I find what I'm looking for, and then sit back down on my bed.

There are a few things I cannot bear to leave behind, even when we're in a rush to leave a town. My mother knows to bring these things, and I usually try to keep them in the same place, all together, so if she needs to just swipe them all up, she can do it fast. One of the things is a small photo album of me and my parents. I left that in my dresser for now. Another thing is a rare *Star Wars* comic book from the original series in 1977. My father got that one for me off eBay, about a year before he died. The last thing, though, the one I'm holding now, is what I consider the key.

It's not a key in the actual, literal sense. It's a metaphorical key. Something I think opens something else. It's my jeweled dagger, in a black-velvet-lined box. It's the dagger I envision when I have to defend myself and slice up my enemies—and I think it belonged to my father.

It's not a hand-me-down. I have no proof my father actually owned this. When he told me about my ability, he never mentioned the dagger, but I always wonder — did he use it the same way I do? I mean, we share the ability, maybe we share the dagger, right? My mother always claims she knows nothing about the dagger. Never saw it before the day I found it inside a cardboard box, a few weeks after my father died. I love my mother, but she's always been a bit of a truth twister.

The hilt of the dagger is embedded with red and green jewels. Rubies and emeralds, maybe. I don't know if they're real or fake. If they're real, the thing is probably priceless, another reason I'm sure my mother knew of its existence. How could such a thing of value be in our possession without her knowing about it?

The blade is gold and shiny and feels cold as I run my fingertips down the middle. There's a connection here. I *feel* a connection with this dagger. Maybe that's why I use it to cut, even if I just use it from inside my memory. If I could only figure out where the thing came from, I know it would answer a lot of questions. Maybe it would explain why I have this ability and why people want to kill me for it. The dagger is what Alexander and the scarred man are looking for, or at least one of the things they're looking for, even though my mother always denies the theory. I'm sure Alexander has mentioned this in one of our fights. Or maybe it was me who stupidly mentioned that I have the dagger.

For a while, I move the dagger around in my hands, searching for something, but I'm not sure what I'm searching for. All I know is that I sense the connection, sense that this is the key, and that my mother, when the time is right, will explain where the dagger came from — what it means and why we have it. Why it's my imaginary weapon.

Closing my eyes, I drift back in time. I see my father sitting in a tan armchair, just across from me. His hair is dark blond and messy. He holds an apple, throws it up in the air,

26

and then catches it. But when the apple comes down, it's different from when it went up. It's sliced from top to bottom, like a knife went through the skin and pulp. The memory is from my thirteenth birthday, the night he told me about my ability — and I didn't believe him. I told him he was just doing a magic trick, messing with me. I was wrong, of course, and not too long after, Alexander and the scarred man killed him.

My father and I share the ability; it only makes sense that we share the dagger. It has to be his. It has to be what Alexander and the scarred man are after, but what else could they possibly want from me?

"Chase?" my mother says from the doorway.

Quickly, I place the dagger back in the box.

"There's someone here to see you," she whispers. "A girl. She says she knows you?"

"A girl in Rockpoint who knows me?"

My mother nods. "I guess she lives in the complex and wanted to bring us a welcome-to-the-neighborhood gift."

Welcome to the neighborhood?

Three guesses who the welcoming committee is at Rockpoint Apartments.

Chapter Three

Melody is standing in my kitchen by the counter. Her braid hangs nearly to her waist, and her hand is curled around the handle of a basket like she's Little Red Riding Hood. Whatever is inside the basket smells so good that I reach right in.

"Chase," my mother reprimands. "Maybe you could wait a second."

Melody chuckles as I pull out a muffin.

"He eats constantly," my mother says. "I can't keep up with his appetite."

"I made them last night," Melody says, pointing to the muffin in my hand. She gives the rest to my mother, who places the basket on the counter. "I heard someone new was in the complex, but I didn't know until this morning that it was you."

"Which apartment do you live in?" my mother asks her as I take a bite of the muffin. I think it's blueberry.

"We're in unit three," Melody says. "The one right in the front of the building. Unit one and two are for the landlord and the maintenance guy."

She goes on to tell us that she's lived in the apartment complex since she was twelve. She says she lives with her father and doesn't say anything about a mother. I've only known her a day, *barely* a day, but I do know that most of the time, she's either greeting people as a one-person welcoming committee or on her phone playing a game. I'm surprised the phone isn't out now, in her hand.

"So I have to go into town," my mother says and grabs her pocketbook off the counter. "Thank you for the muffins, Melody." She smiles at us. I'm pretty sure going into town is just a made-up thing. I'm kind of surprised, actually, that she's encouraging a friendship with Melody. One of our rules has always been to stay away from people I can accidentally cut.

When my mother leaves, Melody stares up at me. I grab another muffin from the basket, and not really knowing what else to do, I invite her to hang out in my room.

As soon as we walk in, I realize my mistake.

"What's this?" she says, going straight for the black box containing my dagger. I left it just sitting on my bed. God, I'm stupid.

"Nothing," I say and try to race ahead of her, but she's too quick.

She opens the box and her jaw drops.

"You just go around touching other people's property?" I say it as kind of a joke, because I'm furious, and that does not always end up well.

"Where did you get this?" she says, completely disregarding the fact that she's in my bedroom, going through my personal possessions.

"It might have been my father's," I tell her. "I don't know."

She sits down on my bed and inspects my dagger, sliding her finger down the blade, eyeing the gems. The inspection goes on for a while.

"Where's your father now?" she asks finally.

"Dead." I breathe in slowly, then blow the breath out into the air. The difficult thing here is not envisioning the dagger when it's just a few feet away from me. If I envision my weapon, there's a chance it will come out of me in anger. Then we'll have to move before we've even settled in. A new record for us.

"I'm sorry," she says. "About your father."

Something in me softens, and I sit down on my bed beside her. "Thanks," I say. "It's been...I don't know. Kind of hard since he...." So much for the outcast bad boy routine, although I'm pretty sure Melody wasn't buying that anyhow.

"I know," she says. "My mother died when I was only three. I mean, I barely remember her, but sometimes...."

Okay. So we're kindred souls or whatever. I may have found a friend for the first time since grammar school. It's no reason to lose my cool.

"You really like the dagger?" I ask.

"Love it." She strokes the blade, the same way I do, gently and with care. "There's this game that I play...."

For a while, she goes on telling me about her games and her apps and her computer Sims. She's not like the girls I've met before. I mean, it's not like I ever knew any girls that well, but I'm sure, from what I've witnessed at school and around the many various neighborhoods I've been in, that Melody is different.

She's reluctant to let go of my dagger, but finally, I place it back in the box and put it in my dresser. When I turn around, Melody is looking around my room. Her braid is wrapped around her neck, and for a second, I wonder what she looks like with her hair down.

"Where did you move from?" she asks, playing with the tip of her braid.

Here's where it gets tricky. Nobody can know too much about me. I have no choice but to lie. "We spent some time in Vermont and Maine," I reply without giving specifics.

"Your mother travels a lot for work?"

"Something like that."

She eyes me with suspicion. It's my bad luck that she's sharp.

"We overhear a lot because we're near the landlord," she says.

"What's that supposed to mean?"

"Just that you're lying." She pulls her cell phone out of the pocket of her jeans. "But I guess it's okay. I mean, if you're in witness protection or something."

Witness protection? What the hell does my mother tell people? I don't know how to respond so I just stare at her. She stares back.

"Want to play Sparkle Rush?" She holds up her phone.

"Sure," I say and grab the phone from her. "I'm pretty sure I can beat you at this one."

Melody laughs as I drop down on the bed beside her. "Don't bet on it," she says.

****

In the morning I decide to take the bus to school. I was going to have my mother bring me in every day, but as long as Melody is on the bus with me and at my stop, I guess it's fine for now. Through the frosty morning air, I head to the end of the apartment complex, where the parking lot meets the main street. I wait for Melody, until I see her coming out of unit three. When she's closer, I can't help but notice that she looks a little different from yesterday, when we sat on my bed for hours playing games on her phone.

"You wearing make-up or something?" I ask.

"No," she says and stuffs her phone into her pocket. "Well, maybe a little. I do that sometimes."

She seems a little uncomfortable, so I change the subject to something she can relate to—apps and video games. We talk until the bus comes, then sit together toward the back. She pulls out her cell and goes right into a routine like we've done this for years together. We play a hidden object game for a few minutes, until she abruptly closes the app.

"I wanted to apologize for yesterday." She leans over as the bus turns a corner, nearly knocking into me. "It was wrong of me to just open that box and look at your dagger."

"My fault for leaving it on my bed."

"Still, I wouldn't expect you to come into my bedroom for

32

the first time and just go through my personal things."

She has a point.

"It's just…." She stares past me, out the window. "It was really something special. The gems and the blade and the hidden triangle. It was like in Kingdom Search, where you have to find the—"

"What hidden triangle?"

She tilts her head. "The triangle with the *I* inside of it. Printed in gold? Beneath one of the rubies?"

I think back over the many times I've inspected that dagger. I've never seen a hidden triangle, but then again, maybe I've never looked so closely at the gems.

"Why would there be a hidden triangle on my dagger?" She seems like the type of girl who would know something about this. And God knows I've been trying to figure out the significance of that dagger since it has landed in my possession.

"If it's hidden, then it's probably something your father did when he owned it, or whoever owned it before him," she says. "It's a symbol, obviously, maybe for a secret society or just a mark of ownership." She tucks her braid into the hood of her jacket. "I could investigate for you, do some online research, but with something as common as a triangle and the letter *I*, it's probably not going to lead you anywhere."

"I'd appreciate if you try, though," I say. Then I remember, because somehow I forget with her, that she really knows nothing about my family and what I actually use the image of that dagger for. "Just…don't tell anyone about this, okay?"

"Not a soul." She sticks her phone out again and opens a farm game. "An update alert!"

She fools around with her game, even as the bus pulls into the loop beside the school and we exit. Having Melody for a friend makes me realize just what I've been missing out on because we've moved around so much. My mother is good company, but she's still my mother. It's not like I could play video games with her, even if I did have a gaming system or a phone capable of downloading apps. Because we move around and change names all the time, my phone has always been a pay-as-you-go piece of crap. Anytime I've played a game, it's been on some random person's phone.

Melody walks me to my locker. She's not really paying attention, nearly bumping into people as she plays her farm game with its new update. I'm just about to close my locker door when Ariana Gracia walks up to us. She looks good today, maybe even better than yesterday. Up close, her skin is tan and sort of glows. Her eyes are dark and shining, like two little ponds in moonlight.

"Hi, Chase," she says to me.

Melody closes her phone. She tucks it into the pocket of her jeans.

"Ariana, right?" I say, knowing perfectly well what her name is.

"Ariana," she confirms, twisting a strand of curly black hair around her finger. "I was just wondering what you were doing tonight."

"Not sure."

"You're doing laundry tonight," Melody says.

I shoot her a look to be quiet. She turns away from us, shrinking out of the conversation, but she still stays by my side.

"There's this place downtown called The Black Crow," Ariana says. "It's a teen club with like, dancing and drinks and snacks." She takes out a tube of red lip-gloss, runs it over her lips, and snaps it shut. "Parents and cops keep trying to get it shut down cause of all the fights down there, but the owner makes his case at town meetings. I guess he says it gives teenagers a place to hang out. It keeps them off the streets."

That's a lot of information. If she's trying to ask me out, I wish she would just do it.

"Sounds like a cool place."

"So you want to like, meet me there tonight?" she says. "Like, seven o'clock?"

"That works."

"Good." She smiles at Melody, who doesn't smile back. "See you then, Chase."

She walks away. I watch. She's wearing a short black leather jacket and tall black boots over tight jeans. Wow.

"Don't you have a boyfriend?" Melody screams after her.

Ariana glances over her shoulder, smiling. "Broke up with Sal last night." She continues to walk until she disappears into a group of students.

"Holy shit," I say to Melody. "Did you just see what happened?"

"Yeah," Melody says. "I was standing right next to you, remember?"

"So?" I say. "What do you think? Good couple, right?"

"Yeah. Good couple." She closes my locker door for me, then starts down the hall. "Just remember what I told you about her boyfriend," she says as we walk. "They break up every other day, Ariana flirts with some other guy, and Sal beats that guy into stew. Then they get back together. It's a weird thing they sort of get off on."

We stop at her locker. "Thanks for the pep talk," I say.

"Just trying to warn you."

My homeroom is just a few doors down, so I wait for her to finish at her locker, and then stand in place as she picks up her book bag.

"See you at break?" she says.

"Yeah." I lean close to her ear. "And if you can find anymore *Star Wars* games...."

She starts laughing.

"You got a problem with that?"

"No," she says. "And may the force be with you until we meet at break, young Jedi."

I laugh with her until she smiles at me, kind of sadly, and turns to walk away. I watch her leave, thinking about how the braid makes her look like Princess Leia in the beginning of *Return of the Jedi*, in the scene when Princess Leia was wearing...not much clothing. But Melody is my friend, so I probably shouldn't go there. Yeah. *Definitely* shouldn't go there.

Chapter Four

The Black Crow might just be the coolest place I've ever been to in my life. As soon as I walk into the club, dark purple lights envelop me. Hip-hop music pumps from a small dance floor in the back of the place, vibrating the walls. In the lobby, a few kids sit on top of lit-up cubes, tossing curse words back and forth. Round, purple plasma lamps line the entranceway, pulsing with strings of electricity. Up by the ceiling, on glowing purple shelving, stuffed black crows scream down at me with open beaks.

At one of the tables by the dance floor, Ariana sits with a group of girls, each one more gorgeous than her neighbor. When Ariana spots me, she waves her friends good-bye, and they scatter to the dance floor. Eminem is playing, some peppier song he does with Rihanna, and the girls start humping the air while watching me. Yes, things are definitely different for me in Rockpoint.

"I ordered you a Black Crow Blackie," Ariana says as I sit down across from her. "It's the house specialty."

"Will it get me drunk?"

"No." She laughs in my face. "It's nonalcoholic. We're fucking sixteen."

I scratch my head. "K," I say. "So what's in it?"

"Magic potion." She smiles across the table, catches the beat, and moves her shoulders around. "After we drink, we dance."

37

"I don't dance."

"Fine," she says. "We'll just press together then."

She moves her hand across the table like a sneaking spider, then drags her fingers over my wrist. I try to play it cool, like I've been touched this way by thousands of girls before. It means nothing to me. But damn, it does mean something. Under the purple light, Ariana glows like a dark queen.

We don't say much while we wait for my drink to arrive. She doesn't really ask where I moved from. She doesn't seem interested in anything except the music and maybe the few guys who sit at a table three away from ours. She takes out her cell phone a few times, texts someone, then stares back at the guys. Maybe I should do something to hold her attention.

"Matching black jackets," I say to her, tugging at my sleeve.

She looks at my leather jacket, then at her own. "Not really," she says. She taps the table with her red fingernails. "Are you going out with Melody Tufts?"

Isn't this a date? Why would I say yes to meeting her here if I was going out with Melody? "We're just friends," I tell her. "She lives by me."

"Got it," she says. "Melody is kind of a loner anyhow. She's kind of a geek."

It happens before I can stop it. As the club beat pumps through the room, I try to pull back, but it's too late.

"Ow!" Ariana says. She slaps the top of her hand. "Something bit me!"

A bead of blood bubbles on top of her skin. This is why it's best that I don't socialize.

She shakes her hand out, spilling the bead of blood onto the tabletop, just as a blond waitress arrives with my Black Crow Blackie.

"Get me a napkin," she says to the waitress.

The waitress places down my Black Crow Blackie, nods, and walks away. The Black Crow Blackie is truly black. It's in a ridiculously tall glass, bubbling and popping like some super-carbonated soda. I guess it does look like a magic potion. When I take a sip from the straw, the drink tastes kind of like cherry syrup and licorice. Like a sweet cough drop.

As I drink, Ariana's gaze continues to roam. The guys three tables over stare back at us. Maybe they're thinking what the hell is a guy like me doing with a girl like her. It doesn't matter what they think, because I'm here with her. She's my date.

"Dance?" she says when I'm half finished with my Black Crow Blackie.

I guess I should just get this over with.

Purple lights flash on the dance floor as Ariana pulls me into a corner. She tucks her fingers into the back pockets of my jeans. She presses her body to mine. I can't even pretend that I've been in this situation before.

I'm not dancing, but I feel her slither against me, doing some dirty dance moves, closing her eyes. I probably should be in heaven right now, euphoric. But I'm not. It's kind of awkward, and though I'll admit that I'm turned on, it's a strange kind of turned on—like being in the wrong place and catching a view of something sexual you shouldn't have seen.

The song hits a thumping crescendo, and Ariana shakes back her hair, exposing the tan skin on her neck. I'm thinking maybe I should kiss her when something hard slams into my right shoulder. Ariana's eyes flash as she moves away from me. Her eyes flash in *delight*.

"Sal!"

The next second, a fist flies through the air, and I'm on my back, staring up into a bar of flashing purple lights. Warm blood trickles from my mouth.

"You shouldn't!" Ariana screams.

From the floor, I see her wrap her arms around who I assume is Sal. He's a tall guy with a shaved head, maybe around my height or an inch taller. He starts kissing Ariana like crazy, like they're in a bedroom or something. The guys

that were three tables over before, the ones Ariana kept looking at, circle around me. I'm kind of dazed and confused.

"Get up, fucker," one of the guys says.

"Let me take care of him," Sal says. "Ari can watch."

Ariana's eyes pulse in pleasure. It's just now that I realize Melody was right. I was used in some sick and twisted bedroom game.

Wiping the blood from my mouth, I try to sit up, only to catch another fist to the side of my head.

"Take it outside!" a deep, older man's voice shouts. "Take it out of my place!"

I'm drag-walked to the front of The Black Crow, a blur of purple lights all around me, the black crows staring down at me, the electricity-filled plasma lamps flashing through my eyes, searing long, jagged lines into my vision. The air outside is like cold, penetrating knives, and right away, I snap back to life and fill with rage.

Little does Sal know he's messed with the wrong guy.

Sal's friends, a big circle of them, try to keep me down so Sal can pummel me, but I'm strong. Probably a lot stronger than they anticipated. Pushing them away, I get to my feet. I shoot Ariana a wicked look as she watches in glee, and then I tighten my shoulders.

"You like my girl?" Sal says to me.

"No," I tell him. "Your girl came on to *me*."

Ariana laughs like there's no way in hell she came on to me. She did. And I was stupid enough to fall for the act.

"She's off-limits," Sal says. "But just so we're clear on that, we're going to play a little game."

"Oh yeah?" I say.

"Yeah," he says back. "Let's see how far you can run before we take you down. Let's see how far you make it before we bloody you up."

I'm not running. I don't need to. Of course, I could just do what he says, play his game, and then maybe it won't come down to what it's going to come down to—what will

40

probably make my mother and I have to pack up and leave again. But it's too late. I'm pissed.

Sal watches me for a minute, thinking I'm going to run. Why wouldn't I run? There's a gang of guys around me, ready to beat me to blood and dust. But when he figures out I'm standing my ground, he cocks his head and curls his fingers into a fist.

Ariana giggles.

"You know," I say to her, "you're kind of a sleazy girl."

And that's when Sal's fist comes down but doesn't make contact. His eyes pop open, and then his body folds and crumples. His gang gazes down at him, confused. It's quiet. Someone asks him if he's okay, and when he doesn't answer, a few guys dash off. Cars in the parking lot speed away—his weaker buddies who just didn't want to get involved in this. At this point, they're lucky to get out.

One of his friends falls. Then another. And another.

"He's got a switchblade!" someone hollers.

Ariana is screaming. Red and blue lights flash in the distance, coming closer. One by one, the friends speed away. I didn't get them too badly. Just a threat, like my mother calls it. Just a warning slice. Stay back.

Sal stands, holding his stomach, slightly hunched as sirens blare close by. He looks down, where an egg-sized spot of red bleeds through his shirt. He's made the connection that I stabbed him and looks at my hand for a weapon.

"Not over," he says, pointing at me.

Ariana grabs his hand and they both run away, jump into a dark car, and drive off.

The cops pull into the parking lot, and just as I get ready to face my punishment—the only one involved in the fight who didn't get away—someone laces their fingers with mine and tugs me hard. They keep pulling, moving through the parking lot, to the back of The Black Crow. Quickly, I'm forced behind a brown dumpster.

"I did try to warn you," Melody says.

41

Chapter Five

"What are you doing here?" I ask, gazing across at Melody.

We're crouched behind the dumpster as red and blue lights flash in front of The Black Crow.

"Nothing," she says.

"Melody."

"Okay," she says and drops all the way down to the pavement. "I just had a bad feeling, so I may have been inside, hiding at a back table, spying on you and Ariana."

Despite what's going on around us, I can't help but laugh. Melody slaps my jacket as a cop car pulls around the back of The Black Crow where we're hidden. The cop flashes a spotlight around the back of the building, so Melody pulls me farther behind the dumpster. Finally, the cop car drives away.

"Are you okay?" she asks.

"Fine."

She eyes me suspiciously. I've seen that look before.

"I guess the owner called the cops."

"*I* called the cops," she says. "But if I'd known you were going to be able to defend yourself against all of them, I wouldn't have done it."

Again, the suspicious look.

"Sometimes you just have to fight back," I say.

"With what?" she asks.

What does she think I used? Obviously, if she was spying

43

on me, she saw what I did. Or, now that I think about it, I guess since she did see, from an outside perspective....

"Let me see it," she says.

"What?"

"The knife. I want to see it."

"It's in the pocket of my — "

She pounces on top of me. Knocks all the breath from my lungs.

"Melody!" I say. "Mel...Melody!"

She frisks me, runs her hands all over me, down my leg and under my shirt. I could probably pull her off me, but I don't, even though I know damn well she's not going to find what she's looking for.

"I ditched it!" I say as she straddles me, pressing my hands back. Her braid whacks me in the face. My head is against the pavement, and I catch a whiff of the dumpster. Cherries and licorice. Old Black Crow Blackies.

Finally, she crawls off me, breathless.

"You didn't use a knife," she says.

"No," I say, giving up the fight. As I sit up, the world spins for a second then rights itself. Vaguely, I hear music from inside The Black Crow. "Why do you have to be in my business all the time?"

"All the time?" she says. "We just met!"

Both of us catch our breath. It takes a minute.

"Okay," I say and lean back on my hands. "I'll tell you the truth, but you have to promise not to tell anyone. Not a soul. Not your father or your friends. Nobody in the world."

"Not a soul," she says back. "Just between you and me."

So I tell her everything. And she's the only one in the world, outside of my mother, my deranged cousin, and the scarred man, who knows. I tell her about the dagger, how I envision it and can cut people. I tell her that I am marked for death, and that's why we move around. I tell her I can't get close to people because I can accidentally slice them if I get too angry. She doesn't seem surprised, not the least bit skeptical, just sits listening like I'm telling her about a new video game.

The only thing I leave out is my true name. She has to know me as Chase Chandler. If we're at school hanging around together and she accidentally calls me Shaw, that would be catastrophic. I just skip over the name change thing entirely and go on about my cousin and the scarred man. When I finish, she sits in thought. Someone comes out of the back door, tosses a bag into the dumpster, and goes back inside.

"So the dagger obviously belonged to your father," she says. "He used it just like you."

"He never mentioned it to me," I reply. "But that's what I think."

She moves us back a few feet, away from the dumpster and the back door. "I did some research on the triangle. It can mean a few different things, like I thought, but my top guesses are that it was used for magical summoning, or as a symbol of the element *fire*. The *I* inside of the triangle might not be the letter *I*, but a Roman numeral, giving you the number one—the first item in a group. And since it's a blade we're talking about, another symbol of fire, I'm going with elemental fire. So it would be the first item in a group of something. Maybe something having to do with the magical elements."

"So what does all of that mean?"

"I'm not sure," she says. "But since you have this gift—"

"It's not a gift." My veins burn, but I have to control myself with her. She's the last person in the world I want to cut. "I've always called it an ability. Not a gift."

"But it *is* a gift," she says. "You're just looking at it negatively."

How could I not look at it negatively? I cut people. It's not like I can read minds or speak to crossed-over loved ones. My whole purpose in life is to wound.

"For every negative, there's a positive," she goes on. "It

makes you unique, so there's a positive already, right?"

I shake my head. I just don't know. I've never had anyone explain it like this before.

"You have to start thinking of it as a positive thing," she says. "Because I have a feeling there's a lot more you need to know about it." She stands up, reaches for my hand, and pulls me up. "Maybe you should text your mom to come pick us up."

I do as she says.

****

Fifteen minutes later, my mother's Jetta pulls into the parking lot of The Black Crow. All signs of a commotion are gone. Ariana and Sal are gone. Their friends are gone. The cops are gone. My mother looks a little surprised to see that I'm with Melody. She dropped me off, thinking I was dating a girl named Ariana. I still haven't apologized to Melody for not listening to her about that. It's actually a little uncomfortable to bring up Ariana now, but I don't really know why. In just a few days, I've connected with Melody like nobody else I've ever known. There really shouldn't be anything uncomfortable between us.

"Do you think you could drive me home, too?" Melody asks my mom. "You know, same place?"

"Of course!" my mother says and waves her into the car. I offer the front seat, but Melody hops into the back. "So what's going on?" my mother asks.

I turn to look at Melody as the car pulls onto the main road. My mother is going to kill me for what I just did. Actually, for a few things I just did.

"I got in a fight," I tell her. "With Ariana's boyfriend and a few other guys."

My mother sighs. Her shoulders drop.

"But I came out of it fine, if you know what I mean."

She tosses me a look to shut up, like I'm crazy for saying this in front of Melody and should know better.

"She knows," I say. "Melody knows."

46

The car comes to a screeching stop, and we all fly forward. Like I haven't had enough blows to the face tonight.

"What?" my mother says—no, shouts. It's quiet for a few seconds, until she realizes what she did and where we are—in the middle of the road. "Oh my God. I'm so sorry, Melody." She glances into the rearview mirror and meets Melody's eyes. They do some silent mind-reading like girls do, and then my mother starts driving again. I'm guessing they just exchanged this pact: *No one will ever know what Chase can do.* They swore it to each other wordlessly.

At home, Melody doesn't go back to her apartment. She heads into my kitchen with my mother, where the two of them put together some kind of ice-filled towel for my mouth. I guess maybe it's still bleeding or swollen. It hurts, but I can't say I'm not used to pain.

"I'll make you two some popcorn," my mother says as Melody sits beside me on the couch. I've already turned on the television.

"French toast and sausages," I tell my mother. "I'm starving."

"Of course you are."

She leaves to the kitchen, and Melody presses her hand to the towel against my mouth. Her pressure makes it feel better. Less painful.

"I'm sorry," I tell her. "For not believing you about Ariana." Truthfully, maybe I did believe her but just didn't want to face the facts. The hottest girl at school, in the real world, would not ask out a guy like me. "I was stupid to think I had a shot with that."

"You're stupid but not for that reason," she says, pressing harder on my towel.

I raise my eyebrows for her to continue. She has a strange way of giving pep talks.

"You're attractive," she says and looks away. "You had a shot with her. She's just a freak, that's all. She's just a flirt."

"Attractive?" I say. It's possible that I'm decent-looking.

How would anyone really know that about themselves? "Like, Luke Skywalker attractive or like Han Solo attractive?"

Melody laughs. "I don't know. Maybe like old Ben Kenobi." She laughs harder as my jaw drops. "I'm kidding. I guess like Anakin Skywalker."

I will take that.

After that, we watch television. There are a few things I want to ask her, a few things I want to do, like maybe research more about the triangle with the Roman numeral inside, but I think it's best to just veg right now. My mother brings us in plates of French toast and sausages, and we eat that while laughing at reruns of *South Park*.

"What are you doing this weekend?" I ask Melody as ten o'clock rolls around.

"Playing The Sims," she replies. "I've got my Sim in the science career and have to level her up. Her name is Penelope Prince. You want to come over and see her?"

"Of course I do," I reply. "But I was also thinking we could look into that triangle stuff. The element stuff?"

My mother walks into the living room, breaking off Melody's response. "What are you two talking about?" she asks. Another thing about my mother is that she does nothing by accident. She came in here at this moment for a specific reason.

"Melody found a gold triangle etched into my dagger," I reply. "It's under one of the rubies. I saw it this afternoon when I looked it over. It has the Roman numeral *I* inside."

"Interesting," my mother says and sits down on the armchair beside the couch. She crosses her leg over her other leg, like she's getting comfortable for a long conversation. "And you think that's something significant?"

"Probably," Melody replies. "That's how these things work. You get one piece of the puzzle, then you go on to the next level."

"It's not a game, Melody," I tell her.

"It's a puzzle, and a puzzle is a game," she says back. "If

it weren't a puzzle, there wouldn't be hidden symbols." She sits back like that's her final word.

I've got Melody pretty much figured out now. I may not have had many friends in my sixteen years, but I people-watch from afar, and I know how they operate. Melody thinks in gaming terms. She sees life as a puzzle, a string of games and level-ups. She tries to get her XP and go on to the next place. She thinks everything works this way when sometimes it just doesn't.

Maybe the triangle with the *I* is just a trademark from whatever company manufactured the dagger. Maybe it's just an image my father liked and had engraved under the stone. Melody is probably over-thinking this, and I went along because a)—she knows more about this stuff, and b)—I was searching for any information about the dagger. Any little fact or detail. It's really all I have left of my father, and even with that, I'm grasping at nothing anyhow. I don't even know if he owned it. That was just a feeling I had because of our shared ability.

"I'm going to say that the Roman numeral *I* stands for the first of a few," Melody says to my mother. "Do you have any information at all about the origin of the dagger?"

Here's where my mother will lie. She will say she knows nothing when I'm sure she has an entire lifetime of stories about that dagger and its history.

"It's just…." Melody starts with hesitation. "Chase says it was in a box that was probably his father's. And since you were married, and since you knew what his father could do…I just assume you two didn't have secrets."

"We didn't have secrets," my mother says back, narrowing her eyes.

Melody is good at playing. She really is.

"I'll be right back," my mother says. She stands from the chair. "I have to show you two something."

She leaves the room and heads for her bedroom. Melody smiles and I smile back at her. With just a few short words,

Melody has opened me up to more information than I've had in years.

A few minutes later, my mother returns, holding a cardboard box. I've seen the box before but thought she kept her jewelry in there. She sits back down on the armchair, closes her eyes, and then starts opening the box. She pauses just before she pulls out whatever is inside.

"Your father and I wanted to wait until the time was right," she tells me. "And please understand that I don't know everything and can't *tell* you everything, but what I do know, I'll tell you now, only so you two don't go off on some wild goose chase." From out of the box, she pulls a huge golden cup—a goblet or chalice. "You can do the honors," my mother says to Melody, carefully handing over the goblet.

Melody inspects the goblet as I lean over her shoulder to get a closer look. The goblet is constructed entirely of gold, with dark, curved etchings around the brim that look like birds in flight. The handle is thick with a circle of rubies just around the base. Melody holds it up by the handle and looks at the etchings. She looks at the handle. She looks inside.

"Roman numeral two," she says to my mother. "It's inside an inverted gold triangle, similar to the one on the dagger." She points inside the goblet, at the very bottom. There, etched right into the goblet, below one lone ruby, is an upside-down gold triangle stamped inside with Roman numeral *II*.

"Your cousin has number three," my mother says to me. "Alexander has the wand. It has a triangle, too, with an imprint of Roman numeral three."

I scratch my head. None of this makes sense to me.

"So we're talking about symbols of the four magical elements," Melody says. "A grouping of them." She fades off into thought. "Fire, water, air, and earth. It's in one of my games."

"Yes," my mother replies. "A dagger, a cup, a wand, and a pentacle—all representative of the four elements. I'm not

50

sure of all the facts, but according to Chase's father, a magic ritual called the Ritual of the Four was done years and years ago, using these four objects. It was done as sort of the opposite of a family curse — it was to give the family bloodline unique gifts and abilities. The four items came together and...I'm not sure of the true history, but I do know that Alexander wants the dagger and the goblet."

"And that's why he's trying to kill me," I say. "For the dagger *and* the goblet."

"Him wanting the dagger and the goblet has a lot to do with it," my mother replies. "Your father had the suspicion, shortly before his death, that Alexander was being guided by someone else, a man who knew the family secret. That man isn't in our family line, but he wants the power. He has it to some extent, by some other means, but in order to do what you can do or to possibly have the abilities represented by all four objects, you would need the four items, and we have two of them."

"What are the abilities?" Melody asks.

"Well," my mother says and sits back. "The power of the dagger is obvious, because Chase has it and his father had it. The dagger can cut and slice. It can stab and wound." She turns to face me, her eyes soft and watery. "That's what you can do, the gift of the dagger your ancestors left for you in your blood and in Alexander's blood. The dagger belonged to your father. He used it just as you do, by visualizing the blade and projecting. He had hoped, when you came into the gift that you would use it the same way he did." She closes her eyes. "He never got to see that happen."

Silence falls, and I find I can't look up, not at Melody and certainly not at my mother. I guess I had the ability all along, before my father even told me. It's in my blood, in Alexander's blood, too. Maybe it's stronger for me because I own the physical dagger.

"The rest of the abilities I'm not certain of, not entirely," my mother continues at length. "But I do know the Terra

51

family who own the pentacle, and they have the gift of great strength." She fades off and closes her eyes again. "Fraser Terra is the only one left in that family line."

"Where is that one?" Melody asks. "The pentacle that represents earth and strength?"

"Connecticut," my mother says. "Fraser Terra, the owner of the pentacle, lives in Connecticut and is my contact and connection. He's who I turn to when I need help. I trust him. He's all that's left of the original four families involved in the Ritual of the Four, besides Chase and his cousin Alexander, of course. The other descendants are dead, and that's how we got the goblet and Alexander got the wand. They were passed to us. But now, like I said, this other man wants all four items."

The scarred man. So that's what he's truly after. Power. The dagger and the goblet. And Alexander was stupid enough to follow. I honestly don't remember Alexander being such a bad kid when we were younger. He was quiet and never really played the same things I did, but he wasn't cruel or messed up. I'm sure the scarred man is responsible for the metamorphosis. He twisted Alexander's mind around somehow. The problem is, something deep down tells me that by following this man, Alexander may have marked himself for death. Evil usually works alone in the end.

"So the goblet was the other thing they were after," I say to my mother. "Right?"

"I think I've answered enough questions for tonight," she replies.

Typical avoidance. But she's told me enough, so I'll let it slide this time.

After that, we all sit in silence. Melody knows more about these things than I do, and I watch her think it out, but it's pretty much a dead end. My mother told us what she knows or what she's willing to tell for now, so at least I have an idea what Alexander and the scarred man are after. At least I know how we got our ability to cut and wound.

Melody yawns and stretches her arms to the ceiling.

"I'll walk you home," I say.

Outside, the air has turned colder. The tip of my nose instantly numbs and freezes. It's chilly in New England in the fall, but being in upstate New York is a different kind of chill. It's deeper and pushes down into your bones.

The water fountain in the center of the apartment complex hums and bubbles as we walk past—the last reminder of warmer days. When we get to unit three, Melody takes her keys out of her pocket. They jingle and the sound through the frosty air reminds me that winter is coming soon. I really hope Alexander and the scarred man don't find me this time. I'd love to see the apartment complex in winter. I would love to spend the holidays with my friend.

"So you'll come over tomorrow afternoon?" Melody asks.

"After lunch," I tell her. "I have to help my mother finish up the laundry and stuff." Her porch light shines into her hair, and I notice a smear of something brown and shiny, just above her forehead. "You have syrup in your—"

We both reach for her hair at the same time. Our hands touch, then stay suspended in the air for a few seconds. I'm not sure why one of us isn't pulling away.

Melody's eyes twinkle, then she steps back. "See you tomorrow," she whispers.

She steps into her apartment. And the porch light goes off.

Chapter Six

Over the weekend, Melody and I played The Sims, watched *Star Wars*, ate pizza and nachos, and sat on a bench by the water fountain, playing games and talking about school. One of the things that troubled her was the fact that I don't just have enemies searching for me in the outside world, but here, right inside Rockpoint, all of Sal's friends are pissed and ready to retaliate. They think I stabbed them, and Melody is sure they're all going to gang up on me at some point. Probably soon. I keep assuring her that I can take care of myself, which leads me to another issue.

My mother and I fought Saturday morning. We fought bad. She came out of it with a bloody forearm and a scratch just under her eye. I'm not proud of what I did to her, but it's not something I can help. She kept going off about how I ruined things by cutting Sal and his friends, that now Alexander can find us with ease, but I kept telling her that's ridiculous. Teenagers fight all the time, and nobody except Melody knows that I didn't really have a knife. It was dark. They all thought I was carrying. Still, my mother says news like this flies through the school and into different towns, over the Internet and stuff. She's worried that someone will find it strange that one guy fought off a gang, even if that one guy had a weapon.

And it didn't end with just that argument. No. I was pissed about something else, too. My mother never told me about the Ritual of the Four and never told me that Alexander had number three—the wand. She never confirmed that Alexander was after my dagger, and never told me about the gold goblet. That would have been useful information, say, when he was slicing me down my neck. Now, just because Melody enters the picture and the truth is kind of out there, she decides to give me some details? Not buying it.

And that doesn't even touch on how pissed I was about the dagger. All this time I suspected it belonged to my father, but she never confirmed that for me. She never told me the truth—it was his dagger, he used it as I do. With him dead and gone, it would have been nice to know for certain that I still had this last piece of him. Doesn't she care at all that I miss him every day? That the one thing that held me to him was in my possession the entire time?

She claims they both decided, around the time my father told me about my ability, that it would be best to keep all the details from me until I was old enough to understand. Until I was old enough to appreciate the dagger and its history. Until it was in my possession. Times like these I wish I could talk to my father, ask him about the Ritual of the Four. Now, without him here to explain this huge thing, it almost feels as though he died all over again.

As soon as Melody and I walk into school Monday morning, it becomes obvious that people know what happened Friday night at The Black Crow. People are staring at me. People are sizing me up, wondering who I am and where I came from and how I was able to take down the school-assigned badass and his gang. I try to ignore the stares as Melody and I walk to my locker. She probably doesn't notice them at all. She's been playing some bubble-popping game since we were on the bus.

"Ariana is coming over here," Melody says, not even looking up from her phone.

"How do you do that?" I say and open my locker.

Melody stuffs her phone in her pocket as Ariana walks up

to us. Ariana's clothing is toned-down today, just a red sweater and low shoes in exchange for her usual black leather jacket and high boots. In contrast, Melody is dressed up today. I noticed at the bus stop but didn't say anything. She's wearing a frilly purple top that's girly and out of character for her. It's underneath her coat, but she had it unzipped so I saw it. It's possible that I only notice girls' clothing when there's some kind of major change.

"I just wanted to say sorry," Ariana says, standing in front of me. "About Friday night."

This might be the real Ariana. It's possible that she's not being fake today, not out for some way to get her boyfriend jealous.

"What you did was kind of impressive," she continues. "Nobody even saw the knife. Did the cops take you in?"

"Melody pulled me away," I say. "She hid me behind the dumpster in the back."

"Good for Melody," Ariana says and shoots a fake smile over. "So," she says, turning back to me. "I know this is going to sound insane, but did you want to maybe do something next weekend? Like go someplace different?"

This is a true date proposal. I won this on my own. Well, maybe not on my own, but with a little help from what Melody calls my "gift." And though it's a confidence booster, I'm pretty sure, now that I've experienced a night of hell on account of Ariana, that she's just not my type.

"I'm going to pass," I say. "I think you should probably just hang out with Sal."

"I don't really care for the fact that Sal like, couldn't fight for me, you know?" She shrugs. "Anyhow, if you change your mind, let me know."

She walks away. I have to admit I'm a little more interested in her now that she's chilled out. But she's still kind of sleazy, based on the fact that she hits on guys who are *not* her boyfriend, and I can't really see myself with that kind of girl, whether she's hot or not. I already had a taste of physical attraction, when I first met her and then on the dance floor. That's probably as far as it will ever go between us. I really don't know how to play her weird jealousy games.

"It's probably best that you don't date her," Melody says. "You know, because of the problems with Sal and all."

"I think I'm going to have problems anyway," I say and close my locker. "And my mother said if I do…you know, my *thing* again, we're going to have to move."

"You can't move!" Melody says.

The look in her eyes reminds me of what I have to lose if I fight back against Sal. My mother is right. I can't do it. Sooner or later, someone will make the connection that I don't have a visual weapon. Melody already made the connection.

"It sucks that I have to move all the time," I tell her. "Especially now when you and I hang out together. So for now I'll do what I can to not use…my *thing*."

She rocks back and forth, probably thinking the same thing I am—I'm damned if I do, damned if I don't. Either way here, I'm screwed.

"I could always just fight back with my fists," I say.

She doesn't even pretend that's a viable solution.

****

Most of the day, I don't see Sal around. I'm pretty sure he's a junior like me, but he's not in any of my classes. And the rest of those guys…I could probably bump right into one of them in the hallway and not remember who he is and that I fought with him Friday night. It was dark in The Black Crow and dark out in the parking lot. All I remember is a lot of fists and some pain.

Just before the last bell, I'm in the locker room in gym, changing back into my jeans and T-shirt. I'm not actually in love with gym and athletics, but I do get by. I think all the running over the past few years has made me pretty quick and agile. As I bend down to tie my sneaker, I notice some kid with bony arms and legs is standing over me. Just standing there.

58

"Can I help you?" I say, straightening.

"I have a message for you," the kid says. "From Sal."

This could be one of those tricks where you ask what the message is, only to get knocked in the jaw. I don't reply. I just stand to my full height, towering over this scrawny kid.

He glances in the direction of the doorway, where the gym teacher, Mr. Girard, stands guard, huge arms crossed over his chest. We're out of earshot, but if a fight were to erupt, Mr. Girard would be over here in a second.

"Sal wants you to meet him in the football field tonight," the bony kid says, pointing toward the window to indicate the field. "Eight o'clock."

"I'm not going to do that," I reply. Seriously. How stupid do they think I am?

"If you don't, then everyone will know you backed out."

How can I back out of something I didn't even agree to? But I get what Sal is trying to do here. He knows damn well I'm not stupid enough to meet him in a dark field at night. He's just trying to pick up his reputation after I shoved it to the ground.

"You can tell Sal that I'm busy tonight, but he could come talk to me anytime at my locker," I say.

"Stupid," the bony kid says back. "Fights don't last five seconds in school."

"I already fought him." I could get cocky and add in the fact that I was triumphant, but I don't want to push this. "As far as I'm concerned, it's over."

"Well, as far as Sal is concerned, it's just begun." He shakes back wiry brown hair. "You be there tonight at eight, or things are going to get ugly."

He turns and walks away to the other side of the locker room. The bell rings and I finish tying my sneakers, then head out to the hall to meet up with Melody. I'm not going to tell her about the invitation to the field tonight. Because I'm still not sure what I'm going to do.

****

59

When I get home, my mother is slouched on the living room couch, reading a paranormal romance novel. I think she decided to take Mondays off from work, because she does a lot of business on Saturday and uses Sunday-Monday as her weekend. She looks relaxed, and I guess it's good to see her like that, but there's still a part of me burning from our argument Saturday morning. Add to that the guilt of cutting her by accident, and I can't even really look at her right now.

"How was school?" she says and puts a finger inside her book to hold her place.

"Fine," I reply. "Ariana asked me out again."

She sits up. "What did you say?"

"No, of course." I toss my book bag into the corner, then drop down on the couch next to her.

"That's good," she replies. "We don't need anymore drama around here." She sets her book down on the coffee table. "So I met Melody's father this morning."

I haven't met Melody's father yet. He's a bank manager and works a lot, and Sunday he didn't come outside much because he was watching a basketball game.

"He's concerned about Melody," my mother continues. "That she's always stuck in these video games and never really faces the real world. He says she doesn't do real-world things."

Melody not in the real world? Really? I guess there are two ways of looking at that. One is that it's a joke, because of course Melody isn't living in the real world. She's forever wrapped up in some kind of game. But the other side is that sometimes I think maybe Melody knows more about the world and how it works than most people think she does.

"It's tough being a teenage girl without a mom around," my mother says. "She was only three when her mother died, and her father said she's never really connected to anyone since then. Not until you moved in."

I'm not really sure what she's getting at here.

"We were both thinking that maybe it would be a good

idea if you...you know, took her somewhere. Maybe this weekend. Get her out of the apartment and away from her phone and computer for a little while."

Now I see where she's going.

"Not a good idea," I tell her. "It's hard for me to think about just leaving Melody behind, and if Alexander shows up, we're gone in a matter of minutes. I'll never see her again."

"She'll understand."

I have to pull back, because I'm starting to feel that burn in my veins. When it comes to Melody, I don't know. It's a sensitive issue. Maybe because she's the first real friend I've had in a while. Maybe because she's a girl.

"Look," my mother says. "I know you've never really had a girlfriend, and you're at the age now where—"

"I don't want Melody as a girlfriend," I say. "We're just friends."

Something snaps inside of me. I'm not sure why it happens or what it means, but my dagger flashes through my mind. I wish I could direct my anger at myself, but it always goes outward. My mother slaps her cheek and pulls away blood on the heel of her hand.

"Damn it, Shaw," she says. "If you like the girl, just ask her out. It's not like you have a chance at blowing it. She's been dropping hints since the first day you met her."

"Hints?"

She sighs. "Honestly."

While my mother tends to the scratch on her cheek, I think this out. I maintain that it's not fair that I can't date and can't have friendships, but at the same time, isn't it already too late? I'm already friends with Melody, and just thinking about leaving her behind, which I will eventually have to do, makes me angry in a way I can't understand. Like I want to punch my fist through the wall. Like I want to cut up everything in sight.

"Fine," I say and stand. "There's some Halloween dance

at school Friday night. I'll ask her to that."

"Good," my mother says.

"But we're just going as friends," I remind her. There are a million reasons to keep it just a friendship between Melody and me. I could cut her by accident if we get into some lover's spat. We could fall in love, only to have to split apart when Alexander and the scarred man find me like they always do. Plus, I really don't want to risk losing what we have now.

My mother picks her book up from the coffee table, so I head to my room. I'd nearly forgotten that I have to make a decision about tonight, if I'm going to meet Sal in some dark field at school. Should I exist at Rockpoint High as a coward, even if the alternative might be pain or even death? Sooner or later, I'm going to have to face up to what's coming. If I don't meet Sal tonight, he'll just find another way to even the score.

But then I think about my mother and how I don't drive yet, so if I ask her to bring me to the field tonight, it will be like asking her to drive me to my doom. Maybe I could fight Sal and hold him off, keep myself from fatal injury, but I can't fight a whole gang of guys. Not without my secret weapon, and I can't use that without risking the truth coming out.

So for my mother and for Melody, I make the final decision to stay home tonight.

Chapter Seven

I told myself there was no way in hell I was wearing a costume to the Halloween bash, but here I am, standing in front of my mirror, my reflection colorful and puffy, dressed as a pirate. Melody, to my surprise, gave me an enthusiastic "Yes!" when I asked her to the Halloween dance. She decided on these matching pirate costumes and went out yesterday to buy them. Now, I'm waiting for her to show up, and I'm pretty sure she's going to laugh when she sees me. Oh, well. It's her fault I look like this.

This week went by pretty fast. I spent most of the time with Melody out shopping or sitting outside on the bench by the fountain. We've even adopted a sitting pose out there, me sitting and facing the fountain, her sort of lying down, leaning the back of her head against my shoulder, facing the opposite direction while she plays a game and we talk. Here I go with every cliché in the book. We are like two peas in a pod, like peanut butter and jelly, like milk and cereal. All that. Basically, we've become inseparable.

I never told her about backing out of the fight with Sal, but she did hear through some rumors at school and was proud of me for not going to fight him. She's the only one who seems to feel that way, though. Most people, the same ones who looked at me with shock and maybe admiration on Monday, were smirking at me when I walked by them. Yeah, Sal got what he was after. He's head badass at Rockpoint

63

High again. But I still get the feeling he's not done punishing me for making people question that even for a few days.

At six-thirty, there's a knock on my front door, and my mother calls out that Melody is here. I take one last look at my ridiculous self in the mirror, adjust my floppy pirate's hat and the red and white scarf around my waist, and step out of my bedroom.

When I get to the living room, there's some hot chick standing by the couch. Like, seriously hot, with a killer body and cascades of brown hair falling over her shoulders in ripples and waves. The hot chick is dressed as a sexy pirate. I'm talking sexy from top to bottom. I have to look three times to realize that the hot chick is Melody.

I open my mouth to greet her, but nothing comes out. My mother laughs, but Melody looks anxious to hear what I have to say about her costume. I mean, God. She's got hardly anything on top, just this push-up black deal over her chest. Her red and white striped skirt is short and all cut up, matching my scarf-belt. Her pirate's hat is lacy and black and slightly askew. And her hair....

"No braid," is all I get out.

"You don't like my hair down?" she asks.

Can't reply.

"He likes it," my mother says. "I believe you've rendered him speechless."

I can tell, because I know Melody so well, that this is not quite the response she was looking for. I'm stupid for not telling her right away how hot she looks. I just don't know how to say it without looking like a pig, because she's stirred up everything that is possible to stir up in me. And she's supposed to be my best friend.

"We'd better get going," my mother says.

In the car, it's quiet. Melody and I are sitting in the backseat, and I can't help but look at her constantly, wondering how I ever missed all the curves of her body and all the sparkles in her eyes. In my defense, it's not too often that I *see* her eyes, because she's always looking down at her phone. Still, I can't get past the transformation. Or the thing that was always there but I didn't see because I was too stupid or too afraid.

My mother drops us off in front of the school, and we head to the gymnasium. As soon as we walk in, male heads turn in our direction. Melody is attracting all sorts of attention, and I'm feeling proud that she's my date. I grab her arm, lock it into mine, and then we find a table.

The gym is decorated for Halloween, with flashing plastic jack-o'-lantern centerpieces on the tables and orange and black streamers and balloons covering the back wall. A computer-printed sign taped to the wall says *A Magical October*. There's some photo opportunity thing in the far corner, where I guess you can get a memento of the night. The dance floor, which is basically the center of the gym, pulses white from an unseen strobe light. Music blasts from a cheap sound system.

"I'll get you a drink?" I ask Melody.

"And a plate of snacks, if you could," she responds. "If I get up...I don't know. It seems like some people are staring at me."

"Can't imagine why," I say and stand.

When I return with punch and a plate of chips and cheese cubes, Melody has her phone out. I place down the food, then reach out, but she pulls the phone away.

"Give it," I say.

"But I have to collect my coins from—"

"Melody."

She tries to move the phone out of my reach, but I'm quick and end up swiping it from her. I mean, she's here at a school dance, dressed to kill, probably breaking at least fifty school dress code rules. Let go and have some fun. Away from the games for one night.

"I hate you," she says and pulls the plate of snacks to her.

After that, we eat and talk. A few kids I recognize from

classes pass by our table on their way to get a photo taken or maybe to dance. Most girls are dressed as witches or like Katniss from *The Hunger Games*. There are a few mermaids and one princess. The guys are dressed a little darker, if they dressed at all, most with blood and guts on their bodies in some form or another. Thankfully, nobody else had the pirate idea, although most people don't seem to have dressed in couple's costumes.

"Do you think Ariana and Sal will be here?" I ask Melody.

She takes a sip of orange punch. "I don't think school functions are their thing," she replies.

That's good news. Part of me wondered if Sal would beat my head in to the backdrop of Michael Jackson's "Thriller" synchronized with the flashing strobe lights while witches and mermaids looked on.

After an hour passes, I see that look in Melody's eyes, like she wants to dance. It's obvious that she's longing for it—she keeps gazing at me and then at the dance floor. I don't dance well, but I could possibly stand there while she dances, kind of like I did with my short-lived dirty dancing with Ariana. For a while I successfully play this off, pretending not to notice her not-so-subtle hints and huffs, then finally stand and offer her my hand.

When we get out on the dance floor, it's actually pretty crowded. Some club song is playing, pumping out a techno beat, one that really doesn't fit with Melody's personality and style, but she doesn't seem to notice or care. She moves her head around with her eyes closed, like she's getting in tune with the music. It's not a slow song, but she still wraps her arms around my shoulders. I drop my hands to her waist. My fingers press into her bare skin.

And we dance. It's not graceful. Melody is on the beat, but she's still kind of out there, moving her head around like she's floating in a cloud somewhere. She's lost in this.

It's a good thing we're already in the position to slow

dance, because the song quickly changes to some moody love song. Melody presses closer, and I move my hand to her hair. I'm going to make another Princess Leia comparison. Melody's hair, all thick and wavy and ripply, looks just like Princess Leia's in *Return of the Jedi* when she was on Endor with the Ewoks.

We sway to the music, and I have to think all these *Star Wars* thoughts to keep myself from falling through to this other place with Melody. It works until I feel her shaking as I hold her. When I grasp her arms and pull her back to look at her, a tear streaks down her cheek. She stares into my eyes, then turns and runs straight across the gym to the girls' locker room, knocking into people in her haste. What the hell just happened?

For a full minute, I stand stranded on the dance floor, gazing toward the girls' locker room until the song changes and I snap myself together. I walk back to our table where our empty snack plate still sits, and Melody's nearly finished cup of punch. Still not knowing what to do, I drop down in the seat and hang my head. I somehow made Melody cry — the very thing I was trying to avoid — but what did I do?

As I sit waiting, figuring out my next move, somebody moves into my side vision. I think it's this kid Franklin who's in my English class. He slips into the chair beside me and shakes out the sleeve of his zombie costume.

"Ariana Gracia wants to talk with you."

"Right now?" I ask. "She's not even here, is she?"

"She's out the back door," he replies. "If you sneak by the chaperones, you can get back there pretty easily."

This is really the last thing I need to deal with. What the hell does Ariana want? She's not here at the dance but wants to speak with me at the back door of the gym?

Successfully avoiding the eyes of the chaperones, I slide into the narrow little hallway that encloses the back gym door. The door leads out to the field, but because it's been cold, we've only gone back there a few times to play football.

When I push on the bar and the door moves open, I see Ariana standing there, all bundled up in some stylish black coat.

"What do you want?" I ask her as she shivers.

"Oh, thank God you're here," she says. "I was hoping you'd come to the dance."

Something feels off here. Not right.

"I was really upset, so I was wondering if you'd like, walk with me for a bit."

Girls like Ariana are seldom upset. And if they are, they usually get over it pretty quickly.

"Sal and I had a big fight," she says. "And I need to talk to someone."

I glance back at the gym, but the doorway area is enclosed so I can't see anything out there except for a few distant lights bouncing around the walls.

"I'm actually here with Melody," I say. "She just...she stepped away for a minute."

"So you can walk with me?"

Her eyes grow wide, even a little tearful. My shoulders fall in submission. And I step outside the door.

"What happened?" I ask as we walk around the back of the school toward the field.

"Oh, you know," she says and waves her gloved hand through the air. "Guys can be jerks." She grabs for my hand, but I move it away.

"Don't," I warn her. "Melody is my date tonight."

"Moved on already?" She laughs.

As the puff of smoke from her laughter flies into the air, pounding footsteps echo behind me. From the side. From the front. They're coming at me from every angle, like a swarm. Yeah. I was stupid to fall for Ariana's trick again.

Chapter Eight

"What have we got here?" Sal says, appearing in front of me like he grew out of the darkness. "Chase Chandler the pirate?"

Laughter rings out in a circle around me. This isn't going to end well.

Ariana wraps her arms around Sal's neck. She holds onto him in a death grip.

"My girl seems to think you bested me at The Black Crow."

"Look," I say, trying to keep calm. "You guys came at me, and I had no choice but to defend myself. It's over and done."

Sal pushes Ariana away and steps toward me. We're about the same height and stare eye to eye. He's got the darkest, coldest eyes I've ever seen.

"I'm going to guess you got no place to stash a knife in that costume," he says. "Unless you have some plastic pirate's sword hidden in there."

Laughter again. It's coming at me from all directions, like I'm on stage and performing for the entertainment of the crowd around me. It's bad enough that I'm surrounded and about to be beaten, but did it really have to happen when I was in a pirate costume?

We're just in front of the football field. The lights are off, but if I go by memory, I could dash through the field and end up near the street on the other side. The only problem is that there are woods back there, too. I could get lost, and it's much too cold out here to get lost in the woods. Melody doesn't even know where I am. No one would find me.

"So what are we going to do tonight?" Sal says. I'm not sure if he's talking to me or if he's talking to his gang. Last time, it was too dark to really make out any of their faces, and even though it's sort of dark now, I can determine that most of these guys are pretty big. Some have shaved heads like Sal. One has long blond hair and is dressed in leather. Two are dark-skinned and have gold chains around their necks. "Weapons or no weapons?" Sal asks.

"No weapons," I say, assuming he's talking to me.

The gang roars in laughter. I guess Sal wasn't talking to me.

"I think since you used weapons last time, it's only fair that we use weapons this time," Sal goes on. "Let's make this nice and even."

"No weapons, Sal," Ariana says.

"Somebody take Ari back to the car," Sal says.

One of the guys—a shaved-head clone of Sal, only shorter—jumps on the demand. Ariana protests, kicking and screaming as the guy drags her off into the darkness. There goes my last shot of getting out of this.

I have a decision to make here, and I have to make it fast. Do I cut these punks up, or do I attempt to keep myself from harming them? It might come out by accident, like it does when I argue with my mother, but there's also a chance I can hold back. It all depends on how angry I get. It all depends on how much I want to control it so we don't have to move again. It all depends on how much I like living in Rockpoint and being with Melody.

Before I can decide what I'm going to do, before I can even develop a plan, Sal lifts his fist and knocks me across the jaw. Remarkably, I stay standing. I'm not furious yet, but I feel the burn in my veins and try to control it as my body sways. Maybe Sal just wanted to threaten me and get in one last punch. Maybe he's all talk. Maybe he doesn't have weapons.

But Sal's punch was like a signal to the others. All of them come at me in blurs of black and gold and leather. Someone pushes me forward, where someone else's knee lands in my gut. Another guy grabs me by the collar of my pirate shirt and jerks me around until I'm disoriented. I end up in front of the blond guy, who whacks me in the ribs. Sal moves through the crowd, and all I see is a fist and then the pavement.

"What you got now?" Sal says, bending over me. "You got nothing." Something hard slams into my shoulder and catches the side of my head. It's not a fist. Maybe a steel pipe or a bat. As pain vibrates through my skull, the lights from the gym windows flicker on and off, on and off, on and off. Then I realize it's not the lights flickering — it's my vision.

I do have something. But my world is turning black. It's too late to use my only weapon. Even as I lie here in a heap, a deep ache in my stomach and a swirl of dizziness spinning through my head, I can't help but feel proud of myself for not cutting them. Somehow, I must have control, because if I can hold off during the worst beating of my life, I can hold off anytime.

Someone drags me by my arms across the pavement, toward the dark field. My dagger bursts into my mind, flashing and jeweled and sharp, but it's too late. I'm too weak now to project.

"Not a word," Sal's voice says from somewhere above me.

"Sal —" one of them starts.

"Not a fucking word!" Sal says back.

Maybe they think I'm dead. It's probably best to just let them keep thinking that so they leave me alone. The pavement changes to cold grass beneath me. They keep pulling and the dirt and grass scrape against my side. Then they run off, and I'm stranded.

My first thought is to call Melody. My phone is stashed

inside my pirate costume, just below my waist belt in a deep pocket. But as I reach inside, I feel not one cell, but two. I have Melody's phone. Now what do I do?

I could call my mother, but how do I explain to an overly protective mom that she has to come pick me up in the middle of a field in the back of the school, and that she should be prepared for what I'm sure is a bloody and bruised mess of a teenager? I rewind the fight in my mind. Or maybe, now that I think about it, the fight wasn't a fight at all, more like a gang of guys messing up one person who was stupid enough to hold back from using their one and only weapon. I could have easily avoided all of this. Now I'm not sure what to do.

For a while, I dip in and out of what I think must be sleep. I'm cold. So cold. My head is throbbing, and I'm so far away from the school that I can't even hear the music playing in the gym. Or maybe the dance is over. I don't know. Did Sal really mean to smash me in the head with a weapon? Or did he just mess up a direct hit to my shoulder and is now worried that he killed me? Does he even care?

My limbs, when I first hit the frosty grass, were icy. Now they're numb. I can't feel much, except for the constant throb in my head. The lights in the distance — the ones I assume are the gym lights — go off. I'm left in complete darkness. What happened to Melody? How did she get home? Maybe she's looking for me. She *has* to be looking for me. I mean, the dance is over, and I just disappeared without a trace. Soon…hopefully soon…she'll come find me.

Minutes pass, maybe hours. Finally, I'm strong enough to text my mother. My hand curls over one of the cell phones, and when I hold it up to my eyes, I see that it's actually Melody's phone. Her game alerts are going off like crazy. She has coins to collect. She has crops to harvest. She has XP to pick up, and her energy is full. Quickly, I pull my own phone from my pocket and text my mother:

"Pick me up. Back of school. Field."

"Lightsaber?" she replies.

"NO."

After that, I can't text anymore. I'm not even sure if she replies. Or what I did with my phone. It might still be in my hand, but I can't feel my fingers so I don't know. I gaze up at the sky, where clusters of stars glitter above me. As I inhale and exhale, puffs of smoke rise into the air, chase each other, and then dissolve. For as dim as the world looked moments ago, now it seems overly sharp. Wicked dazzling. The stars shape-shift and explode. The sky bends and twists in blacks and blues and purples.

And then I fall asleep again.

Chapter Nine

I'm in my bed and warm, but when I try to open my eyes, a searing pain races across my brain. A hand cups my forehead and gently rubs.

"Shaw?" my mother says. "Try to stay awake, okay?"

I nod, but just the effort sends another jolt of pain through my head.

Memory rewind: Headlights cut through a field. My mother screams. My mother drags me to the car. A groggy explanation of what happened to me. A vague refusal of the hospital. And then my bed. That could have been minutes ago or days ago.

"Can you sit up?" she whispers. "I need you to drink some tea."

Slowly, I get myself into an upright position and sip some tea. It's herbal and gross, so I shake my head, which was a bad idea because I can't help but moan when the pain hits me.

"The tea will help," my mother says. "I've put some anti-inflammatory and nerve-relaxing herbs in there."

It takes a while but I get the tea down and instantly feel better. My head still hurts, but it's a dull pain now, and I'm more relaxed.

"Where's Melody?" I ask. "What happened?"

My mother grabs my empty teacup and places it down on my nightstand. "I guess Melody didn't know what happened

75

to you. She thought you left the dance." She sighs. "Her father came to pick her up."

"I had her cellphone, though."

"She used someone else's phone to call him."

Another memory rewind: A slow dance with Melody. Melody in tears. Melody running to the girls' locker room.

"She thinks I ditched her, doesn't she?"

My mother closes her eyes. She nods.

"Great."

I fall back onto my pillow. All of this was for nothing. Melody hates me now, and I took a beating just so I could stay in Rockpoint with her.

"Shaw," my mother says and brushes back my hair. "Why didn't you just—"

"I was going to," I tell her. "But you told me we'd have to move if I did."

"So you controlled it?"

"Somehow," I explain. "I mean, I know Dad could, but I could never do it until now."

My mother lifts herself from my bed. She stands over me, and her eyes fill with tears. I was stupid to mention my father. That always gets her going, especially with me in this condition.

"Your father controlled it because he didn't have it quite as powerfully as you have it."

"That's not true," I say. "He could do things I could never do." I remember him cutting up the apple. Just tossing it up in the air and slicing it, using only the power of his mind. Superb control.

"You can do everything he could do and more. You've just always chosen to look at it as a curse. Your father thought of it in more positive ways."

I honestly don't think my mother is right here. My father was better than me. He had control, and I never had that. Not until now.

"Anyhow, it's almost morning, and I've been up all night

with you." She yawns, covers her mouth. "Can I trust that you won't fall asleep? You might have a concussion."

"I won't."

She kisses my forehead and leaves my room.

Then I close my eyes and drift away.

****

It's Saturday, around noon. A few things have become clear to me—one kind of embarrassing. I'm not wearing my pirate costume anymore, so that means my mother, at some point, must have undressed me and slipped me into my sweatpants. Yeah, she's my mother, but that doesn't mean I want her doing things that were meant to happen when I was three. The other thing is that I still have Melody's phone. She must be furious with me. So furious, she's not coming over to pick up her phone or even talk with me. I mean, nothing in the world could really come between Melody and her phone.

My mother gave me a tiny bell, and I'm supposed to ring it when I want something. So far, she's brought in cereal and eggs, soup and crackers, and a can of soda. The last few times I've rang the bell, she hasn't come into my room. I guess she's getting sick of the routine, even though it was her idea. What did she really think I was going to do with this kind of power? But now I really need to speak with her, so I keep ringing and ringing until my ears hurt.

"What?" she says, stopping in the doorway of my room.

"Can you go over and get Melody and tell her to come over here?"

She presses her eyes closed. It's not like she hasn't done enough for me today. She's missing work just to bring me food and tend to my head and all the other various pains in my body. Without a response, she turns for the living room. A minute later, the apartment door opens and closes.

With the house quiet, all alone and in my bed, I think back on my time so far in Rockpoint. I think about my ultimate goal—living someplace for longer than a month. Living without fear of Alexander and the scarred man. And lately, I've also wanted to find out more about the dagger, the cup, the wand, and the pentacle. Maybe there's a way to break this cycle so if I ever have a kid someday, he doesn't have to run around the country chased by lunatics.

It took a while, so I'm guessing my mother really had to persuade Melody to come over. Finally, the door opens out in the living room, and I hear two female voices. One is Melody's, and just hearing it, my stomach does this weird jumping thing. I sit up and try to look all manly and less like a patient.

When Melody walks into my room, her hair is still down. She's wearing jeans and a loose T-shirt that says *Rockpoint Savings and Loan 1953*. She has on a smudge of makeup that might be leftover from the dance last night. Her eyes are all crinkled up, mad at me. I don't know if she has ever looked as beautiful as she looks right now.

"Oh my God," she says when she sees me in bed. "It's true?"

"That I was beaten to within an inch of my life and left for dead?" I say. "Yeah. True."

She rushes to my bed and sits down beside me. I tell her all about what happened, how Ariana tricked me into going outside and that Sal and his gang were waiting for me out there. There was no stopping the beating and no talking my way through. They had in mind to beat me and they beat me.

"Your head," she says. She lifts her hand to touch me but then pauses and stops. "I mean, they must have used something pretty sharp."

"Probably a pipe." Based on the injury, it seems Sal hit me with a pipe, wanting to bust up my shoulder, but the open end of the pipe struck the side of my head and scraped me. I'm still not sure if he meant that to happen, but he did sound a little scared when he thought I was dead. And that doesn't even count the gut kicks his gang sent at me. Whether he meant to or not, he messed me up good.

Melody's eyes get all glassy. Then she does something

unexpected. She moves up the bed, lies back, and rests her head next to mine on my pillow.

For a while, we don't say anything, we just stare across at each other. Her hair smells flowery, like a million gardens.

"Why did you cry and run away at the dance?" I whisper.

"I don't know," she replies. "I mean, I do know. I'd just rather not say."

"I didn't leave you," I tell her. "It's just...Ariana tricked me. I thought I was going right back inside."

She nods and shifts in the bed. Her hair is so long that it spills over my arm.

"I've had a constant pain in my stomach since you moved here," she says. "I guess at the dance, it just overwhelmed me. You know, dancing that close."

Confirmation is a killer.

"Listen," I say and grab her hand. "You know that I move a lot. I might be here another month, or I might be gone tomorrow. It's not fair to start something up with that hanging over us."

"What if I don't care?"

"I care." I roll into her and look down, meeting eyes. My head throbs but I ignore it. "Even if I didn't have to move, I'd still feel awful if someday I cut you by accident. I controlled it last night, but I can't say I'll be able to control it another time."

"It's just a cut," she says back. "It's not like you're Anakin Skywalker and you'll death grip me or something."

At that, I laugh. She laughs, too. Then it turns serious again.

"I like you way too much to be more than friends with you," I say.

"I understand," she says back.

It kills me to move away from her, especially with the hurt look in her eyes, but I have to. I fall back onto my pillow and stare up at the ceiling. She doesn't move and she doesn't cry. She understands, but I still feel like the worst person in the world. I wish it didn't have to be this way.

We stay in my bed for a while, quiet at first until I start talking about what happened after I left the dance. She tells me how she came back from the locker room and thought I'd ditched her. She said nobody really knew where I went, so she figured her crying sent me away. She wasn't so upset about her phone because she wasn't in the mood to play anything last night or this morning. That makes me feel even worse.

With Melody taking over, my mother decides to go into work for a few hours. After my mother leaves, Melody quickly tires of the bell-ringing routine. I have her bring me in more soda, some Cheez-Its, a box of Pop-Tarts, and a few slices of cheese. It's just after the request for hot dogs that Melody takes the bell and chucks it under my bed. After that, she helps me limp to the bathroom. I really could have done this myself, it's just funny to watch Melody huff and puff and try to carry my weight.

We play a few games, passing her phone back and forth until the battery pretty much dies. Then we just lie back on my bed and stare at each other again. I have to keep telling myself it's best to stay just friends, not to make a move that I'll regret, but it's difficult to keep myself focused. Girls have a tendency to whack all the smart out of you. I found that out the hard way with Ariana.

"It could be different," she says.

"What?"

"Instead of always running from them, maybe you could try running *to* them."

Not sure what she's getting at here. I assume she's talking about Alexander and the scarred man. Melody can be random sometimes, stuffing conversations into strange places. But now that she's on the subject, I'm wondering why she thinks I should go running toward two people who want to kill me.

"Think about it," she says. "If you were to figure out the truth behind all this and then just face them head on, maybe it would all be over."

"Or I'd be dead."

"I don't think so." She spins onto her side. "You're more powerful than they are. The scarred man? He doesn't even have the gift in his blood like you do. And you said your cousin isn't as strong, either. You could win. But first, we need to find out more about the Ritual of the Four."

"What are you suggesting?"

She sits up. "Road trip," she says. "To Connecticut. Let's find number four, the pentacle, and learn what we can from there."

Melody might be crazy. She might be random and daring and completely out of her mind. But she also might be right about this. I've wanted to stop running for a long time. I want to stay in Rockpoint, even though I have enemies here. I also have a friend.

"I'll have a talk with my mother later," I tell her.

"Same here," she says. "With my father."

Not sure where it will go from here. Will my mother drive us to Connecticut? Will she let us go alone on a bus or a train? I'm kind of hoping she'll let us go alone. Somehow, I get the feeling this is something I need to do on my own. Or alone with Melody, to be exact.

"There's something I need to tell you before we do this," I say.

Melody smiles. "Your name isn't really Chase Chandler."

"How the hell did you know—"

"You would be stupid to use your real name when hiding out," she says. "I knew your name wasn't Chase from almost the beginning." She laughs at my shocked expression. "So?" she says. "What's your real name?"

"Shaw," I reach out for her hand and hold it in mine. "Shaw Huntley."

"Shaw Huntley," she repeats. "I like that."

I can't stop myself, and without thinking, I pull her down in a hug.

81

The Ritual of the Four

Chapter Ten

Sunday morning, when I wake up at eight, my mother isn't in the apartment. I try calling for her but get no response, even though she's always up by at least six. She's never exactly been a target for Alexander or the scarred man, but still, a missing mother is worrisome. When I stagger out of bed, still sore from my fight with Sal and his gang, I find a note on the table that says: *Went for a walk – Mom*. It's been a long time since she's gone out early for a walk, and it's especially odd since the temperature would have to rise about twenty degrees just to hit arctic chill.

Yesterday, I never mustered the courage to ask my mother about my road trip with Melody. I was thinking that today I would do it, just throw it out there and hope for the best. Melody is waiting to talk to her father about the whole thing, because we're still not sure how we're going to word it so it doesn't sound crazy or like we're running away to do bad things. I've never had to face a pissed-off father before, but if anything is going to make this guy hate me before he even meets me, it's asking to go out-of-state with his little girl on some secret quest.

I sit at the table and wait for my mother for what seems like forever. Finally, she comes through the door, closes it, and rests her back against the wood. Her eyes are bright but far away. Strange. Maybe it's the icy weather? She's wearing a huge white coat and stupid white earmuffs, but otherwise,

83

shows no signs that she's been out in the cold for at least a half hour.

"What's the matter?" I ask.

She doesn't reply right away. Just stands against the door. Then she sort of floats into the kitchen and pulls a box of frozen pancakes out of the freezer. She drops two on a plate, but forgets to heat them in the microwave and just sets the plate down in front of me.

"Mom?"

She snaps back a little. Catches my eye and shrugs.

"What's the matter?" I ask again.

She falls into the chair across from me as I pound on my frozen pancakes to show her what she did.

"Melody's father just asked me to go out for coffee this afternoon," she says.

It takes me at least a minute to process that. A date? With Melody's father? That's not even in the ballpark of what I expected her to tell me, and creepy and disturbing on so many levels, when my mind finally does a follow-through on the information. Dancing with Melody. Admiring Melody's body when she dressed as a sexy pirate. Envisioning Melody as Princess Leia. Holding Melody's hand. Melody confessing her feelings for me. And there's a chance, however slim, that she could someday become my stepsister?

"That's not happening," I say to my mother.

Without waiting to see her expression, I carry my pancakes to the microwave and stick them in. I set the timer on a minute.

"Shaw," my mother says from the table.

"Not happening," I say again.

Leaving my pancakes spinning in the microwave, I stomp to my room and slam my door. I drop down on the bed and ball my fists. And that's when the true reason I don't want Melody's father dating my mother surfaces.

Flashback a few years, to my parents in our old dining room. Nightly, my father would at some point grab my mother around the waist and drop her down on his lap. She would laugh, throw her head back so her hair slapped him in the face, and he would laugh, too. Then I would roll my eyes and excuse myself, but not before witnessing their affection for each other. Kissing. Lots of kissing. They were in love like nobody I've ever seen. And Melody's father — no matter what kind of guy he is — will never slip into the vacant spot left by my dad. Not for me and certainly not for my mother.

My mother knocks on my door just as I fall back on my bed and stare up at the ceiling. I don't reply, but she pushes the door open, steps in, and closes it behind her like somebody else is in the apartment, but nobody is. It's just the two of us. That's how it is now, and that's how it will always be.

"You really don't have a right to tell me what to do with my own life," she says.

"Got it," I reply, still looking upward.

"And for the record, I didn't say yes to Stephen yet." She walks closer, and the bed dips as she sits down. "I told him I'd think about it and call him in a little while."

From the corner of my eye, I see her spin her wedding ring. Spin and spin and spin. Then she stops and looks over at me like I remind her of what she's up against — the memory of my dad.

"It's been a few years," she whispers. "And besides that, if anyone knows how it feels to lose a spouse, it's Melody's father. He's just as interested in taking things slow as I am."

"And did it ever occur to you that I might have feelings for Melody that go beyond brother and sister stuff?"

"Whoa." She puts her hands up. "We're not talking marriage here. We're talking about a possible — *possible* — afternoon of coffee and chatting."

"Good," I tell her and sit up. "Because nobody will ever take Dad's place."

There's something else I don't think she's factoring in. I mean, she nods in agreement, like of course nobody will ever take Dad's place, but it really shouldn't even have gone this far, to where she's considering a date. Because if I go backward in time, to around when my father died, I can honestly say that my mother never grieved him. She cried, but she didn't grieve. What she did in place of that was run and hide with me, over and over, so she wouldn't have to face the grief. I know this because I went along for the ride, and it hit me at one point, while looking at my photo album, that my dad was truly gone. He wasn't going to be back in Connecticut where we left him. He wasn't going to be waiting for us at some rendezvous point. He was murdered — didn't have a heart attack like she told her family, wasn't mauled by a bear like she told the hospital. He was murdered, and he isn't coming back. There's no ghost of him around, not truly. There are empty places where he once laughed or breathed, that's all. And it's probably time my mother realizes that.

When I tell her all of this, she shoots up from my bed.

"You have no idea how I handled your father's death," she says. "I needed to be strong for you, as your mother, so maybe I hid the times I would break down. That's none of your business. All you need to know is that we both lost someone we loved, and now we have to move on from that."

"We've been moving for two years!" I shout. "Moving here and moving there…trying to run away from it, but it's always behind us!" I stand up too, so I'm just in front of her, towering over her. In these moments, when I'm fighting away the burn in my veins, she looks so frail. Easy prey for the stupid teenage boy who can't control his anger. My eyes press closed and I try so hard to keep my dagger from forming.

"Control it," she says.

And that's when the window breaks. No, not breaks. Shatters. Bits and pieces of glass everywhere. I controlled it but only from cutting my mother. The dagger went straight into the window.

"Damn it," she whispers. "This place is rented."

After that, we clean up the glass, not speaking. Cold air

86

pours in through the busted window, until she finally tapes up a bunch of plastic and closes down the blinds. We meet up again in the living room, where I've decided that round two will begin, because now I'm going to ask about my road trip with Melody.

She drops down on the couch, and I notice that her thumb is bleeding. Great. I controlled myself enough to finally spare my mother from my cutting, but she ended up getting cut anyhow on the glass from the window. Guilt rises in my throat again, burning and acidic, until I tear my eyes away from her bloody thumb and just settle onto the couch, beside her.

"I need to know everything," I tell her as my opening. I'd wanted to sound forceful but the thumb thing really bothered me, so my words are meek. "I need to know about the Ritual of the Four, and who the scarred man is, and why he and Alexander are trying to kill me. It's important to me because I want to stay in Rockpoint with Melody, and I can't do that if Alexander will eventually find me here. I want to get him before he gets me. I want to see if I can reverse the stupid Ritual and take it all away. I want this to end."

My mother doesn't get mad. She doesn't go off, even though she has always been the shorter-fused parent. It's weird that my father could cut and kill someone with just the power of his mind, but he was never full of rage, was a genuinely soft guy. My mother on the other hand….

"Okay," she says, surprising me. "You have a right to know and a right to fight."

So I go on to tell her, while I have her calm, about my plan to find the pentacle with Melody. That the owner of the pentacle, Fraser Terra, might have the answers I'm looking for. My mother agrees. She says we can trust Fraser and that he's all that's left of the descendants involved in the original Ritual of the Four. He knew my father. He knows the history and the situation as it stands now. He is our only hope.

"I will think about allowing this," my mother starts, "but

only if you promise me a few things."

I tell her to list her conditions.

"First," she says, "I need you to stay in school until the next long break, which is Thanksgiving. Over that break, I will — *possibly* — drive you and Melody to the train station and tell Fraser to pick you up in Connecticut."

Thanksgiving break is still a few weeks away, and that's wasting precious time, but I have no choice, so I agree. When it comes to school, there is no getting around her issue with me staying in. She's gone through a lot to keep me educated over the last few years, even when it would have been easier to just pull me out of school and travel.

"I will agree to that," I say. "Next?"

"You agree to protect Melody," she says. "She's all her father has left."

That's not a problem either. If there's danger involved, which there might be depending on how far we get, I will protect Melody. I nod to my mother and let her continue.

"And," she says, staring me right in the eyes, "you don't hate me when I call Stephen in five minutes and tell him that I've decided to meet him for coffee this afternoon."

Well, two promises out of three isn't bad.

****

Monday morning at school, I don't exactly get a warm reception when Sal spots me walking down the hallway. I get the impression he waited in the hall purposely, just to see if I was alive and functional, because he probably sent one of his friends back to the field to check on my status and found out my body was missing. You would think the sight of me would be a relief to him, so he wouldn't have to go to jail or something for murdering me, but no. He just pierces me with his cold eyes, stiffens his shoulders, and carries on down the hall. Melody lets out a huff of disbelief, and we head to her locker.

After my mother spent the afternoon laughing it up with Stephen at the coffee place yesterday, my mood was not the best, so I didn't bother calling Melody last night or hanging out with her. She didn't say anything about this on the bus this morning, so I assume she understands that I was pissed off about the whole thing and needed time to myself. It's really not her father I hate, just the idea of him. In my mind, my parents are forever etched as one being. Stephen threatens to shake that image around until it's unrecognizable.

I didn't have to stop at my locker this morning, but as I wait for Melody to get her stuff out of hers, I see Ariana break away from Sal and watch him until he's out of the hallway. Then she heads over to Melody and me. Melody pulls out her history book, and when she spots Ariana coming toward us, she slams the locker door closed so hard that the floor vibrates.

"I might slap her," she says. "Just so you know."

"You're not slapping anybody," I tell her. It's a gamble with Melody. You would think she's all talk, but that's not really the case. She can get fired up, and I would really hate to be the person on the receiving end of the fury.

"Hi," Ariana says, stopping in front of us.

"What do you want?" I ask.

"To apologize," she says. "I really didn't know they were going to hurt you so bad."

"No harm done," I say as my ribs lock up in pain.

"You could have killed Chase," Melody says, pushing herself to full height. She remembered to use my fake name. I'm very proud of her for that. "And it's kind of pathetic that your boyfriend had to trick him just to get him outside," she continues. "Without something to defend himself against a group of guys."

"Maybe it's pathetic that he stabbed a bunch of people without warning," Ariana says back.

"Oh, that's rich," Melody replies. "You guys dragged him outside The Black Crow and ganged up on him."

And then they're off on some back and forth girl spat that it's probably best I stay out of. I just stand here, drumming my fingers against the locker and wondering how far this will go, until finally the fighting stops and Ariana points her finger at Melody.

"We don't talk again," she says. "You and I. We're done."

"That just made my week!" Melody says as Ariana spins around and stomps away.

As soon as Ariana is gone, something strikes me as funny, and I lose it. Granted, it's not a funny situation, but here I am, hysterical. Melody lifts an eyebrow.

"Remind me to never piss you off," I tell her, holding my ribs.

"You pissed me off last night," she says, and I stop laughing. "It's not like I don't know what's going on between my father and your mother."

The warning bell rings, and I think maybe I'll be late to homeroom this morning just so Melody and I can get this over with now.

"I'm against it," I tell her.

"I like your mother," she says and starts walking to her homeroom. "So I'm not really against it. But my mother has been gone a lot longer than your father."

There's really no way to reply without diminishing the pain she feels over her mother. Yeah, her mother died years and years ago, when she was only three, but who am I to say the wound isn't just as deep as mine, the loss just as suffocating.

"Besides," she says, stopping in front of her homeroom. "I finally have something in common with my father now."

"What?" I ask.

She lets out a little sigh. "We're both chasing a Chandler."

By the time I've worked out what she said, she has disappeared into her homeroom, and the final bell rings.

Part II
Clue And Map

Chapter Eleven

Thanksgiving morning, Melody and her father Stephen arrive at my apartment just past eight o'clock. My mother already has a turkey in the oven, so I guess she's spending the holiday, after she drives Melody and me to the train station, with Stephen. Part of me wants to "accidentally" turn off the oven when I walk by, but the part of me that wants my mother to be happy keeps me from doing the evil deed. That and I'm sure Stephen, babysitting our apartment while we're at the train station, will check the turkey and do whatever needs to be done so he and my mother can have a quiet Thanksgiving without the kids. Just the thought of what will go on in my absence makes my stomach do a pretzel knot. Now I know how parents feel when they leave teenagers alone.

The past few weeks, Melody and I passed the time by watching movies and playing games. We have regularly scheduled "geek out" sessions where we talk about computers and comics and *Star Wars*. She's mostly just into computers and video games, but admits she has always liked *Star Wars*. Not so much into comics, but I let that slide, because she's pretty much the perfect girl with all the other matches we have going for us.

Her father, Stephen Tufts, is difficult to dislike, but I still manage to pull it off. He's one of those laid-back, casual guys that probably all women desire because he's single, dedicated to work and family, and I guess charming if my mother's assessment is correct. He's in his late thirties and still has a full head of hair, brown like Melody's, but maybe a shade darker. He has a permanent look of loss in his eyes, the same look my mother has, and sometimes I feel sorry for the guy for losing his wife. Not too much information on Melody's mother yet, how she died, and who she was, but I have a feeling it will come up eventually. Bad stuff always does.

"So it's a bit of a drive to the city," my mother tells Stephen. "I probably won't be back until this afternoon."

"That's fine," Stephen replies and smiles at her. "I already have my morning here planned out. Watch the parade, then flip to the sports channel for updates on the game."

My mother is nervous about the whole trip but hides it well. Stephen thinks this weekend trip is just Melody and me going to visit my Uncle Fraser in Connecticut, who is alone for Thanksgiving. Stephen probably only agreed to it because my mother offered up the turkey dinner and who knows what else. I shake away the thought and actually shiver in revulsion.

"Bye, Dad," Melody says and hugs him around the waist.

Here's where I see a bit of hesitation. Stephen probably hasn't let her go too far from him, and I can tell by the way he presses his hand to her back that he's having second thoughts. I know how it is with an overprotective parent who calls all the shots—one who has already lost part of the family. He closes his eyes like he's praying for her safety, and that makes me guilty because I'm actually taking Melody into a situation that is probably not safe. Still, I know I'll protect her. If my mother is right and I'm more powerful than Alexander, even if we meet up with him somehow, I might have the upper hand. I feel much more in control than I did at my last meeting with Alexander.

"Have a fun time," Melody's father says, letting go of her. He turns to me. "Be safe, Chase." Translation: *Guard my daughter with your life.*

"We will," I say. I almost add *Be safe with my mom,*" but thank God I catch myself on that one.

"And we're off," my mother says.

There is no direct train from Rockpoint to Connecticut. We're taking something called the Metro North, a train that runs out of New York City into Connecticut. Once we're on there, we're supposed to get off in a town called Stratford, where Fraser will be waiting to pick us up and bring us back to his house. Honestly, I'm kind of excited to meet this guy. From what my mother says, he knows a lot about the Ritual of the Four and my dagger—two things that will always remind me of my dad.

Melody and I spend the car ride—you guessed it—playing games on her phone. Passing the thing back and forth. This is probably a bad idea, because who knows what we'll do on the train now that we're getting bored of trying to beat each other's high scores. Maybe we can pass the time by watching the scenery blow by. Melody has mentioned a few times how pumped up she is that we're going on the Hogwarts Express. I haven't had the heart to tell her the train actually looks nothing like the Hogwarts Express. I saw it online, and it's kind of a glorified bus.

Soon, the New York City skyline appears on the horizon. Melody stops playing on her phone and takes in the skyscrapers in the distance. It's a gray Thanksgiving morning, so the buildings blend right into the clouds. My mother gets off the highway a little too soon. I'm just about to ask her if she's stopping for gas when she pulls into a McDonald's parking lot and parks the car in the back.

"Snacks?" I ask her.

She turns around and shakes her head. "I have something to give you two."

Melody and I lock eyes, expressing our confusion to each other, while my mother digs through the duffel bag she packed for me. I'm surprised when she pulls out two wrapped packages. Both are in red Christmas paper and tied

95

up with white ribbon.

"They're disguised," my mother says. "Obviously, they're not presents. You just need to keep them hidden in your bag until you're safe with Fraser."

"What are they?" Melody asks.

My mother hands one of the boxes, the smaller, longer one, to me.

"Inside is something you're already very familiar with," she tells me. "It's your gold dagger, number one in the Ritual of the Four. The dagger that belonged to your father and your grandfather and the rest of your ancestors."

I hold the package on my lap. It's comforting to have my dagger with me for this journey, even if I've only ever used it by imagining the blade. My real curiosity is what she's giving Melody.

"And to Melody," my mother says, handing her the bigger, square box. "I hereby bequeath to you, on behalf of the deceased Marrin family, the gold goblet. Number two in the Ritual of the Four."

Melody takes the box and locks her hands around it. She holds on like the contents are fragile as thin glass. Then she narrows her eyes and looks across at my mother.

"I'm not in that family line," Melody says. "So I assume the goblet is just a symbolic gift? A way for me to be a part of it all?"

"Not necessarily," my mother responds. "You're not in the Marrin family line — they are all deceased — but the goblet is still very old and carries its own power when activated properly. Fraser will explain everything." She reaches back and touches Melody's shoulder. "When I met Shaw's father, I knew what I was getting into and knew it would be dangerous to carry on with the relationship. I had knowledge of the dagger and knew that someday, the ability might be challenged by other people in his family or even outside the family. But one thing I didn't have was a way to get involved, a way to become a part of what he was and what he did. The goblet came to us later, and...well, now I feel it's best that it belongs to you."

I've seen Melody cry before, but I've never seen her so overwhelmed. She reaches out to my mother, and they share a clumsy front seat to backseat hug. This goes on for a while, so I just smile and hold onto my boxed dagger, letting them have this moment. My mother must really trust Melody if she's handing over something that's been in our family awhile, something so old and powerful. But I do see where she's coming from. Melody belonged to that goblet from the moment she held it in her hands and inspected it for the first time. The goblet almost seems a part of her already, just as the dagger is a part of me.

A half hour later, Melody and I are on the Metro North, sitting on cushiony seats, speeding toward Connecticut. Holiday travelers surround us, though most people seem like they are only heading to Connecticut for the day, maybe to share Thanksgiving dinner and then head back home to New York. Melody is quiet. She hasn't taken out her phone; she's just staring out the window. It's really not safe to talk about what happened with my mother. Not here. We have to wait until we're at Fraser's for that, so for now I just open up a comic book and sit back and relax as the train rumbles toward our destination.

Spiderman doesn't hold my attention. Something keeps nagging at me, and it's not until Melody shifts beside me that I realize what's causing the disturbance. If Melody has the goblet, that must mean my mother assumes Melody will be in my life for a long time. The speech she gave Melody suggested that Melody is to me what my mother was to my father—a romantic interest. I haven't let myself push through that wall yet. I can't. Not until everything is settled. Fixed to my liking. Safe and sound. Whenever I think about Melody and how much I like her, I change gears and control the thought, and that pretty much takes the same amount of effort and concentration it takes to control my dagger. It's nearly impossible.

The flip side explanation is that my mother might be so interested in Stephen that she assumes they'll end up married, and Melody will become part of our family. Either way, it's a safe bet that I'll have Melody in my life for a while. Maybe forever.

I reach over and grasp Melody's hand. We do this a lot, but today it means something different. It means it's possible, if things go right, that maybe I'll be able to care about her in a different way than I care about her now. It would hurt her too much if I told her that, so I just squeeze her hand, keeping the thought tucked inside.

"Nervous?" she whispers.

"About meeting Fraser?" I ask. "A little." I put my Spiderman comic facedown on my lap and stare over Melody, out the window. "We just went by Bridgeport, so I think it'll be any minute now."

"Good," she says, kind of distant. "I have a lot to talk to you about once we're there. I assume we'll have some time alone?"

"Possibly," I reply. "I'm not sure what the sleeping arrangements will be, but I guess we could hang out after the guy goes to sleep."

The train speeds along, and then slows at the Stratford station. We gather our belongings and make our way out the door of the Metro North into a gray Connecticut Thanksgiving midday.

Chapter Twelve

My mother didn't really describe Fraser in any great detail, but I assume he knows what I look like and that I'll be exiting the train with a teenage girl. For a few minutes, Melody and I just stand outside the station, holding our bags, glancing around at the people and the parking lot. It's not until Melody grabs hold of my arm that I notice the figure heading toward us. I assume the figure is Fraser and that Melody grabbed hold of my arm because his appearance is frightening as deep, dark hell.

He's wearing a black hooded cape. Through the grayness of the day, it's like watching the Grim Reaper appear on the screen of an old movie. I can't see a face, so I'm thinking he's just as protective of his hidden identity as I am. Only...it seems to me it's a bit more obvious showing up in public dressed as the Grim Reaper. I mean, in regular clothes you blend in, but what he's got going on would be more appropriate for Halloween. It's not a getup you usually see on Thanksgiving. People in the parking lot are looking over in our direction with expressions of mixed interest and fright.

"Chase Chandler?" he says. His voice is gruff and throaty.

"That's me," I say back.

Without lifting his hood, he gestures for us to follow him. Melody squeezes my arm to the point where I have to shake her off a little for fear of losing circulation to my fingers. We continue to the parking lot, following behind Fraser's thick dragging cape, until we end up beside an old beige clunker.

"You should confirm who I am," Fraser says, still not revealing his face.

Oh. He's got a point.

"And you are?" I ask.

"Fraser Terra," he whispers back. His head moves back and forth, as though searching the area from under his hood. "I will tell you something only your mother and you know. Is that fair?"

It occurs to me that Alexander, if I'd been played here, would know things about my family just as this strange hooded man would. Maybe Alexander would know even more. But I nod my head for him to continue.

"The girl was given the goblet," Fraser says. "Just this morning."

Yes, that piece of information was gold. And I automatically trust him. Nobody knows what just happened in the car with my mother. Nobody but my mother, Melody, and me.

"That's right," Melody squeaks out.

"Then we have a match," Fraser returns. "Get in."

Melody and I slide into the backseat of the car, while Fraser instructs us to duck down until we're away from the parking lot. From this position, I can't see if he's removed his hood or even if his audience in the parking lot has receded. I can't buckle my seatbelt, and I can't find a comfortable position. I'm just crammed against my duffel bag, watching across as Melody stares at me like she's both pissed and amused that we're in this situation.

After a few rough turns and abrupt stops, the car gains speed. Fraser tells us we can get up, and when I lift my head, I see that we're on the highway and that the Grim Reaper is still wearing his hood. Melody clicks in her seatbelt and taps her fingers against her knee. I get her point. We should all be talking here, getting acquainted.

"So where do you live?" I ask Fraser to get some conversation going.

"Classified," he returns.

That's an odd response, seeing as we're going to his house.

"Let's just say we're going to my summer home," he continues. "I have some things there to show you, and later we'll eat dinner before I take you back to your hotel."

Melody and I glance at each other. Nobody said anything about a hotel. I just assumed we were staying with Fraser the whole time. My mother gave me money for an emergency, but not enough to pay for an expensive hotel room.

"So we're not staying with you?" Melody asks.

Fraser slides the car into the fast lane. "Shaw's mother thought it best that the two of you were split from me as much as possible. That way, if someone finds us, they only kill one or two of us instead of all three. We're in possession of items and gifts that are the last in a line, so we have to be extremely careful when we get together. Or not get together at all, as it's been."

He goes on to explain that he paid in advance for Melody and I to share a hotel room in a town a few away from whatever town his "summer home" is in. Staying in a hotel will be much more comfortable than staying in some strange guy's house, but it also means I'll be sleeping in the same location as Melody, unsupervised. I often wonder what my mother's real plans are when she sets this stuff up.

When we finally arrive at Fraser's street, we're instructed to put our heads down again. Melody takes a few minutes before she actually does this, so long, that the car slows before she even ducks down. I'm not sure if Fraser knows she isn't following his directions or if he's just too busy keeping an eye out for trouble. I know how that can be. Every time I come home from school, or from anyplace, really, I check to make sure my surroundings are secure.

Even though we're going to the hotel later, Fraser still

tells us to take our luggage out of the car and carry it into his house. Or, now that I'm walking toward the place, I guess I wouldn't call it a house. More like an oversized shed. Maybe a small cottage.

The cottage is earthy brown with tan shutters. It's set back off the road, nestled in the woods. The driveway is just a long runway of reddish dirt that twists and turns toward the main road in the distance. There's not much back here as far as scenery, just the gray of an overcast day and the whisper of a November breeze through the trees. But the surroundings are thickly wooded, and unless you knew the place was here, it would be impossible to find.

There are empty miniature flowerpots below the windows, which would make the place look sort of homey if the pots were actually filled. The long railing that leads to the front steps is all intertwined wood, like tree branches in a wrestling match. I'm guessing that even if my mother didn't suggest our splitting up, Melody and I still wouldn't have found room to sleep here. I'd be amazed if the place even had a bedroom.

"I'll be making tacos for dinner," Fraser says, holding the front door open for Melody.

"Interesting choice for Thanksgiving dinner," I say.

Fraser lets out a gruff laugh. "They're turkey tacos," he replies.

Inside, the place is a little larger than I imagined, and the scent isn't quite what I anticipated. I thought maybe floral or woody, but it actually smells like mold and old books. There's no bedroom in sight, just a kitchen with a few appliances and a little oak table. Just ahead is a closed wood door that I assume is the bathroom. I think what we're standing in right now, as small as it is, must be the living room. I guess that's why the place smells like old books. The majority of space in the living room is filled with bookcases.

"Have a seat," Fraser says, indicating the two wooden rocking chairs toward the back of the room.

As we settle in, Fraser locks the front door. He makes the rounds, securing windows and peeking outside. Then he turns to us, stands tall in the middle of the room, and lifts his hands to remove his hood.

It's kind of weird. The guy looks just as I imagined him — maybe from his voice or his actions or just my own intuition. He's old, at least in his seventies, with deep lines and crisscrosses of wrinkles beneath his eyes and over his forehead. His hair is white and wavy, just a touch longer in the back. He has a thick, white mustache that blends into a long, scruffy goatee.

"Let's see what you can do," he says to me. "Now that we're finally together, I'm sure we'd both like to see each other in action."

Melody turns to me and raises her eyebrows. She's been on my case for a while now to practice using my dagger for purposes other than just slicing up people when I'm angry or shooting the thing at glass.

"I assume you mean my ability," I say. "But I can only do it when I'm mad."

"That's very untrue," Fraser says. "But if that's where you are right now, then that's where you are."

Melody gives me a look like she's disappointed. Only my mother and Melody have the power to melt my entire being with guilt from their disappointment in me. It's not my fault, though. It's always been the same way. I can only extend the dagger from my mind when I'm in a rage.

"Let's see what *you* can do," I say to Fraser.

Fraser gives me a sideways smile. He takes two swift strides toward Melody, then lifts her right off the rocking chair. While she screams in shock and possibly pain, the old dude hoists her over his head like she's no heavier than a scrap of paper.

"Impressive," I say over Melody's shrieks and complaints.

Fraser sits Melody back down, apologizes, and then

settles himself into a green armchair by one of the bookcases. He lets out a long breath like what he just did took some effort.

"You have it much stronger than your father had it," he says to me. "That's why you have a difficult time controlling it. That's what your mother tells me, and what I've gathered from all the information I've been given."

"I want to get rid of it." I want to get this right out there, before he gets any impression that I love having the ability, or I want to learn to use it the right way, or a *different* way. "The reason we're here—well, one of the reasons we're here—is to find out how to change all this so I don't have this in my bloodline anymore."

"I see," Fraser tells me. "So you really want to know about the Ritual of the Four—how it started and how it can possibly end."

I sit back in the rocking chair and nod, slowly tilting the chair back and forth.

"Well," Fraser says. "I guess it's probably best to start at the beginning." He clears his throat as though gearing up for a long tale. "Centuries ago, four magical items were forged of gold, metal, gems, wood, and crystal. These four magical items—the dagger, the goblet, the wand, and the pentacle— were extremely powerful, extremely valuable, and extremely secretive. Our ancestors were in what we would today call a secret society or perhaps a coven. In those times, similar to today, anything thought of as pagan or magical went against the Catholic Church, and anyone involved would be outcast or even met with death."

"But they went against all that," Melody says. "And they did a ritual with these four items?"

"Exactly," Fraser says. "And I'm sure you know by now that each item holds the power of the element it represents."

"That's where I sometimes get confused," Melody says. "Because I get that the dagger is used for cutting and wounding, but the dagger, during the Ritual, was obviously used as a symbol for elemental fire. So how would the power of the dagger translate to the power of fire?"

Fraser gives her a grin of approval. "How indeed?" he replies. He turns to me. "Let's talk about the anger issues in conjunction with your dagger. You say you can only use it when you're vengeful, mad, upset, or passionate. Is that correct?"

He's sort of right. I never said any of those things except for "mad," but I guess the other words are accurate. Maybe not passionate, though. I don't recall a singular moment in my life when I've felt passionate about something, so I guess I wouldn't know about that one. I nod to him anyhow.

"So we have two things to play around with here." He joins his hands, steeples them to his chin. "One of them is controlling the dagger. Making it listen to you, instead of you listening to *it*. This will take great concentration. The other thing I'd like you to explore is taking the ability a step further. Finding the latent ability." He arches a brow. "Playing with fire."

I don't reply. I think I might have an idea of what he's getting at here. The ability is greater than I thought it was. It goes further than just cutting things. And that makes me all the more pissed off.

"So you're saying that Shaw has the ability to raise fire," Melody says. "I kind of suspected that."

"His abilities are unique to him, and he has to learn about them on his own," Fraser returns. "But, in short, yes. The power of the dagger is associated with the power of fire. His father had it too, but again, not as strongly as Shaw has it, I suspect."

"I can only use the dagger for cutting," I say. "Nothing else."

He shakes his head. "Remember, Shaw, that the power of the dagger lies not only in the visual, but also the symbolic."

"Excuse me," I say and stand.

I'm not really sure where I'm going, but I have to get

away from this, and I need to do it fast. The front door looks like an inviting escape, but then I remember I'm not supposed to be outside of the cottage. Danger at every turn out there, according to Fraser. The only other door is to the bathroom, so I turn and head that way. When I'm in there, I shut the door behind me, not looking back at Melody or Fraser. I need some time to absorb this.

I lean my back against the door. In front of me, the tiny bathroom assaults me with lemon yellow walls and ugly bronze fixtures. Stuff swims around in front of my eyes, the old sink and the rusty yellow tub. I'm not sure what I expected from my trip to Fraser's, but it sure as hell wasn't this. I'm supposed to learn how to lose this ability, not how to gain another one. And why didn't my mother tell me any of this? Why doesn't she tell me *anything*?

After a while, there's a faint knock on the bathroom door. Melody whispers my name, and I pull open the door to let her in.

"Why do you always insist on pouting over things that make you so special?" she says, closing the door.

"Not what I came here for," I return. "I came here to get rid of all this. Make it go away."

"Maybe your mother had a different plan," Melody says. "Because it sure looks like she wants you to keep your gift."

I'm not sure what she means. Maybe Melody understands something about my mother that I don't. Maybe because they're both girls, or because I'm too close to the situation to read everything the way I'm intended to read it. Whatever. What it really comes down to is I went through all this so Alexander and the scarred man would leave me alone. So I could be a normal human being. So I wouldn't have to fight for my life every month. So I wouldn't have to keep moving around. So I could stay in Rockpoint. So I could be with Melody.

"Come on," she says and grabs my hand. "Let's hear the rest of what Fraser has to say."

When we go back out to the living room, Fraser is still in the green armchair. I try to express my apology in silence, just shoot him a look that says, *"I'm pissed, but that's not your fault,"* and then sit back down in the rocking chair.

"Your mother warned me that might be your reaction," he says and waves the whole thing off. "I just wanted you to have all the facts before you decided to reverse the Ritual."

"So that can be done?" I ask. "I can reverse the Ritual?"

"I use the term 'reverse' loosely," he replies. "Or really, for lack of any other term. What you *can* do is a different or new ritual. But you would need a few things in order to do that." He lets out a sigh. Not a good sign. "You already have two of those things," he continues. "The dagger and of course the goblet that was given to the girl just today. If you were to obtain the other items, I would of course consider loaning you my pentacle. I have little use for great strength nowadays."

Melody lists off the four items in the Ritual of the Four, then she closes her eyes in despair. "By that math, we would need the wand," she says. "And that would be impossible to get."

"You would need all four items in the original Ritual of the Four to perform another related ritual," he confirms. "You would need the dagger, the goblet, the wand, and the pentacle. Those represent the four elements, and admittedly, the wand would be difficult to obtain. But if the waves moved smoothly for the two of you, and the universe opened its lucky doors, I have no doubt you could obtain the wand from Alexander. That is actually not my primary concern with Shaw's plan to perform another ritual."

That's the primary concern for me. I really should have realized this. In order to reverse the Ritual, I'll need all the stupid gold and gem items, and Alexander is not just going to hand his wand over to me. Plus, I don't know where he is, and I don't want him knowing where *I* am. It's an impossible feat.

"What's your primary concern?" Melody asks Fraser.

"The fifth piece," Fraser says. "Of course you'll need the power of fire, water, air, and earth, but you'll also need the power of spirit. The human element. The Ritual of the Four, when it was performed centuries ago, used the four elemental items but also the supreme power of a human being. And human beings, in rituals, add their power to the mix by using something very specific — an incantation." He sits back and crosses his arms. "And in order to change or renew the Ritual of the Four, or 'reverse' it as you call it, you would need the original wording of the original incantation."

"And that's from centuries ago," Melody says and sighs.

"And that's from centuries ago," Fraser echoes.

So, that's it. I'm stuck with this ability, and now I have *another* ability, too, and there's no way to take it all back. My father was killed for the ability, my life is in danger because of it, and someday, if I have a kid, *his* life will always be in danger. Not to mention the constant guilt I battle when I cut someone I love, or when I bust up a window, or I slice up a group of kids.

Balling my fists, I start to get up again. This time, I'm going outside. I'm going to scream to the world that my name is Shaw Huntley, not Chase Chandler or Johnny Ray or Lee Greznick. If Alexander wants to find me, I wish he would so I can just get this over with. I'm sick of running. If I'm marked for death, so be it. There's no way out of it now.

"May I ask you to sit down?" Fraser says to me.

I'm kind of hovering over the rocking chair, but his tone startles me enough to sit down again. Before his tone was despaired, now it's something else. Stern, but hopeful.

"As I was saying," Fraser goes on, "you would need the original wording of the original incantation from the Ritual of the Four. That particular incantation was buried with the high priest who performed the Ritual of the Four. His burial location is secret, but his descendants did leave something of a map to the burial location, should any successors of the original Ritual of the Four need to use it in an emergency situation."

I lean forward in the rocking chair, nearly falling over. The incantation I need is out there somewhere.

"So how do we find the map to the burial location?" Melody asks.

"You would need to decode a clue to find the map," Fraser replies. "As I said, this was only to be done in an emergency situation, a situation where you would have to really, *really* want or need the incantation. The descendants of the high priest did not make it easy." With a crack of bones, he gets himself to a standing position. "Let me make us some turkey tacos," he says. "And while we eat, I'll show you the clue."

Chapter Thirteen

While Fraser makes the turkey tacos, Melody and I huddle in a corner in the living room, discussing what just happened. There's not much privacy in the little cottage, but we keep our voices low as Fraser bangs around pots and pans. Melody's eyes are ablaze from hearing we have to decode some kind of clue. She lives for this kind of thing. It's the supreme game, the real-life equivalent of one of her search and find apps.

"Whatever it is, we can figure it out," she whispers.

"But you forget that we still need the wand," I whisper back. "So you're talking about stealing the wand from Alexander, plus using clues and maps to find some burial place from like, over a hundred years ago."

"We can do it," she says. "We just need a plan. And we have all night together to figure one out."

Oh yeah. I almost forgot that I'm spending the night with Melody in a hotel room. Just the thought makes my hands sticky. I try to push away every steamy thought I've ever had about her, like when I imagined her as Princess Leia or on Halloween when she dressed as a sexy pirate. But just when I get the thoughts safely tucked away, new ones take their place. What does Melody wear to bed? What do her sleeping breaths sound like? I close my eyes and think about her hair down and all over a pillow. How she might smell in the morning....

"Shaw?" she says and waves her hand in front of my face.

"With you," I say.

She goes on to make some guesses about what kind of clues were left behind. She suspects the year of burial was around the 1800s. Maybe the original coven involved in the Ritual of the Four were European immigrants. From Ireland, maybe. Someplace where magic was primarily a clandestine endeavor but nonetheless powerful. She suggests we're dealing with intelligent, knowledgeable magic men and magic women—pagans or the descendants of great warriors or wizards. Yeah, Melody can get carried away sometimes. But this time, I actually believe most of what she's guessing.

The scent of spicy Mexican food floods my nostrils, and Fraser calls us in for Thanksgiving dinner. The little oak table is set in the kitchen with three plain white plates and three folded-up paper towels. We tuck in, and I realize how ravenous I am, like a starved bear. Without minding my manners, I pull the bowl of meat toward my plate and start shoveling spoonfuls of shredded, spiced turkey into a taco shell.

"He eats a lot," Melody says, laughing at me.

"I'm noticing that," Fraser responds.

"Melody plays games on her phone a lot," I say. "If we're getting into bad habits here."

"Oh, so we're telling our faults now?" she returns. "Because I've got a long list going for yours." We both laugh as I pull over a bowl of grated yellow cheese.

Fraser looks at Melody. Then he turns to me, back to her, and this goes on in some kind of silent assessment. "Anyhow," he says finally, not making up his plate, "I wanted to make you aware of the power associated with the wand, should you attain it."

Melody spoons some lettuce into her taco shell. "The wand would be associated with the element *air*," she says. "So if I had to guess, I would say the owner of the wand would have the power of wind and flight."

Fraser nods in confirmation. "But remember that even though Alexander has the wand, he is not a direct descendent of the original wand owner. He has no power for flight. That power belonged to the Solan family. The descendants in that family line have unfortunately passed on, so unless the Ritual of the Four is renewed, the power of the wand is just about as useless as the power of the goblet."

Melody stops spooning toppings into her taco. She makes a little noise, kind of like a hurt squeal, but covers it up nicely with a fake cough.

Then the thought occurs to me, and I feel like such a selfish ass for not having it sooner. I should have asked right from the beginning what kind of power Melody would have if she were the true holder of the goblet and in the bloodline. I was too focused on myself to remember that Melody was given something special, and my mother said Fraser could give us more information about the specific power.

"Would you like to know the ability associated with the goblet?" Fraser asks Melody.

"I'm sorry," I say to her. "I've been so wrapped up in getting rid of what I have, I didn't think to ask what you might have had."

I can tell she's hurt, because she does that shrug-and-turn-away thing that girls do. But then something else occurs to me, something Melody said in the bathroom about my mother wanting me to keep my ability, even making some kind of plan to swing me in that direction. My mother gave Melody the goblet so I would have to make a choice—renew the Ritual of the Four, naming Melody as the new bloodline for the power of the goblet, or take the power away from both of us by reversing the Ritual entirely. My mother stuck Melody in the same hotel room as me for one reason—to make us fall in love, give us time alone to do that. Because once you're in love, you'll do anything for the other person.

"I have to admit I'm stumped," Melody says to Fraser. "I know the goblet represents the element water, but how would that translate into a unique power?"

"Very simple," Fraser replies. He breaks a taco shell in half and starts spooning turkey on top of each piece. "Water translates to emotions. Have you ever heard of an empath?"

Melody shakes her head. The word sounds vaguely familiar to me. Maybe my mother used the term once.

"Empaths have the ability to sense emotions in other people," Fraser says. "You can call it extreme sensitivity and intuition, dancing the line of psychic ability. Even when people hide their feelings, an empath knows what's going on deep down. The power of the goblet might just be the most powerful of all the items involved in the Ritual of the Four."

"Wow," Melody whispers.

I concur.

"And of course, like the dagger and elemental fire, you'd have the latent ability of elemental water," Fraser continues. He dumps healthy mounds of sour cream onto his taco halves. "It would be up to you to find that ability and use it in your own unique way."

When Melody turns to me, the desire in her eyes is unmistakable. I'd known she would want the power of the goblet before I even knew what that power was. My mother knew she would want it, too. That's what this entire trip was all about.

Fraser goes on to tell us about the power associated with the pentacle. He has great strength, like he already demonstrated to us, but he also has a direct link to the power of the earth. His latent ability is gathering strength from plants and trees and forming strong bonds with animals. His greatest sadness is that he doesn't have a pet. He didn't feel it would be fair to an animal to drag it around while he bounced from hiding place to hiding place, so while he feeds wildlife and as many stray animals as he can, he doesn't have one as a companion.

After dinner, Melody excuses herself to freshen up in the bathroom. She carries her plate over to the sink, then disappears through the bathroom door.

"The clue to the map?" I ask Fraser.

"Dinner conversation got the better of us," he says. "It seems it has been a while since I've had people to talk to." He takes my empty plate and puts it on top of his. "I'll show it to the two of you after I clean up, and then I'll take you over to your hotel room."

"Sounds like a plan," I reply. "I know Melody can't wait to see the clue."

"Smart girl, she is," he says. "A bit of a firecracker. A lot like your mother, actually."

"Gross," I return. I've already had to think of Melody as my sister.

Fraser rolls his knuckles against the table. "I booked the one hotel room on your mother's advice and because she assured me you two were just good friends," he says in a low voice. "And also, quite frankly, because I'm cheap."

I kind of laugh. I'm not sure what he's trying to say, if he's making a joke or not.

"The girl is in love with you," he says in a lower voice still. "You're aware of that?"

"It's complicated," I reply. "I've done some mean things to her."

We don't have much time to discuss this because I'm sure Melody won't be long in the bathroom. It sucks, because since I've been an older teenager, I haven't had a male presence in my life, and I've had a lot of questions about the opposite sex. Girls are confusing as hell. Yeah, I talk to my mother, but she's a girl, and I always feel like she's on their side, not mine. I know to treat girls with respect, but somehow I end up doing something piggish. Like when Melody wore the pirate costume. I'm sure Melody thinks I only dropped my jaw on the floor that night because she was showing so much skin. And plus, there was the whole Ariana thing. Melody and I have never really gotten into what happened at The Black Crow that night. Melody watched me sexy-dance with

Ariana. And Melody may have already been in love with me at that point.

"It doesn't matter if you've done some questionable things to her," Fraser says. "She's in that painful kind of love that only teenage girls can be in. And that, my friend, is pretty powerful stuff."

"Noted," I reply. I'm about to tell him that one of the reasons I want to end the Ritual of the Four is because of Melody and my desire to be with her. Like really, really be with her. But Melody comes out of the bathroom and starts cleaning up dinner, so maybe tomorrow I'll find a few minutes alone with Fraser. He seems to have my relationship with Melody all figured out, and the guy did it in about two minutes, while I still haven't figured it all out yet.

After dinner cleanup, we all go back to the living room and sit. Fraser goes on for a while with pointless conversation, things like trains and television and something about warm pajamas, but I let it slide because I know he doesn't have many people to talk to. He's on the run and doesn't have the luxury of running with another person to keep him company. Not even a pet, and the guy so desperately wants one. Maybe that's why he's so interested in helping me reverse the Ritual. He's probably tired of running, just as I am.

Finally, he turns serious and starts talking about my dagger. He wants to see it, so I carefully remove it from the box my mother wrapped it in and show it to him. Melody shows him her goblet. He finally starts referring to Melody as "Melody" instead of "the girl." I think maybe he's not sure how to address her. I can't imagine it's easy for an old guy to talk to a teenage girl. *I* have a difficult time talking to teenage girls.

"The pentacle," Melody says. "You have it here with you?"

"Of course," he says. "It never leaves my side."

He stands up and walks to one of the bookcases, then

pulls a book out from the bottom. It's a chunky, red book, as big as a dictionary, with a hard cover but no title. He opens it, exposing a deep, book-sized secret hiding place. The pentacle sparkles from inside.

"The power and connection are from the wood beneath," he says. "The gold and gems are actually over the wood, just like the dagger is primarily constructed of a stronger metal beneath the gold plating." He hands me the gold-plated pentacle.

I examine the pentacle—a star with a circle around it—five-pointed and heavy. I find the number *IV* beneath a ruby in the dead center, inside an inverted triangle, just above an etched straight line. I recognize the inverted triangle and straight line as the elemental symbol for earth. Melody showed me these symbols online.

"The dagger and goblet are gold, metal, and gemstones," Fraser says. "But the pentacle and wand, numbers three and four in the Ritual, are different. The pentacle, as I said, is wood with gold and gems; and the wand, I believe, is made of crystal quartz. It's supposed to be very stunning. A band of gold twists around the base in a snaky ring, and the diamond in the center is supposedly blue. The wand is probably worth millions."

"Wow," Melody says. "I would love to see that."

"Few people have," Fraser replies.

I hand the pentacle over to Melody for her examination. Of all the items in the Ritual of the Four, the pentacle is the least impressive. It looks like anything you could buy in an occult shop, like the pendant of a clunky gold necklace, maybe. My dagger is much more impressive, and the wand sounds incredible.

"I have the clue here with me," Fraser says. "Please keep in mind that Alexander and Lomidus would kill for this clue."

"Lomidus?" I say. "Is that the scarred man?"

"Yes, very scarred, I'd say," Fraser replies. "He's

practiced slicing too much. Even practiced on himself in a mirror."

That's kind of sick. Pretty disgusting. The guy wanted the power so much he practiced using it on himself?

"I have much to tell you about Lomidus and his family, but we'll save that for tomorrow," Fraser says. He takes the pentacle from Melody, places it back into the book, and secures it in the bookcase. "I'll be right back," he says.

Melody can barely contain her excitement. Her foot taps against the floor. She squirms in the rocking chair. Maybe the clue will be easy. Hopefully, it will be easy. But I'm guessing it's still going to give her gamer's mind a workout.

Fraser dons his Grim Reaper cape, then slithers out the front door.

"He hid it outside," I say. "Smart."

"Very," Melody says back.

We sit for a few minutes, until finally, Fraser steps back inside, bringing a gust of frosty wind with him. He shuts and locks the door, then sits down in the armchair. He pulls down the hood of his cape and stares at the cylindrical item in his hand.

"I buried it in the herb garden out back," he says. "Wherever I happen to stay, I split up the pentacle and the clue. The pentacle stays by my side, and the clue gets a resting place in a backyard for the duration of my stay. I was given the clue directly from the dying hands of Tomas Rane, one of the last living descendants of the high priest Abraham Rane."

Melody's hands shake as Fraser hands her the cylindrical tube. The tube is black and looks like a thermos you'd carry lunch in for school. If someone were to accidentally dig the tube up, it really shows no signs of being anything extraordinary or holding some valuable clue to a map. It just looks like someone's old lunch thermos or maybe a time capsule. Melody holds the tube for a second, takes a breath, and unscrews the top.

She pulls out a slip of yellowing paper. The paper is about the size of a credit card, and something is written on it, but I can't see what it is. Melody inspects it, and to my surprise, she frowns. It's not going to be an easy one. She's already stumped.

"Not to discourage you," Fraser starts, "but I could never figure it out."

"Cryptogram?" she asks. "Some kind of shifted alphabet code?"

"Maybe," Fraser returns. "It would have to be something difficult enough to pose a challenge, but not indecipherable."

She hands me the slip of paper. On it, written in brownish, bold lettering, are the letters:

FCU XRKV TVDVKVIP WRZITYVJKVI, DRJJ.

There's a circle near the top of the paper, and above that, it says, *North, E.*

"That must be a direction," I say. "Like a compass point. Northeast."

"We're in the Northeast," Melody says. "So that's kind of pointless information."

Fraser shakes his head. "Nothing is pointless," he says. "Plus, they would have wanted to make this information available to descendants who may have migrated away from New England. If you happened to be living in Texas, for instance, knowing the map to the burial site was in the Northeast would help you immensely."

I study the paper for a few minutes, but I get nothing. Melody is probably right that it's some kind of shifted alphabet code, and Fraser is probably right in saying that it must be decipherable, it's just a matter of sitting down and figuring it out. That's not my strong point, but that's mostly out of laziness. If I have a true and urgent need to figure something out, I'll give it my all. Luckily, in my case, I have somebody beside me who can, once she sits down and puts her gamer brain on, figure this out like it's just some fun game on the back of a cereal box.

Melody takes the paper from me, sits back in the rocking chair, and gets to it. She scratches her head, rocks and rocks, then pauses and sits forward.

"A lot of *Vs*," she says. "I'm going to say, if this were a cryptogram, that the *V* would be a stand-in for the letter *E* or maybe *R* or *S* or *L*. Those are common letters." She studies it some more. "And since the *V* is the second letter in the third word, I'm going with an *E* or an *R*. Probably rule out an *S*."

She goes on about this, thinking out loud, while Fraser listens. I lose my concentration and stare out the back window. The days are getting shorter, and it's already shifted to full dark outside. The cottage is not well insulated, and the chill that seeps in from under the door and around the windows is strong and unpleasant. Thank God we don't have to sleep here tonight.

After a while, Melody sighs and just sits with the clue in her lap. She rubs her forehead with the ball of her palm. Great. She's out of brainpower.

"How many years have you been trying to figure this out?" she asks Fraser.

"Off and on since I obtained it, probably fifteen years ago," he replies. "But please keep in mind that I never truly needed the information. Anytime I sat and pondered the clue, it was mostly out of fun or boredom."

Melody nods and closes her eyes to recharge. Then she does something that's typical Melody. She fires up an app and jumps right into a game. I would question this, but I think I know what she's doing—giving her mind a break from figuring out the clue. Letting it digest what she has put into it so she's ready for another go later on. Gaming is her outlet. It's how she rests and relaxes, how she keeps her mind away from things that are bothering her or she just doesn't want to face or she has to push away for now.

While she's doing that, I talk with Fraser about where he actually lives. No place. He's a nowhere man, just like me. He moves around from place to place and just happened upon this cottage in one of his travels years ago. I guess the true owners spend most of their time in Florida, so the place just sits here. Fraser says he likes Vermont the best, and in the warmer months he camps out in the mountains there and lives off the land. He has no problem with that and says it's how humans originally lived, although now that he's getting older, it does wear him down. He has some money in a bank account, so he's able to purchase extra things he might need, like the turkey tacos for dinner, for instance. He again tells me that he wants a pet. A dog, mostly. I make a mental note to pick one up for him at an animal shelter after I reverse the Ritual and we don't have to worry about Alexander and Lomidus anymore.

Around eight o'clock, we've all settled into our own thing. Fraser is reading, Melody is working on the clue, and I'm playing this wicked cool *Star Wars* game on her phone. Fraser shuts his book and yawns. He announces that it's time to drive us over to the hotel and that we'll talk more in the morning.

"Can I take it with me?" Melody says, lifting the clue. "Or can I take a picture of it with my phone?"

"No duplicates," Fraser says. "No pictures or photocopies."

Melody gives him her best pleading, disappointed look. Fraser stands from his armchair, sighs, then nods, relenting. "You can take it with you, but it goes without saying that it can under no circumstances leave your possession." He puts his book into the bookcase. "And I'll need it back in the morning."

Fraser slides on his black cape while Melody and I gather all our things. Melody sends a quick text to her father that we're both fine, then we make our way outside to Fraser's old car.

Once we're safely inside the car, Fraser instructs us to lower our heads. Melody doesn't listen again. But as Fraser backs down the twisting driveway, he catches Melody, and she finally obeys, ducking her head down and giving me a look like she doesn't like not knowing what's going on around us. There's really nothing here, so I don't know what the big deal is. It's just woods.

"Oxford," she says when we're finally told we can pop up again.

"How did you know that?" Fraser says.

Melody doesn't reply but lifts her phone to show me our whereabouts on the GPS on her phone. I get the impression Fraser doesn't know much about technology, but I'm sure he wouldn't like it if he knew Melody was tracking his exact location on her phone. I grab her phone and click the GPS map off, then hand it to her. Hopefully, she'll get the message.

After that, we jump on the highway, then pass a few exits until Fraser pulls off and drives into the parking lot of a hotel. It's a classy hotel, not huge and towering like in the city, but newer and cozier. Fraser asks us if he should wear his cape to pick up our room card in the lobby, and we both respond with a screaming *No!* He tells us we're probably right, chuckles, then lowers his head and gets out of the car, telling us he'll be right back.

"I like him," Melody says. "He's weird, but he seems pretty honest and knows a lot."

I nod in response. I can't wait until tomorrow when I can sit down with Fraser and maybe talk to him about my life. Today we talked mostly about him and what he knows about the Ritual of the Four, but I do need to hear more about Lomidus and would love to hear some things about my father, too. A verbal instruction manual on the opposite sex wouldn't hurt, either. Fraser is a bachelor, never married, so I assume he's had his share of relationships over the years.

When Fraser returns, he hands me the card key to our room.

"I'll be back at ten o'clock tomorrow morning," he says. "Then we'll talk about Lomidus and his family, and we'll see what Melody comes up with as far as that clue." He glances at her, like he's still unsure if he should leave the clue with her. I can understand his hesitation. Leaving something irreplaceable with a person he just met must be excruciating. "In all honesty, between us, I'm hoping you find the burial site with the incantation, so I can live out the rest of my years in warmth and peace."

"Shaw's mother wants otherwise," Melody says.

"I cannot betray her trust by admitting to that," Fraser says, but his tone says it all. My mother doesn't want me to reverse the Ritual. She wants me to renew it, keep my ability, and give Melody one as well. I guess it all comes down to the actual incantation. When we find it, we'll see what we can do with the Ritual. "And remember," Fraser continues. "Both of you are to stay inside the hotel. No leaving under any circumstances, and keep the clue with you at all times."

"Got it," I tell him.

Melody grabs her carry-bag and opens the car door. I tell her I'll be right there, and she looks at me in confusion but then understands and closes the door, leaving me with Fraser.

"Between you and me," I say, taking note of Melody standing far enough away from the car that she can't hear me, "I'm a little nervous to be alone with her all night."

"I did get two beds for you," Fraser says. "It's not as though I've set you up in a honeymoon suite."

I let out a shaky laugh. "I don't know," I say. "I mean, what if when we get in the room, I just tell her I want to be with her and we spend the night . . ."

"Well," he says, "for one, you'd never work out the clue."

He winks at me, and I smile. "Thanks," I tell him.

It's not like I'm really going to spend the night making out with Melody or whatever. But the thought does occur to me. It occurs in vivid color and light. But it's not time yet. It's all or nothing, and I can't give her my all yet. It wouldn't be fair to let her think that I could.

"I'll see you at ten tomorrow," Fraser says and claps me

on the shoulder. "I'll just come right to your room and get you. Remember to make sure it's me before you open your door."

"Got it," I say.

I pick up my duffel bag, wave to Fraser, and step out into the parking lot of the hotel.

"Ready to work out those letters?" I ask Melody as we walk to the hotel door.

"Oh, I've already figured out how to decode the letters," she says. "It's the rest of the clue I'm worried about."

Chapter Fourteen

I don't really want to say more about the clue while Melody and I are outside the hotel, so I wait until we're safely inside our room. The room is nice, two double beds like Fraser told me, a table by the window, a TV, and a refrigerator. It smells like cleaning detergents and stale air, but I'm used to hotel rooms, so it really just feels like home to me. Melody drops her bag on the bed, then heads right over to the table, holding the clue in her hand.

"So how do you decode the letters?" I ask and sit down on the bed.

"It's a shifted alphabet code," she replies. "Fraser was right—it needed to be simple enough to carry over the ages for other generations to figure out with ease, but not *too* much ease. I've done some shifting in my head, but still haven't found where the shift starts. It'll come down to what *A* equals. It could be a shift of only a few letters, like *A* equals *C* or *D*, or it could be as far as *A* equals *X* or *Y*. I could probably do it in two seconds online, but I don't think Fraser would want me typing the clue in anywhere."

I'm still not entirely sure what she means, but the alphabet code wasn't her biggest worry anyway. "Why are you worried about the rest of the clue?" I ask. "That was pretty simple. Just a location."

"Not so much the location," she responds. She grabs the notepad of paper provided by the hotel and starts scribbling

125

down the alphabet. "But the circle below the location. I have no idea what that means."

Maybe I can be of some use here. I grab her phone from out of her bag and start Googling *symbols + circle*. It's a degree sign, like I sort of knew, but it's also a symbol of unity or infinity, sometimes protection. After telling Melody this information and getting little response, I turn back to the alphabet code and try to help her there. At least we already have an idea about that one.

"Maybe the letter *A* equals some relevant letter," I tell her. "Like a *D* for dagger or something."

"I tried *D*," she mumbles. "I've shifted quite a few over now." She taps her finger on the desk. I wonder if maybe I should tell her to give it a break for now, that we should settle into our room, but it looks as though she's on a mission. "What was the high priest's name?" she asks.

"Abraham something," I reply.

"Abraham Rane?"

"Yeah, I think."

She nods. "*R* for Ritual of the Four, or *R* for Rane," she whispers. "I'm going to try *A* equals *R*."

I stand and lean over her shoulder while she goes back and forth with the alphabet. Onto the paper, she writes down the letters: *O-L-D*.

She turns her head up to me and smiles. "I think we've got the first word."

It comes fast after that:

OLD GATE CEMETERY.

"Holy shit," I say.

Melody shoots me a stern look. She doesn't really like it when I swear. My mother doesn't either, but sometimes it's necessary to express what you're feeling. And what I'm feeling now is, Holy shit! Melody figured it out!

There are still two words left. "Finish it," I tell her.

Melody writes in the last part of the clue:

WRZITYVJKVI, DRJJ.

126

When she starts to decode it, I narrow my eyes. Then I say, "Holy shit," and get another disapproving look. WRZITYVJKVI, DRJJ translates to: FAIRCHESTER, MASS.

"I just moved from Fairchester," I say. "Before we came to Rockpoint."

"Do you remember an Old Gate Cemetery?" she asks.

"Yeah," I say, thinking back. "It was near this carnival I went to, the one where Alexander showed up with Lomidus."

I go on to tell her what I remember about Old Gate Cemetery. Here's where it helps to have a pretty good map of New England in your head from moving around so damn much. The cemetery is old, with oval brown crumbling stones for grave markers. The place is set back from the road, and any time we drove by it, no one was there. I don't even think you could drive through it, you just had to park on the street and walk in.

"So we have to go there with Fraser," Melody says. "He could drive us tomorrow or Saturday and we'll just have to see if we can figure out the rest of the clue from there."

"Sounds like a plan," I tell her. "I bet the map is somewhere in the cemetery and probably even Abraham's burial site with the incantation." It's starting to look good and doable, but then I remember. "And then all we have to do is…."

"Find your cousin and the wand," she says and sighs.

"Yeah."

I drop back down on the bed, then fall onto my back. Not only do I not know how to find Alexander and Lomidus, but doing that will also be dangerous. Plus, the only way to do it is to have Fraser drive us around, and maybe the old guy isn't in such a state for fighting with two villainous slicers. If it came down to it, though, I know he would take us. There are a few things I've learned from Fraser so far: 1) the history of the Ritual of the Four and the knowledge that there's an incantation out there somewhere to change or end it; 2) each item in the Ritual is uniquely powerful; 3) turkey tacos for

Thanksgiving dinner rocks; and 4) Fraser wants me to end the Ritual of the Four just as badly as I want to end it.

Melody sits down beside me. "You realize, too, that we're eventually going to have to dig up an old grave to find the incantation."

"Haven't gotten that far in my thought process," I admit. "Still working on the clue and how I'll find Alexander. If I *want* to find Alexander."

"He's probably looking for you in New England," she says. "So that narrows it down to—"

"Six states," I say and playfully tug her braid. "Not exactly narrowing it down."

We sit in thought for a few minutes, and then she goes back to the clue while I sink into some uncomfortable mixture of weariness and hunger. Yeah, I ate a plethora of turkey tacos, but that seems like forever ago. Melody watches me rub my stomach for a while, then huffs and walks to her carry-bag.

"Here," she says and pulls something out of her bag. "I thought you could wait until tomorrow at least, but that appetite of yours...."

She tosses a box of Pop-Tarts onto the bed beside me. The big box of Pop-Tarts—brown sugar cinnamon, my favorite flavor. I could so marry this girl. I thank her, stuff a few Pop-Tarts into my mouth, and then go inspect the hotel room. There's not much to see, or nothing that I haven't seen before in hotel rooms, so I just click on the television and decide to watch for a while until it's time to go to sleep. I take the bed by the door, just in case Melody likes to be closer to the window and away from the bathroom.

It's close to midnight when Melody finally stops fiddling around with the clue and checking things on her phone. Or maybe she was playing games all that time, I don't know. All I know is that I'm beyond tired. She tells me she's going to get ready for bed, so I turn off the show about alien invasions I was watching, and slip under the covers. I'd already brushed my teeth and changed into sweatpants around eleven, thinking it must be time for Melody to give in to the night and go to sleep. Sometimes I forget how tenacious she is when it comes to figuring out any kind of puzzle.

Ten minutes later, when she comes out of the bathroom, her hair is down. It's all flowing and ripply, just like it was at the Halloween dance. She's wearing a purple nightgown with the words *Kool Kat* printed on the front. Her bare legs shimmer as she walks by my bed.

"Goodnight," she says and clicks off the light.

For a minute it's dark and quiet. Her bed squeaks when she slides in, and my heart speeds up. "Goodnight," I whisper back.

Back to dark and quiet. She doesn't make a sound. I listen for a while. I imagine for a while. What would it be like with her? If we took all these steps past friendship, and we kissed every morning at the bus stop, and we fell asleep texting or talking? What would it be like to hold her on my couch back in Rockpoint? Feel her ripply hair through my fingers or....

"Shaw?" she whispers.

"Yeah?"

"Can you...can you come sleep with me?"

All my blood rushes to my chest, warm and explosive. God. Is she kidding?

"Yeah," I whisper back. "I can."

I'm not really sure what to do next. I mean, I already told her I'd come sleep with her, but does she really mean sleep? *All or nothing,* I remind myself. *Can't give her my all yet.* But still, I slide out from my covers and slide under hers. The scent of minty toothpaste and a million gardens falls over me.

"Thanks," she whispers as I settle in. "It's just...I never told you, but I get nightmares. Bad ones. About my mom and my sister."

"Your sister?"

She rolls around to face me. The room is dark, but my eyes adjust enough to make out the outline of her face, her shadowy hair all around her.

"My mom was pregnant with my sister when she died," she says. "I was really young when it happened, but the two of them still sometimes, you know, come to me at night. I used to sleep with a teddy bear, but when I turned sixteen, I told my father to get rid of it because I was too old."

"It's okay," I tell her. "You can hold on to me. I'll be your teddy bear."

She laughs, and the next thing I know, our bodies are entwined.

"How did they die?" I ask. "Your mother and your sister?"

"My mom was a musician," she starts. "My dad met her one night when she was singing at a bar. I guess he was just out of college and they...I guess a lot of guys came on to her, but she fell for my dad really fast. They fell in love and had me and then they started having problems because of her band." Melody is pretty close to me, in my arms, but she holds on tighter, like she needs my touch. "He didn't want her in the band anymore," she continues, "because she was a mom, and he didn't want her to work so late at night. When she was pregnant with my sister Harmony, she was coming back from a gig at four in the morning with the rest of her band, and some drunk guy slammed head-on into their van. She died instantly."

"God," I whisper. "I'm so sorry."

Melody sucks in a crying breath. I can't hold her any closer than I'm holding her now.

"So sometimes they come to me," she whispers. "At night. In my dreams."

"Maybe it's not supposed to be a nightmare thing," I tell her. "Maybe it's supposed to be comforting."

She pulls away. "When you see your mother and your baby sister covered in blood at night, it's not at all comforting."

"Sorry," I say again. I hope she understands that I'm just

trying to help. I know exactly what she's going through. So many times I've had visions of my father's last moments. It's not pretty, and it's almost something that's so difficult to process that my mind automatically deletes the thought. Melody's mind must keep the thoughts going while she sleeps. "Try to get some sleep, okay?" I stroke her hair. "You need to be fresh for tomorrow. We have a lot to do."

"I know," she says. "I'm doing all I can to help you."

She closes her eyes and rests her head against the pillow. I'm still holding her, thinking about how much she has done for me and how she's pretty much sacrificing the power of the goblet just so she can reverse the Ritual for me. From the beginning, all she has ever done is help me. She helped me escape the police at The Black Crow, she tried to warn me about Sal and Ariana, she constantly makes sure I have food and I'm comfortable, and she went with me on this trip, knowing the danger involved. What can I possibly do to make all that up to her? Because it sure as hell isn't telling her I just want to be friends when I know damn well she's in love with me.

It's difficult to sleep. For a while, I go in and out, listening as Melody's breaths grow heavy with sleep and dreams. She squirms and twitches, so I pull her closer just in case she's in the middle of a nightmare. Finally, my body gives in, and I slip away, Melody's warmth filling both the bed and my dreams.

Chapter Fifteen

Waking up next to a girl does not suck. The bed is hot and flowery, like I'm balled up inside a sweet-smelling cocoon. Heat radiates from Melody's core, and her legs brush against mine. Somewhere in the middle of the night, our hold on each other loosened and broke, so as soon as I realize we're no longer entwined, I wrap my arms around her and she opens her eyes. She smiles. And that's when I realize I'm falling in love with her.

"Morning," she whispers.

"Morning," I say back.

We stare at each other for a few minutes. I think she knows. I think she sees it.

"Funny," she whispers. "Usually when I wake up, I think a thousand thoughts about you before I even open my eyes. Today I didn't need to. You're right next to me."

"What are the thoughts?" I ask. "Like, just a few. You don't need to tell me all thousand."

She giggles. "I just think about seeing you at the bus stop, how you'll look, if your hair will be all messy, or if you'll be wearing your leather jacket. I think about sitting with you on the bus and how our shoulders knock into each other when the bus hits a bump. I think about *Star Wars* and Anakin and Padmé and imagine that we're them."

"Anakin and Padmé didn't exactly have a happy ending," I remind her. "I seem to recall something about a

133

death grip and twin babies that Anakin didn't know about. Oh, and didn't Anakin turn into more machine than man?"

"It's possible," she returns. "Somebody called Darth Vader?"

We both laugh and she reaches out to me. She smoothes my hair, then gives me that look like Ariana gave me on the dance floor, or like Selena Gomez gives the camera in a music video. I move away.

All or nothing.

She wasn't expecting me to move away. She thought I was all in. I see the hurt in her eyes.

"Sorry," I say and push the covers aside. For some reason my veins start to burn, but I keep the image of my dagger from forming, focus on some random thought of a blue spinning ball. "I need to walk." I find my leather jacket thrown over the back of a chair and pull it on, running a hand through my hair. Then I open my duffel bag and find a few bucks. "I'll be back."

"Wait!" she says as I grab the room key. "Fraser said we're not supposed to leave the hotel room. Where are you going?"

"I saw a Dunkin Donuts next to the hotel when we pulled in last night," I reply. "And I can take care of myself. I have so far." With that, I leave the hotel room, gasping for full, calming breaths as I jog down the stairwell and speed out the hotel door.

It might have snowed a little last night. It's hard to tell. It could be frost coating the grass, or a dusting of snow. The air smells like snow, like that wintery mix of pine and chill, so I'm going with snow. Last night, while I held Melody and we both dreamed, flakes of snow fell over the hotel and blew by our window.

I spot the orange and pink lights of Dunkin Donuts up ahead, then kick the curb and keep on going. It's just now that I realize I'm a little uncomfortable. Majorly sweaty. I didn't brush my teeth or use the bathroom or take a shower. I just needed to walk so I hopped out of bed and walked.

I didn't think that falling in love was going to feel like this. I thought maybe I'd feel it in my head, where my thoughts rage and settle, where I think about girls and how they look and how they smell. Or maybe I would feel it in my heart, because that's what all the songs say. Or maybe I'd feel it down there, because that's where I feel girls like Ariana. But I didn't know I would feel love all over like this. Running through my entire being and hurting from top to bottom. Why the hell does it hurt?

All or nothing.

To hell with all or nothing.

When I get inside Dunkin Donuts, warm air wraps around me, and the scent of fresh coffee and sugary donuts puts me in a better mood. I head for the bathroom, pee and wash, then go back to the counter and order two bagels with cream cheese and two coffees. Now that I think about it, the hotel did provide some kind of continental breakfast, so I really could have eaten for free. Melody probably thinks I'm insane for going out in the cold when I could have just as easily stayed inside the warmth of the hotel and eaten a feast. But at least this got me away from her for now. It gave me a chance to organize my thoughts and make peace with what's going on inside of me. If I'd stayed in bed with her, doing what she obviously thought we were going to do....

I must be insane.

When I get back to the hotel room, Melody is in the shower. She cleaned the room a little, and the table is cleared off, so I set down the bag of bagels and the tray of coffees. Then I sit on the edge of the bed, and I hear singing. The most beautiful, sad singing I've ever heard in my life.

I think Melody is singing the song we danced to at the Halloween dance. It's some song about learning how to love, or maybe it's a breakup song, now that I focus on the lyrics. Cascades of sorrowful notes echo around the room until goosebumps run up my arm. All this time, hours and hours

135

spent together, and I never knew Melody could sing. I remember at the dance thinking she was on the beat and wondering how that could be because she didn't seem like the kind of girl who knew how to stay on the beat. Not only did I break her heart, I know nothing about her, who she really is beneath the brains and the gaming.

When she finally comes out of the bathroom, her hair in a long, wet braid, she pretends nothing is wrong. She just thanks me for the Dunkin Donuts, sits down and palms her coffee, then pulls the clue out of her carry-bag. I will play along with this game of avoidance until I physically can't.

"I'm thinking that once we get to Old Gate Cemetery, we'll see this circle printed somewhere," she says, pointing to the little circle drawn below North, E. "The only thing that bothers me is that this is supposed to be a clue for the map, not the actual burial site. It would make more sense, being in a cemetery, if this were a clue to the burial site."

"I'm telling you, the burial site is at the cemetery." I switch on the television, but she gives me a look like she's trying to concentrate, so I flip it back off. "The clue leads us right to Old Gate Cemetery, and then we use the circle as the map, or to take us to the map. It would make no sense for someone to take us to a cemetery that's not also the burial site."

"Especially since it's an *old* cemetery," she says.

"Mmm," I say back.

It's close to nine, so I guess I should start packing up my things. I'm not sure where we'll stay tonight, but Fraser did say he was checking us out of here, and knowing him, he'll think it's best to choose a different location for each night. The guy might be more paranoid than I am.

I'm psyched to tell him that Melody decoded the shifted alphabet code, but still kind of bummed that we didn't figure out the entire thing. We both have the feeling, though, that it will all come clear once we're at the cemetery. I'm a little nervous to head back to Fairchester. That's the last place I saw Alexander and Lomidus, where they both tried to kill me. But they'd have to be long gone from there by now, knowing my mother and I fled the town. Actually, it might be the safest place in New England right now. I would be stupid to head back there.

At ten o'clock, Melody and I pick up our bags and stand by the beds. She glances at the bed where we slept, then turns away from me. Yeah, I've decided to throw my all or nothing mantra out the window. And as soon as I need to tell her how I really feel, I will do it. But that time is not right now. Plus, I'm scared as hell of the way I really feel.

"Did you call your dad this morning?" I ask.

She nods.

"So I guess Thanksgiving dinner went well for them last night?"

"Probably best that you don't know," she replies.

Yeah. Great. My mother and Melody's father hooked up last night. Yay for that.

"Not like that," she says, probably reading my expression. "Well, I don't know. I mean, it's not like my father would tell me if things went *that* well between them. I just meant that he seemed happy."

"Things went *that* well then," I say.

"Yeah, cause a guy couldn't possibly be happy with a girl unless sex was involved."

Here we go.

"Hey," I say. "You put it out there this morning, and I didn't take it."

"Excuse me?" She sticks her hands on her hips. "All I wanted...what I *thought*, was that we would...." She drops down on the bed and crushes her carry-bag to her chest. "Forget it."

What the hell? I'm getting mixed signals, right?

Just past ten o'clock, Melody heads for the room door. She stands there, away from me, and shuffles her feet back and forth. I tap my finger on the table, reminding myself to get my head in the game. My goal is to find the incantation and reverse the Ritual of the Four. I can worry about my love life later.

Ten-fifteen. Melody takes her phone out of her bag. She glances at it, then at me.

Ten-thirty. Fraser is ridiculously late.

"He did say ten, right?" Melody says.

"Yeah, he said it a few times," I say back. "Maybe he overslept?"

"Old people rarely oversleep," she says. She walks to the window, pushes the curtains aside, and peers down into the parking lot. She shakes her head.

Ten forty-five. I offer to go check downstairs, thinking maybe he forgot our room number. Melody nods, and I'm off. I check the parking lot. I check the lobby. I check all the hallways in the hotel. No Fraser. And checkout time is eleven.

When I get back to the room, Melody is flush with worry. We need to check out of the hotel, and we need a ride away from the hotel, back to Fraser's. We're pretty much stranded until Fraser comes to get us. Our parents are hours away in New York.

"I'm going to go check us out of the hotel," I say. "Before they try to charge us for another night. We'll just have to wait down in the parking lot."

"Why would he do this?" she says. "Why would he be so late?"

I shrug, then tell her I'll meet her in the parking lot. I tell her to be careful and on guard. Not to talk to strangers. I finally get a little smile on that one.

It's nearly eleven-thirty when Melody suggests that something might be wrong. It's not like I wasn't thinking it, I just tried to tell myself it was all okay. Maybe Fraser overslept or forgot about us or lost track of time. But now that it's way past the time where any of those things would be applicable, I'm getting a shiver deep in my bones.

"Should we call your mom?" Melody asks.

We're sitting on the curb in the parking lot of the hotel, a slant of early winter sunshine falling over us. It's warm on my cheeks, but my limbs are still freezing.

"We said we were going to do as much of this alone as we could," I remind her.

"Right," she says. She takes her cell out of her pocket and starts typing away on Google. "I'm calling us a taxi."

"What?"

But she's on a mission, as usual. She knows what she's doing or has formulated her own plan, so I let her do it. She talks to someone, gives our location and where we're headed, then hangs up.

"I just gave them the street name," she says. "I'll have them drop us off near Fraser's, but we don't want a trail of exactly where we're headed."

"What are you trying to say?"

She sighs. "It's probably nothing," she says. "But...."

All sorts of catastrophes move through my mind. Fraser is nearly two hours late. Something is majorly wrong. Maybe he had some medical issue and we need to get to him as soon as we can. Maybe he fell. Maybe he has something wrong with his mind, some old person's disease, and completely forgot about us. Or maybe....

"Thank God you paid attention to where he actually lived," I say. "I have no idea where we were yesterday."

"I know exactly where we were," she says. "I just hope Fraser is okay."

By the time Metro Taxi shows up, I can no longer feel my flesh. Even with my leather jacket on, sitting in direct sunlight, my body feels like cold gel. Melody must be freezing, but at least she thought to bring gloves. I guide her toward the taxi, taking note that she pulls away from me a little. I can't believe only hours ago we were so close in the hotel bed.

The taxi driver is an excessively hairy, middle-aged guy who flashes us a friendly wave as we get situated inside. We head off for Fraser's street, our bags on our laps in the taxi. I whisper to Melody that I don't exactly have a ton of money to pay this guy, but Melody says she has emergency cash in her bag. Good thing, because when we finally get to Fraser's road, the taxi driver asks us for a whopping thirty bucks for a fifteen-minute ride.

He lets us off in front of a white ranch-style house that borders the woods. These are probably the same woods in the back of Fraser's cottage; they run behind the neighborhood. Melody and I glance at each other as the taxi drives off. Then we turn to the woods.

"If there's trouble...." she says, finally saying aloud what we're both thinking.

"Probably the woods are our best bet," I say. "Fraser's cottage must be only four or five houses down."

We find a path to the woods between two houses. Melody watches to make sure nobody in the neighborhood comes outside, while I step onto the dirt pathway. It's a wooded neighborhood, the houses pretty spread out, so that works in our favor. What doesn't work in our favor is that it's the day after Thanksgiving, so most people are home from work or school. We spot a red-haired lady from the neighboring house as she exits her car, holding a few shopping bags. Melody freezes, then slips behind a pine tree, tugging my jacket sleeve. We carry on down the path, until we're fully ensconced in the woods.

"This way," she whispers.

Melody's nose is Rudolph-red. Her cheeks are bluish-white. I know I must look just as cold, just as hyper-exposed to the elements. In the woods, with the lack of direct sunlight, it's even colder. We trample through dead leaves and dropped pine needles, watching the backyards of houses, counting down to the cottage.

We're only about two houses away from Fraser's cottage when the scent hits me.

I throw my arm across Melody's chest, holding her back.

"What?" she whispers.

"They're here," I whisper, taking a few steps backward. "I don't know how they found me, but they're here."

Melody shivers. Her eyes dart around the woods. "Are you sure?"

I nod, pulling her off the path and behind a tall, thick tree trunk. "When they're close to me, I can smell them," I say. "Blood, like a metallic scent. I'm not sure why, but I've always been able to smell when they're close. That's probably how they know I'm close, too."

"Fraser," she says, still shivering. "Do you think he's okay?"

"He would have shown up at the hotel if he was okay."

"Maybe he knew they were coming and didn't want them to follow him," Melody says. "God, Shaw."

"I know."

We stare at each other for a full minute, eyes wide in alarm and despair. Here's where I have to take over. Melody does the brainwork, but I need to be the protector. If something happens to Melody, I'll kill someone. I swear I will.

"I have to make sure Fraser is okay," I say. "So you stay here, okay?"

She shakes her head.

"There's no time to argue," I say. "Stay hidden here, and I'll come back and get you when I can." I grab her hand and squeeze. "If you see anyone except me coming back, you run as fast as you can and call the police."

"And if you don't come back?"

"Call the police," I say. "And then my mom."

Before I can process the pleading, terrified look in her eyes, I drop my bag beside her and jog off toward Fraser's cottage. It's difficult to navigate in a place you've never been before. It does not help that my body is numb from cold air and fear. I dash over exposed tree roots, hop over silver rocks and fallen branches, the whole time wondering if I should be

141

doing this at all. Adrenalin runs through my veins like icy fire, and I'm pretty sure that's the only thing keeping me moving. I'm not sure what I'll find at the cottage, but Fraser might need my help. Either that or I'm running right into a big fat trap, set by Alexander and Lomidus.

I suspected we were four or five houses away from Fraser's, and that initial estimate wasn't too far off. By the time I've passed a few more backyards, the woods have thinned and I can tell, by instinct or by some kind of inner navigation that I'm close to the cottage. I cut through to the sparsest part of the woods, closer to the main road, then pause when the back of the cottage comes into view. Fraser's car is in the driveway.

There are no signs of a disturbance. I'm hovering between storming inside the cottage or just viewing it from afar. But standing back here isn't going to do Fraser any good. Not if he's inside and in trouble. The scent of blood still hangs in the air but about the same strength as it was back in the woods. It's not overpowering like I thought it would be when I was this close. Like it always is when I'm close to Alexander.

Last time I faced Alexander and Lomidus, my mother was only a few minutes away. I sent a code word, she gathered our things and jumped in the car, and we fled. Fast. But now my mother is miles away. *Hours* away. And my kind-of girlfriend or my friend that's a girl—hell, the girl I'm in love with—is hiding in the woods, shivering, waiting for my safe return. If I'm going to back out for any of those reasons, now would be the time to do it.

But I don't. Something pulls me ahead, and I keep going, sneaking toward the cottage, praying that Alexander isn't inside waiting. I'm just to the front door when I hear the crunch of leaves behind me, trampled underfoot. I spin around—and see Melody standing in the walkway.

"Don't go in," she whispers.

"I told you to stay in the woods!"

"Listen." She steps closer, and I point toward the woods

142

for her to retreat, but she doesn't pay attention. The girl really thinks she's some kind of kick-ass *Star Wars* princess. "If you go inside, do not touch a thing," she says. "Understand?"

"He's fine," I say. "He has to be fine."

Melody shakes her head. She presses her eyes closed. Yeah. Fraser probably isn't okay.

She snakes past me. I try to grab her waist but she's much too quick. With her gloved hand, she gives the door a gentle pull, and it opens freely. I push past her, just in case Alexander is ready and waiting, positioned to strike and slice whoever he sees first. But the cottage is empty. The bathroom door is ajar, so I can see the entire cottage. Nobody is in here.

Quietly, I step all the way inside and sense that Melody is right behind me. The kitchen holds the faint scent of coffee, and there's a loaf of bread set on the counter, like Fraser was just starting to fix up his morning breakfast. An odd silence falls over me, and I turn to make sure Melody is okay.

And then she screams. No, not screams. Shrieks. Wails. It's ear-piercing and shoots through every part of my body.

"Fraser!" she gasps. "Fraser!"

And then I see him.

Lying on the living room floor in front of the bookcases. In a pool of blood.

Chapter Sixteen

Melody holds me back as I try to run to Fraser's body. It's a blur of screams and arms and tears, until I finally have the sense to rest my hand over Melody's mouth to shut her up. If Alexander is close by—and I'm sure he is—I don't want him hearing her scream. Or the neighbors, for that matter, even though most of them are too far from the cottage to hear anything.

"Don't touch anything!" she says. "It's a murder scene."

One look at Fraser and I know she's right. He's facedown, but what I can see of the side of his face is a horrifying gray-white. Dead. Not to mention there's enough blood around him to fill a gallon milk container. Nobody could live through that.

"They killed him," I say.

"Oh my God," Melody whispers. Her limbs start flying around, and I have no choice but to hold her arms to her sides. Tears stream down her cheeks, and her body is twitching, kind of like it was last night when she was in one of her nightmares.

"We have to get out of here," she says, tugging my arm.

I'm with her. But then I remember something.

"The pentacle," I say. "We have to take it with us."

"Don't step in the blood!" she says as I race for the bookcase. "And don't touch anything with your fingers!"

Carefully, I avoid stepping in the pool of blood around

145

Fraser. The blood is dark against the wood floor, thick and fresh. They probably killed him just this morning, while he was setting up his breakfast. Maybe when I was at Dunkin Donuts, moaning and pissy over my Melody issue. But how did they know I was with Fraser yesterday? It's not a coincidence that they killed him now, just a day after I finally met him.

Melody is in the kitchen, wandering and crying as I stretch my arm into the bookcase and knock the back of my hand against the book with the secret hiding place. It falls open on the floor. Empty.

"Damn!" I say. "They have the pentacle!"

Melody pulls a set of keys off a hook by the cabinet. "We'll have to worry about it later," she says as the keys jingle through the cottage. "We have to go."

She races for the door where I meet her, and then we both spin and take one last look back at Fraser. She closes her eyes in a silent prayer, and even though we need to leave, I close my eyes, too. I think about Fraser in his crazy black cape and how he fed us turkey tacos and told us everything about the Ritual of the Four. How he trusted us with the clue. How he planned to tell us so much more today, all about Lomidus and some things about my father. Now, I will never know.

"Goodbye, Fraser," Melody whispers.

She tugs me out the door, runs around the cottage to where she's stashed our bags, and then pulls me by my hand back to the driveway and Fraser's car.

I didn't really think about what she was doing with the keys. Now I know.

"You're crazy," I say as she opens the driver's door. "You don't have a license!"

"No time to discuss it," she says and disappears inside the car.

I hop in beside her, into the passenger's seat, as she starts the engine.

The car lurches in reverse, snapping my neck against the

seat.

"Sorry," she says. "Not real good in reverse."

"You know how to drive?" I ask. "*Please* tell me you know how to drive."

She reverses in a semicircle, swinging the car around, obviously realizing she's not going to make it in reverse all the way down the twisting driveway. We end up about an inch away from the frame of the cottage. Then she spins the wheel and slams the car into drive. We speed forward, racing down the driveway.

"My father takes me driving on Sundays," she says. "It's one of the few things we actually do together."

I click in my seatbelt. I have a feeling this is going to be a bumpy ride.

****

Somehow, we make it onto the highway. Melody remembered how to get back to the main road, and then we found a sign for some highway called Route 8. Now, we're driving in the slow lane—exceptionally slow, like, noticeably too slow—and Melody is rubbing her head. She's checking the rearview mirror, adjusting the seat, pretty much doing all the things she should have done *before* attempting to drive on the highway.

"I'll need you to type Fairchester into my phone GPS," she says. "Navigate me to Massachusetts."

She's all business, so I do as she says. Even though we're in a car we stole from a dead guy. Even though Melody doesn't have a license. Even though her driving skills are iffy at best.

"Um…." I say, tilting her phone to look through the map. "It looks tricky. We need to get on to something called eighty-four and then ninety-one." She nods and keeps driving. I watch us as the little blue dot on her phone, heading to intersect with the eighty-four highway or whatever it is. "I need to call my mom," I say. "We can't just leave…I mean, someone has to take care of Fraser's…you know…his body."

"I agree," she says as cars zoom by us. "Once we're close to Fairchester, we'll take a breather."

So we keep going, me trying not to wet myself as cars pass by us on the highway and Melody grips the steering wheel. Me, navigating us toward Fairchester, Massachusetts. Me, hanging onto the dashboard for dear life when Melody gets too close to the car in front of us. Me, making sure the seatbelt is clicked in and tight and secure. Me, picturing Fraser in a pool of blood. Me, wondering where Alexander is now and if he's hunting for me in Connecticut. Me, thanking every last lucky star that Melody is as insane as she is.

After an hour of illegal and possibly reckless driving, Melody pulls off the highway and into the parking lot of a Burger King. She drives around the back and parks.

And then she falls into my arms, crying.

Okay, so the adrenalin or fear or whatever was driving her has worn off, and she's feeling it all now—all the fright, all the sadness, all the shock. I stroke her hair, holding her, wanting to tell her it's all going to be okay but knowing that I can't really do that. My mind flashes back to when I first moved to Rockpoint and wanted more than anything to not have to move again. To not have to worry about Alexander and all this violence and death. Maybe I didn't even realize how badly I wanted that back then, but I do now.

"Why did they kill him?" she says, sobbing. "He was just an old man."

"Because they're twisted and evil," I say, still stroking her hair.

"Did he suffer?" she asks. "Did he know he was going to...."

"I don't know."

All evidence points to Fraser knowing. Maybe trying to keep his pentacle safe. He was making breakfast, it seemed, setting up his coffee and his toast, when he probably heard them coming and made a run for it into the living room. But maybe still...maybe he didn't know they were going to kill him. Maybe he thought he could bargain with them. I didn't examine Fraser, but I could tell it was Alexander's work. Lomidus does not have that strength. Not to cut deep into veins or arteries. Even when they killed my dad, I'm almost sure it was Alexander. My dad. *Please, God, do not let my dad have looked the way Fraser looked.*

Melody is still crying, so I keep holding her as the car vibrates and hums beneath us. Pretty soon, we're going to need gas, and we're going to need to eat. All we ate all day was a bagel this morning, and that seems like years ago.

"Hey," I say. "Let's go through the drive-thru and order some burgers, okay?"

"Shaw Huntley," she says and picks her head up. "You eat more than anyone else I've ever known."

Her cheeks are streaked in tears. I smile at her, not really going into the fact that anyone in the world would be hungry right now. A flipping bagel. Hours and hours ago.

So we pull ourselves together and order two burgers, two fries, and two milkshakes. Heaven.

****

Making it all the way to Fairchester is quite a feat. In the process, we made five wrong turns, got off the wrong exit three times, and once headed back in the wrong direction when Melody lost focus. Or maybe it was me who lost focus, I'm not sure. But still, we're here. And now I have to call my mother before Melody and I can even begin to formulate a plan.

"Anything look familiar?" she says.

"You'll want to pull into Allen's Hardware," I say, pointing as we pull off the exit ramp. "We can figure out what we'll do from there."

Allen's Hardware is closed on Fridays and Mondays. Still, I don't want to hang around the empty parking lot too long. Anything we can do to avoid the police right now is a plus. The thought of getting pulled over or questioned by the cops makes me so shaky that I don't even let the image wander through my mind. Just pretend like I'm with my mother and we're just fine. All legal. License and registration perfect.

"I assume you want to go right to Old Gate Cemetery?" she says.

I shake my head. "We'll be here for the night, so we should probably check into a motel first. Get settled."

"Do you know any motels around here with…looser policies?"

I know what she means. If we go to a fancier hotel, not only will we not have enough money to foot the bill, but also, they'll ask a lot of questions. We're not legal adults yet. We're not with parents. We don't have a credit card.

"Some kids from school used to go to this motel on the far side of Fairchester," I say. "It was called the Rowboat Inn or something like that."

"Sounds nice and fancy," she says and smiles.

"Yeah," I say. "Real fancy. Broken windows, peeling paint, and an old rowboat out front that's covered in graffiti. Most of the kids went there after school dances and proms to…."

"I get it," she says. "You want to go there now, or should we call your mom first?"

After a minute of contemplation, I decide we should get someplace safer, even if that place is on the far side of Fairchester. At least inside the Rowboat Inn, we're not doing anything illegal. Well, not really. I just hope the place still caters to underage kids willing to pay the forty-buck fee for some privacy.

After directing Melody to the Rowboat Inn, we pull into a parking space and decide that I'll go in alone to secure our room. She's too nervous, and us going in together will probably be uncomfortable, seeing as the place has a reputation as a hot spot for teens in love. I tell her to lock the car doors, then I gather up the little bit of money we have collectively, and hop out of Fraser's car.

The Rowboat Inn looks exactly as I remember it. There's an old rowboat in front of the place, corroded and written-over. The blue paint on the outside of the building is peeling off in hand-sized shreds. A few broken plastic chairs are positioned in front of the first-floor rooms, on mock porches. I hadn't seen the motel too many times, just driving by on the way to a shopping center my mother used to like. My mother and I, when we lived in Fairchester or anywhere really, stayed inside as much as we could. It has only been since Rockpoint that we've ventured out. Normally, my mother would just go to work, and I would go to school. Even when I went to the carnival in Fairchester, it was a rare event. The autumn carnival was a huge thing in Fairchester, so I went.

Inside the Rowboat Inn, the lobby is littered with old brochures and ripped-up travel magazines. It smells old and stagnant, even though there's a full coffeepot set up right by the front desk, which makes me think the coffee was brewed like, yesterday. The man sitting behind the front desk is tattooed and bald, with a red mustache and a scruffy red beard. Bald men with tons of facial hair have always struck me as funny. It will probably be my karma to end up looking that way when I'm fifty. If I make it that long, that is.

"Can I help you?" he says, standing.

My shoulders stiffen, and I slap forty bucks down on the desk. "Need a room for tonight," I say.

He looks me over. I'm wearing my leather jacket, and my hair is probably all messed up, like it usually is. Not that he looks much classier.

Right next to my forty bucks, he slaps down a piece of paper.

"I'll need your personal information," he says.

"Personal information?"

He smirks. "K, kid," he says. "Here's the deal. The room's forty bucks straight if ya fill out the paperwork. Gimme sixty straight, and we call off the paperwork."

Sixty straight? What does that mean? Where's Melody

when you need her?

"I only have forty." Melody has more, but I just want to get this over with. I drag the paper toward me and fill out as much personal information as I can—which is mostly just fabrication and gibberish. My name is Lee Greznick, and I'm from Fairchester (I was both, once upon a time). I live at Autumn's Circle (made up—it reminded me of the autumn carnival), and my phone number is a bunch of random numbers that popped into my head. Wow. Maybe I'm getting just as good as my mother at this kind of thing.

The man inspects the paper and narrows his eyes. He knows it's all made up. Still, he reaches beneath the counter and pulls out a room key. It's a big green keychain, shaped like the number one, but it's stamped with the number seventeen. A silver key dangles from the key ring. He tells me the room is located around the back of the building, on the second floor.

"When's checkout?" I say, grabbing the key from him.

He laughs. Like out loud and hearty, like hold your stomach kind of laughing. "Most people only stay a few hours, kid, so I don't know," he says. "You can come back tomorrow by noon, I guess."

Okay, then.

Back at the car, I check my surroundings, then hop in and tell Melody to drive around the motel. It's actually a good thing that the car will be in the far back of the place. Melody even finds a parking space that's pretty much hidden, toward the far edge of the lot.

"No trouble?" I ask her.

"No," she replies. She lets out a little laugh, which is good to hear. "Believe me, I checked the rearview mirror constantly, so I'm positive nobody followed us here. All I saw in the rearview were hundreds of cars passing by us."

"Maybe because you were doing thirty in a fifty-five zone for like two hours," I say, pulling up my duffel bag.

"Possibly," she says and laughs again. "But I got us here,

152

right?"

"Better than I could have done."

When we step out of Fraser's car with our bags, heading for the outside staircase that leads to the second floor of the motel, I notice the sky is inky with nightfall. Cars and trucks zoom ahead on the main road, their headlights slicing through the motel and the parking lot. The air is just as cold as it was earlier, but now the chill is somehow draining and intolerable. I think I need a few hours to relax. My body is taxed.

Oh. Now I know what he meant by sixty straight. Sixty bucks, without tax.

Room number seventeen is the last room on the top floor. I play around with the key in the lock until the door pops open and a wave of foul motel scents wash over me — cheap cleaners, dusty carpets, and stale cigarettes. Melody steps in behind me, and I search for a light switch but can't find one. I fumble around in the dark until I finally find a lamp and click it on.

"Okay," Melody says, looking around. "Officially grossed out."

Not as nice as the hotel room Fraser got for us. Not even close. There's no refrigerator. The television looks like it might be from the eighties. There's only one bed, and it's covered in what looks like an old blue sleeping bag, spread open. Even the remote control is nasty. It's all faded and looks like rats have chewed on the buttons for years.

"Forty bucks was way too much for this dump," Melody says, dropping her carry-bag on the floor by the television.

I don't even tell her the guy tried to get sixty straight from me.

"I need to freshen up," she says, heading for the bathroom. "If that's even possible in this place."

"I'll call my mom."

"Use my phone!"

She closes the bathroom door, and I search around in her

153

bag until I find her phone. She's got all kinds of food in here—my open box of Pop-Tarts, a small bag of mixed nuts, and an apple. I try not to look at her clothes, because maybe she's got like, bras and stuff in here, but my eyes do dance over the contents of her bag. When I inhale, I can smell Melody all over. God.

My mother's cell is already programmed in Melody's phone, so I sit down on the edge of the bed and call. It rings three times. My stomach contracts just thinking about what I have to tell her. It's not good news.

"Hello?" my mother says. "Melody?"

She sounds nervous already.

"It's me," I say.

"Is everything okay?"

I rub the back of my neck. "No," I say. "Fraser is dead."

Silence.

"Mom?"

"I'm here," she whispers. "Are you sure?"

I'm kind of afraid to lean back on the bed. Really don't want to rest my head on this nylon blanket or sleeping bag or whatever it is. But I'm exhausted, so I do it anyway. I tell my mother what happened with Fraser, that Melody and I are safe for now, and that we're in a motel. When I get to the Fairchester part, she stops me.

"So you have it," she says in a low voice. "You know where you're going."

Why am I not surprised that my mother knows about the clue?

"Mom," I say. "If you know something about any of this, now would be the time to tell me."

She sighs. "Hold on a sec," she replies.

I hear her walking around, then some glass things banging together like she's cleaning up the nail polishes at the place she does her manicures. I guess it's late Friday evening, so she'd be just finishing up with her clients.

"Okay," she says, coming back on the line. "I just wanted

to make sure nobody was around. How's everything going with Melody? Is she okay?"

Way to change the subject. I glance at the closed bathroom door, then stand and walk toward the back of the motel room by a junky old table with a junky old chair. "She's fine," I reply. "She was a little shaken up about Fraser."

"Understandable," my mother says. "But you've been comforting her, right?"

"We've been alone in hotel rooms, what do you think I've been doing?"

"Falling in love with her maybe?"

"Something like that." I glance at the bathroom door again, then pull out the chair and fall in. "So what do you know about Fairchester? About the clue?"

"Fraser was supposed to tell you all of this," she says.

"Well, he can't now," I say, full-out angry like I usually am when I talk to my mother. "Alexander took care of that. And he took the pentacle, which makes my life even more difficult right now." Melody comes out of the bathroom. She sits down on the bed, on the edge, so I move from the table and sit down next to her. "Tell me, Mom," I say. "We need to know what's going on."

"Fine," she says as Melody moves closer to hear what my mother is saying. "The clue, as you probably now realize, is what Alexander is after. Your grandfather knew about the clue and decoded it in the seventies, years before it was handed over to Fraser."

My grandfather on my father's side died of lung cancer when I was only one or two. I've seen some black-and-white pictures of him posing in a dark hat, a cigar in his mouth, maybe taken in the fifties or sixties. That's all I know of him.

"He told your father about the clue and the map," my mother continues, "so your father always knew where the map was located. Alexander and Lomidus killed your father because of the clue." She exhales through the phone. "I guess what I'm trying to say here is that they tortured your father, but he wouldn't give them the information they wanted. That's why they keep asking you for something you don't have. They thought your father passed the clue down to you."

Tortured my father. My dagger pops into my mind, but I change the thought so quickly it makes me dizzy. Melody is the only one here, and if I get angry....

"So that's why they've been trying to kill me all this time," I say. "Because they think I have the clue to the map and want to torture me for it, just like Dad."

"Yes," my mother replies. "And because they want the dagger, of course, with no strings attached. It seems they've always stopped just shy of killing you, though, because if they killed you, there went one of their last hopes of getting the incantation. Lomidus wants all four items, and he wants the incantation. He wants all that power and feels it rightfully belongs to him."

"Why were we in Fairchester before we went to Rockpoint?" I ask her. "That wasn't just a coincidence."

She pauses. "Because I knew the map was in an old cemetery, but I didn't know the town or state the cemetery was in," she replies finally. "Your father never told me the name of the cemetery straight-out, but over the years, I did hear bits and pieces of things when your grandfather was alive. All the towns you and I went to in New England when we moved around...those were all the towns that had a cemetery with a name similar to the name I overheard. I wanted to keep you safe, wanted it all to end, just as you do. So finally, in Fairchester, I was pretty sure I'd hit the right place. I was ready to find the map to the incantation and try to end it all."

Melody eyes me in confusion. There are a few things that don't make sense. Why did my mother give Melody the goblet then? Why did she want me to fall in love with Melody so I wouldn't reverse the Ritual?

"I'm not sure I get it," I say. "You didn't find the

156

incantation?"

"I didn't try, Shaw," my mother replies. "When I got that close to finding the map, I realized that your father would have wanted you to keep the gift in the family line. He loved what he had, loved what he could do and that his son shared the gift with him. You know he always thought of it as something special, even if it got him killed, and he knew eventually it would. *I* knew eventually it would."

Melody rests her arm around my shoulder. I fall into her. My mother knew everything, all this time. She knew about the cemetery and moved around until she found the one that seemed most likely, or the one that matched up with whatever else she knew.

"Shaw, we really should cut off now," my mother says.

"What about Fraser?" I ask. "We can't just leave him there in the cottage."

"I'll take care of it," she says. "But not for a few days. I'm sorry. But if you have the car, and the authorities get involved...."

Melody nods in agreement as though my mother can see her.

"One last thing," I say to my mom. "Why didn't you ever tell me any of this?"

Another long pause. "Because I knew you would do exactly what you're doing right now," she replies finally. "Off and running toward a dangerous situation."

She's got a point. If I'd known there was a way to turn all of it around, to end the Ritual, I would have tried to do this a long time ago.

"So do what you feel is right," my mother says. "And take care of each other. Be safe and good luck."

We both say "bye" into the phone. Then Melody takes the phone from my hand and plugs it into her charger. We sit in silence for a few minutes. The room is so dark and shadowy, even with the lamp on.

"Cemetery tonight?" Melody asks.

"First thing tomorrow morning," I say. "I just…I can't."

Melody nods and fishes the box of Pop-Tarts out of her carry-bag. We share one, quiet while we eat, and then she cleans up the wrapper and crumbs and sits back down on the bed beside me.

"I know it's not the best situation," she says. "But I'm glad that we're together."

"So you're not still mad at me for this morning?"

"Depends," she says and smiles. "Do you still think I wanted sex?"

"Yeah," I say. "Because that's what all the girls want from me."

We laugh, and just for a few seconds, I forget all the bad things.

****

Around seven, Melody drops a round, red apple down in front of me on the bed. I'd been complaining—probably for at least an hour—that I was hungry. What I had in mind was more like two turkey subs from Subway, which I know for a fact is just down the road from the Rowboat Inn, in the little group of shops my mother used to love. I don't have anything against healthy foods, they're usually just not enough to fill me up. They just make me hungrier and crankier.

"Thanks," I tell her. "But I think we've already established that I'm more a meat and potatoes guy."

"Actually, you're a junk food and fast food kind of guy," she says, sitting down beside me on the bed. "But the apple isn't for eating." She lifts the apple in front of my eyes. "Try to slice it."

"What?"

"You said your father used to do it."

I stare at the apple for a few seconds, thinking about my father and how he had the sort of control over his ability that I will never have. I remember him tossing the apple into the air and the thing coming back down all sliced up. Something I will never be able to do.

"Just cause my dad could do it doesn't mean I can," I say.

"Try it," she demands. "Focus on the dagger, and just imagine it cutting up the apple."

"I need to be angry."

"Fine," she says. She stands up, drops the apple on the bed, and places her hands on her hips. "Here are some things to be angry about. Alexander and Lomidus killed your father. They killed Fraser."

"Melody," I warn. "Don't do this."

But she keeps going. Alexander and Lomidus took Fraser's pentacle. My mother lied to me about everything. Sal and Ariana plotted to beat me to near-death at the Halloween dance. Everything that gets me going, Melody knows about.

And it works.

My veins burn and boil, and soon I'm trying to control my anger but realize that's not my objective here. I focus on my dagger, keeping the vision right in the front of my mind, then project both the dagger and my anger at the apple resting on the bed. With a loud *crunch*, the thing slices right in half, all the way down, separating into two parts.

Melody smiles.

"Happy?" I say.

"Very," she says back.

"Good." I stand up. "I'm going out to get dinner."

"Wait...what?" She runs to me as I pull on my leather jacket.

"There's a Subway just down the street," I say. "I'll get us some subs and drinks." I grab the room key and some money from my bag. My cash stash — small to begin with — is really dwindling.

"You just had a major breakthrough with your gift," she says. "And you're just walking out now? Plus, it could be dangerous out there, and if anything happens to you, I'll just die."

I reach down and grab her hand. "That's why we can't be together," I say and squeeze her hand to near crushing. "And

159

us not being together is also one of the things you missed when you listed all the things in my life that piss me off." With that, I turn for the door and open it. "Don't let anyone in," I say.

I walk out into the cold, and as I turn to close and lock the door, Melody's eyes fill with tears.

Chapter Seventeen

It always feels better when I walk. When I'm angry or upset, or just plain hating the world, I walk, and things seem to grow clearer in my mind. My thoughts settle. My anger ebbs. In the case right now, though, I'm not really angry anymore. I told Melody how I feel—finally told her—so now it seems like at least I've done something that might make her happy. Cry tears of joy or whatever, not that I'm all that special but she seems to think so. Telling her is not enough to make up for everything she's sacrificed for me and everything she's done for me—and that includes what she did for me tonight. I never thought I would be able to slice up an apple the way my dad did. I never even thought to try.

As I walk down the sidewalk, away from the Rowboat Inn and toward the shopping center, I'm careful to keep my face out of the sight of oncoming traffic. It's dark, so that helps, but some of the surrounding stores and gas stations do illuminate the road. I keep my head down, moving in a straight line, until I see the yellow lights of Subway just up ahead. And then I notice, right next to Subway, the Fairchester Gift Shop. I'd nearly forgotten how much my mother loved that place.

An idea comes to me. A gift shop—a gift for Melody. It seems like the right thing to do. I'll buy her a little gift; that way, she has proof that I'm falling for her, plus it's a way to thank her for all she does for me. And if memory serves, the

161

Fairchester Gift Shop has something perfect.

Inside, the place smells just as I remember, like candles and soaps and spice. I head for the back where a wall of teddy bears looms in front of me. Under the golden glow of the shop, I pick out the perfect bear, which is also the cheapest bear and the ugliest bear. He's pudgy, and his eyes are crossed. His nose is stitched on sideways. His mouth is twisted. I laugh to myself and carry him to the counter.

The cashier is an older woman with short gray hair. She's wearing those thick, oversized round glasses that remind me of librarians and grade-school teachers. She rings me up and takes my twenty, then hands me back nine bucks and change. That's all I have left to buy dinner with. I guess Melody and I will have to share a foot-long turkey sub and a soda.

"Benji Bear," the lady behind the counter says, placing the bear into a paper bag. "He's been here for ages."

"It's for a girl," I say, wanting to get it right out in the open that I'm not buying the thing for myself.

She chuckles. "Lucky girl, then."

"Depends on how you look at things right now."

We share a smile, and I can tell that me buying Benji Bear has just made her night.

****

When I get back to the Rowboat Inn, Melody is resting on the bed on her stomach, looking down at the clue. She's dressed for bed already, wearing her purple nightgown. Her legs are bare, and her hair is down and flowing. I swear she does this stuff to drive me insane.

"Thank God," she says as I close and lock the door. "I was going nuts worrying."

I hold the Benji Bear bag behind my back. "We have to split a turkey sub," I tell her, balancing both the Subway bag and the soda in one hand. "Money was a little tight once I got there."

"What's going on?" She narrows her eyes. "Are you hiding something?"

I jerk my head for her to come to me. I can tell she thinks something is wrong, so as she gets closer I smile. Then I pull Benji Bear from the bag and hold him out for her. Like I needed to see her cry again.

"For me?" she says.

"You said your father got rid of yours," I reply. "So I got you a new one."

"Oh!" She squeezes Benji Bear to her chest. "He's so...he's so ugly!"

"I know, right?"

We laugh, and then she thanks me a million times. When I tell her his name, she hugs me, Benji Bear smooshed between us, and the plastic Subway bag against her back. I inhale her hair, because I love it when she wears it down. I love how it smells like a million gardens.

"You smell good," I tell her.

"I do?" she whispers, holding me. I don't think she's going to let go, I really don't. I let her hold on for as long as she wants, which because I'm starving, feels like an hour.

Finally, we separate and set ourselves up on the bed with our sub and our soda. While I was gone, Melody pulled the nasty blue sleeping bag off the bed and tossed it into a corner. Thank God, because that thing was really making my skin crawl.

"So, first thing in the morning we're going to the cemetery," I remind her.

"Are you nervous?" she asks, biting into her half of the turkey sub.

"Mostly about not finding out what the rest of the clue means."

She sighs and puts her sub down on the plastic bag. "Me too," she says. "I've been over it a thousand times, and I still can't figure out what that little circle means."

"Guess we'll find out tomorrow." I sip my soda. "Maybe. Hopefully."

As we eat, we discuss the clue again, come up with

nothing, then we play some games on her phone. I get ready for bed in the bathroom, which is one of the worst experiences of my life—there's hair on the floor and black mold in the tub, not to mention the toilet water is murky from I don't know what—then meet up with Melody in bed around midnight. The blue sleeping bag is over us for warmth, but Melody put it toward the bottom of the bed so it doesn't touch our skin or faces.

We snuggle under the covers, combating the draft as chilly air moves around us in an endless circle of coldness. Melody pulls closer, squishing Benji Bear's soft paws and fat belly between us. My stomach rumbles in hunger, but I try to ignore it. I ate the last Pop-Tart around nine. Now, just knowing our food supply is low makes me even hungrier.

"I heard you singing this morning," I tell her. "In the shower."

"Great," she replies.

"You sounded good," I say. "I didn't know you could sing."

"My father kind of banned singing," she says. "I mean, he didn't officially say I couldn't sing in the apartment, it's just when I was younger I was singing a song from *High School Musical*, and he flipped out."

"Maybe he doesn't like *High School Musical*."

"*Everyone* likes *High School Musical*."

I will not readily admit to that so I just laugh. The bed shakes. It's a cheap bed, I mean, like really cheap. I can't believe the thing hasn't broken just from me laughing.

"It's because of my mom," Melody says. "He doesn't like me singing because it reminds him of my mom."

I know what she means. Most of the time, I feel like that with my mother. Like everything I do reminds her of my father. I'm the last piece she has of him, and for Melody's dad, it's probably the same way. Melody is all he has left of his dead wife. Kind of sad that we're both forever mirrors of dead people.

164

"You should sing if you want," I tell her. "Because you sound really good."

"Thanks," she whispers, sleepy.

She presses closer. I resist the urge to kiss her.

We fall asleep, entwined.

****

"We need to be back before checkout," Melody says in the early sunlight, glancing back at the Rowboat Inn as we walk to Fraser's car. "So he doesn't give our room to someone else."

We made the decision this morning, while we ate the last of the bag of nuts for breakfast that we would stay one more night at the inn. We need to be home tomorrow, because school is Monday and that's when Melody's dad expects her home. My mother expects me home, too, but at least she would understand why we couldn't be back in time. Forces out of our control or whatever.

Time is running short. We have two days to do the impossible—decode a clue, find a map, dig up a body to obtain an incantation, steal the wand and pentacle from Alexander, and work some kind of old magic to reverse the Ritual of the Four. Melody hasn't mentioned yet how impossible the feat is, probably to keep me positive and moving forward, but sometimes I see the despair in her eyes.

"I don't see why we wouldn't be back to the motel before noon," I tell her as we hop into the car and throw our bags in the back. Melody didn't trust leaving a single thing at the motel. "The cemetery is right in Fairchester."

"And if we run into trouble?"

"If we run into trouble, we're screwed anyhow," I reply.

She sighs, starts up the car, and reverses. My head jerks back. She's still not very good in reverse.

I direct her to Old Gate Cemetery, my stomach growling as we pass every fast food place. Finally, she pulls up in front of a brown wood fence. She parks the car near the curb, on a slant, and we glance at each other once, then exit the car.

"I'm not taking out the clue," she says as we walk toward the wood cemetery gate. "I mean, we really have it memorized anyhow."

"True," I reply.

We pass through the open gate into the cemetery. The ground below us is covered in dead pine needles and frosted brown grass that crunches underfoot. The gravestones are pretty spread out, not in any particular row or order, just randomly stuck in the ground. Most of them are eroding. Some are sprinkled with moss. A few are broken.

"Any ideas?" I ask as we move around.

She bends down to inspect a tombstone. "No," she replies. "Well, I don't know. Maybe." She takes out her phone, opens up her compass, and moves it around. "Northeast is this way," she says, pointing.

"You do realize that the little circle symbol is on the compass, by those numbers that keep going up and down?"

"I studied how to read a compass last night, while you were at Subway," she says. "I was curious because of the Northeast thing and the little circle that could mean degrees."

"And?"

She doesn't answer, she just moves ahead, weaving in and out of tombstones, glancing at each one as she walks by. The cemetery isn't huge, not like fields and fields of graves, but I still don't think we've looked at each grave, if that's what she's trying to accomplish.

"A circle with a dot in the middle is a symbol of the sun," she says as I follow behind her. "Maybe that's what the clue means. Maybe the dot in the middle just wore away over time because the clue was written so long ago."

"Lost me," I reply.

"Maybe we're supposed to head northeast, toward the sun, or something like that?" She stops short. "You go that way and look," she demands, pointing to the far side of the cemetery. "We'll cover more ground if we split up."

I jog off in the opposite direction of the sun. I'm trying to use my brain here, think of everything I know about the sun, moon, stars, and direction. The sun rises in the east. It sets in the west. The North Star…I guess that's in the north? I never really think of myself as stupid until I try to figure these things out.

Melody is in the distance, bending down to read tombstones, moving her phone around, shuffling through the cemetery. I'm almost positive she's in the right location and I'm in the wrong one, but still, it's important that we check every grave for some kind of clue.

Most of these tombstones are from the 1700s and 1800s. Not too many from the 1900s and nothing recent at all. I keep reading the names as I pass by, not really knowing what I'm looking for but hoping something will pop up as different or unusual.

I'm just about ready to head back to Melody when I notice a grave toward the back of the cemetery, just in front of a row of dead trees and thin woods, hidden by fallen leaves. The leaves are scattered around, covering up most of the gravestone, but I can see the top curve of the oval stone sticking out like a reaching hand. There's a house back there that neighbors the cemetery, so I make sure nobody is outside in the yard and keep moving.

When I get to the grave, I turn back to gauge my distance. The road is so far off that I can barely see Fraser's car. Melody isn't in my direct line of vision. I bend down and push aside some leaves, exposing the name carved into the gravestone — Edgar North. The name doesn't ring a bell or seem important, but still, I play the name over and over in my mind, just to be sure. North…Edgar North…North, Edgar….

North, E.

"Melody!" I call.

I get a little nervous when she doesn't come right away. Then I see her slip through some skeletal old trees and rush to me. I stand up to greet her, so excited I can barely keep my limbs still.

167

"It wasn't a direction," I say, pointing down at the grave. "North, E. doesn't mean northeast. It's a person."

Melody squats to read the name on the gravestone. She glances up at me, eyes wide. "Good job," she says.

"You're not the only one good with clues."

She rolls her eyes. "Don't get cocky." She pushes aside the leaves at the base of the grave. I help her, and the deeper we go, the wetter and heavier the leaves become. When we get to the bottom, she gasps.

On the very bottom of the gravestone, just to the right, is a carved little circle.

"Holy shit," I say. "What does that mean?"

Melody stands and paces in front of Edgar North's grave. She shakes out her hands, thinking. "I'm not sure," she says finally. "I mean, we have everything now. We have all the things listed on the clue. We should be seeing something now. We should have the map."

"Maybe the circle is like a pointer or indicator," I say, thinking of the compass. "Maybe the map is in the direction of the circle."

We look around. If the circle is pointing toward the back of Edgar North's grave, it's indicating the row of dead trees, or the house beyond. If it's pointing ahead of his grave, it's indicating the road in the distance, which really makes no sense at all. Or maybe there was once a grave in front of Edgar North, but that grave is long gone. Maybe that grave was engraved with the words *The Map Is Here*.

"It could be the house," I say. "The map might be inside."

Melody casts her gaze at the house, a shamrock-green New England colonial, inspects it as only Melody can, and shakes her head. "The house is too new," she says. "See the bottom? The foundation isn't stone, it's cement."

She's right. Most of the historical houses I've seen in New England have stone foundations and look much older. And any house that would have been used in the clue would date back to the 1800s, possibly making it historical property.

"Unless they tore down the original house," Melody says. "In that case...."

"They wouldn't put the map in a house."

She thinks on that, then turns toward the row of dead trees. A spiral of smoke lifts from the chimney of the house, and the scent of fire tingles the inside of my nose. Someone must have recently lit a fire, which means that someone is inside right now.

"We should go into those woods," Melody says, indicating the trees. "You know, walk away from the circle in a straight line."

"Be careful," I say, pointing to the smoke. "Someone is inside."

"It's a cemetery," Melody replies. "Public property."

"That doesn't mean teenagers should be traipsing around in the woods behind an old gravestone."

"Traipsing?" she says.

"It's a word."

We move forward, in between the trees, directly behind the gravestone. There's nothing on the ground, even as I kick aside some fallen branches, and Melody bends down and brushes her hand against the dead grass. I even look upward through the tangled mass of tree limbs, but get nothing but a partial view of pearly sky. Melody rubs her hand against a tree trunk. She holds her arm out straight, parallel to the gravestone, to get an accurate location.

"This is wrong," she says.

I'm beginning to agree with her. There's nothing here but trees.

After a few more minutes of searching, which we're really only doing out of despair and frustration, we go back to Edgar North's grave. Melody kneels in front of it, her eyes moving back and forth over the words on the tombstone. *Edgar North 1783-1839*. That's it. Plain and simple. Just the name, the dates, and the little circle at the bottom. She rests her hand at the base of the gravestone, then she places her

169

finger in the center of the carved circle and presses. She turns back and shrugs like it was stupid but all she had left for a guess.

I point to the street, then back at the woods. Then I switch. East and west. North and south. Left and right. Up and down.

"Melody," I say. "Maybe…maybe the circle is supposed to be a marker for something down beneath, like X marks the spot. Maybe the map is just below the circle."

She smacks her forehead. "You're right!" she says. "Help me start digging!"

I don't think the map is going to be right on the surface. It had to survive years and years of storms and erosion and landscaping. It could be as far down as the coffin itself.

Melody lifts an eyebrow when I don't start digging right away.

"We're going to get caught," I say. "The people in that house…."

If they call the cops and the police come here, we're double screwed. No, not double screwed, *quadruple* screwed. Desecrating a grave. Grave robbing. Driving without a license. Leaving the scene of a crime back in Connecticut.

"Do you trust me?" Melody says.

"With my life," I reply.

"Then just start digging with your hands," she says. "I've got it under control."

So I listen to her. I always do. I wish I could explain why I always do what she says, even when I know the outcome is a million shades of awful.

"Did you know that Abraham Lincoln was the first president to be embalmed?" Melody says as we dig.

"That fact slipped by me."

"It's true," she says.

Like I would challenge her. She's probably right, plus I get the sense that she's just talking in random facts to avoid facing reality. We're not making much progress with just our hands. The ground below the circle marker is wet and pliable from the pile of leaves we pushed away, but as we go a little deeper, hands and fingernails covered in earth, it's difficult to dig. I haven't told her yet that I suspect the map is closer to the coffin than to the tombstone, but because she's Melody, the thought has probably occurred to her.

When we get the hole about the size a dog would dig down a bone, my hands are stiff and frozen. Melody stops when I do, and I'm just about to tell her we need to come back with a shovel and some gloves when she puts a dirt-covered finger to her lips. Her eyes shift to the left at the trees behind the grave.

"Don't move," she whispers. "Somebody is coming."

Chapter Eighteen

Don't move? Melody must be crazy. No, Melody *is* crazy. Somebody is coming into the cemetery and she's telling me not to move?

In the distance, I hear faint footsteps and rustling leaves. My first instinct, when I sense trouble, is to smell the air for any touch of blood or metal. As I breathe in, the air smells just like it did before, like burning wood and fire. My muscles stiffen, and my blood pulses in my throat as the footsteps get closer to the cemetery.

"Let me talk," Melody says. "Just stay quiet."

A second later, a middle-aged man rushes through the trees, coming at us like a storm. He's dressed in a denim jacket and faded jeans, a cool and casual sort of guy, only he's really not cool and casual right now. Curls of gray-black hair stick out from the brim of a blue baseball cap, and he adjusts the cap as his eyes fix on us like he can't believe what he's witnessing.

"What the hell do you kids think you're doing?" he says, stopping just behind the grave.

Melody scratches the corner of her eye, nonchalant. "Geocaching," she says.

"Excuse me?"

"Geocaching," she says again. She stands up and holds out her phone. "You know, geocaching?"

Her attempt to smooth this over may have pissed this guy

off even more. His bushy gray-black eyebrows push together, and his mouth grows thin.

"People hide containers in public locations," Melody says. "They put the locations or the coordinates of the containers online and then you go and find them and leave behind a little something for the next person to find. It's like a treasure hunt." She smiles at him. "And it's perfectly legal."

"You're going to have to leave," he says, glancing down at the grave. "You can't do what you're doing."

"The law says I can," she says back. "This is a public area."

"So if I call the caretaker and tell him some kids are digging up an old grave, you're saying he'll just let you go about your business?"

They go back and forth debating this for at least five minutes. Melody claims geocaching is legal. Baseball-hat guy says it's not legal to dig up a grave. Melody says it's public property, baseball-hat guy says she can't *destroy* public property. The guy isn't an ass, he's just honestly trying to keep the graveyard free of vandalism. He's probably the owner of the neighboring house and spotted trouble, even if it's not his job to take care of the cemetery.

I've had just about enough of the back and forth talk of legal rights, so I stand up and grab Melody's hand.

"We'll just get going," I say, tugging her away from her argument.

"Chase," she says, using my fake name and eyeing me. "We have every right to—"

"Let's just go," I say. I turn to baseball-hat guy. "Sorry for any inconvenience."

Melody protests as I pull her away, back to the road. I have a plan, though, and I really should have thought of it sooner. We need tools, and we need darkness. That's my grand plan. Come back later when it's dark and bring a shovel. It sucks that we don't have time on our side, and we have no choice but to come back later when the sun goes down.

"You weren't going to win," I say as she pulls the car away from the curb.

"I know that," she says. "I just hate when people tell me I can't do things."

"We were digging up a grave."

"I know!"

She stops at a red light but doesn't quite judge it right, so we skid for a couple seconds before landing a few feet past the white line.

"We need to eat something," I say. "We're both cranky because all we've eaten since last night is a bag of nuts."

"I'm trying to save the little bit of money we have left." She stares up at the red light. "We need gas money to get back home or Fraser's or wherever the hell we're going next, plus we need at least forty for another night at Motel Nasty. And that doesn't even count the money we'll need for a stupid shovel."

Wow. She's hit an entirely new level of crankiness. Best to back off.

The light turns green and she jets ahead, out of the intersection. As she drives, cooling down a touch, we discuss what we're going to do about eating and decide we'll stop and buy as much as we can at a drugstore. Melody says they're cheaper than convenience stores. We decide that tonight, we'll eat dinner at McDonalds, and split what we can of a value meal. We'll need energy for the dig, so we can splurge on burgers. Then, after dinner, we'll head back to the cemetery.

We pull into the parking lot of the inn, check our surroundings, and lug the bags of food and our carry-bags back to Room 17. Part of me hates to think this, but I really should have checked to see if Fraser had any money stashed in the cottage back in Connecticut. We were in a hurry to get out of there, but it would have taken me only a second to run back to Fraser's coat or find his wallet. God, I'm a horrible person.

Melody dumps the food onto the bed and tears right into a box of granola bars. She stuffs one in her mouth, eating savagely like I eat, and I try not to laugh because her temperament is iffy right now. Unfortunately, I can't hold my hysterics in, and I burst out laughing, almost in her face. She shoots me a look and I stop. Then I drop down beside her and rip open a bag of Doritos.

"Did you know that in Japan, watermelons are square?" she says.

"Maybe I'll move there someday, then," I say and crunch on one of the Doritos. "You know you say these random facts when you feel like there's no hope, right?"

"I don't know," she says. "Maybe."

It's the first time she's admitting defeat. Not a good sign.

"It's just that I hoped we'd be farther by now," she says. "I thought last night we'd figure out the clue part and find the map, today we'd be at the burial place, and tomorrow we'd...."

"There's no way we're going to find Alexander," I admit. "We should probably just give it up for now, or just find the map and come back another time to dig up the incantation. He'll probably find me in Rockpoint soon, anyhow. He always finds me eventually."

"That's it!" she says. She stands and starts pacing. "You said that he always finds you, but you don't know how. You can sense him, too, when he's near you...you said you smell blood or metal?"

I nod. "I'm not sure why, but whenever he's close, I smell it. At Fraser's, he must have just left, because the scent was faint but still there."

"So why can't you find him that way?" she says. "By following that trace or scent of blood in the air?"

"Because it would take me months, that's why," I reply. "And in case you haven't noticed, we only have two days."

"Well, we know he was just in Connecticut yesterday,"

she says. "And we know he somehow found you, we just don't know how he found you at Fraser's, but he hadn't yet found you in Rockpoint."

Seems kind of strange, now that I'm looking at it like that. It usually takes Alexander and Lomidus at least a month to find me, but I was only at Fraser's house for a day. I'm starting to wonder if maybe Alexander always knows where I am but just holds back for whatever reason.

"Maybe he's waiting for me to make some kind of move," I say. "Like when I was at the carnival, they came to find me that night. Maybe they thought I was at the carnival because—"

"You were searching for the incantation at some old fairground in Fairchester," she finishes. "Same with Fraser's. They knew the two of you would discuss it and probably knew Fraser had the physical clue."

"But in Rockpoint—"

"They probably know the incantation is in New England," she says. "That's why your mother took you out of New England and to New York. They probably knew you were in Rockpoint all along but just waited until you went back to New England."

Please don't let that be true. If they know where my mother is…not that she's ever been a target, but it still doesn't sit well with me. And if they know Melody is traveling with me and knows about the clue and all of this, then she's a target, too.

"You shouldn't have accepted the goblet," I say. "You shouldn't have gotten involved in any of this."

"Too late," she replies. "Plus, the goblet means a lot to me."

"Why?" I hop off the bed and stand near the table. "You can't do anything with it. It's just a paperweight. A decoration."

She looks at me like I just slapped her in the face. "Nice," she says.

177

"That's not what I meant," I say. "But now that we're on the subject, why haven't you asked me about it? I could just as easily renew the Ritual and give you all that power. You're just fine with me ending the whole thing?"

She shrugs and turns away from me. "I just wanted whatever you wanted," she whispers. "But yes, of course I would have liked to have the power of the goblet."

"Why didn't you tell me then?"

"Because I went along with you to help you find out about the Ritual," she replies. She spins around, splotches of pink on her cheeks. "And then we found out for sure that you could end it or break it, and all I wanted to do from the beginning was keep you safe." She lowers her head. "Even if I honestly don't agree with what you're doing."

"Oh no?"

"No," she says back. "In fact, you're stupid for wanting to get rid of such a unique gift. It's been in your family forever. Your father would have been upset if he knew."

"People are trying to kill me!" I shout. "They killed Fraser! They killed my *father!*"

The blood in my veins boils and burns. It's the same sensation I have in fights with my mother, when my mother usually ends up....

Melody gasps. She grabs her thumb, wraps her fingers around and squeezes.

"Melody," I say. "Please tell me I didn't...."

She shakes her head and turns away from me. I press my eyes closed.

"Come here," I say. "Let me see."

Slowly, she spins and walks to the table. I grab her thumb. It's sliced down the padding, bleeding.

"Damn it," I say.

"It's okay," she whispers. "We both knew it might happen."

That's not good enough for me. I don't want to hear that it's okay, and I hate that she just expected I would cut her by accident someday. Holding her thumb, I smooth some of the blood with my finger. Wipe it away as best I can. Then I raise her thumb to my mouth and rest it against my lips. I taste her blood, warm and salty. She rolls her eyes up at me, and I drop down in the chair and pull her down with me. Right onto my lap, just like my dad used to do with my mom.

And then we're kissing.

It's not normal kissing. Melody is just as insane with kissing as she is with everything else. She's fast—I can't even keep up with her lip movements, can't keep her contained or soft or even. It's just fast kissing. Frantic. Electric.

We break apart and we're panting. Seriously panting, like we just ran for miles.

"Where did you...learn to kiss...like that?" I say, gasping out the words.

"The Internet," she replies.

I'm not even going to try to figure that one out.

"I'm sorry," she whispers and dips her head to my shoulder.

"It's okay," I tell her. "That's been building up for a long time."

She moves away and drops down on the bed, on her back.

Focus, Shaw.

My mind is spinning. I think I might have just screwed up a million things, not to mention my kissing sucks, and Melody is probably thinking that right now. I never mastered the long kiss. In eighth grade, I kissed two girls in one day, but since then, it's been kind of slow going. I remember that day in middle school, our gym teacher decided not to show up, so we were all just hanging out in the stairwell near the gym. Someone came up with this brilliant idea to play a kissing game, only there really wasn't a game. We just switched and kissed. Victoria Cohen and Krystal...I don't remember Krystal's last name. But her hair was honey, and she smelled like vanilla cookies. I do remember that.

Melody stares up at the ceiling. Her stomach moves up and down as she breathes. I can't stop thinking that I messed up our first kiss.

I want another shot.

I move to the bed and rest myself beside her, slide my hand across her cheek, and kiss her again. Slower. In control.

And it's not half bad.

Chapter Nineteen

It's twilight when Melody pulls the car up to Old Gate Cemetery. We bought a shovel at Allen's Hardware and stashed it in the trunk. Now, we just have to get inside the cemetery, carrying a shovel without being noticed by any passing cars or the baseball-hat guy who lives in the neighboring house. Yeah. That should be easy.

I'm still trying to get my head in the game after my afternoon with Melody. After we kissed, we played some games on her phone, then watched YouTube for a while. Then we kissed again before leaving for McDonald's and the hardware store. I told her I wanted to wait until all of this was over before we became an official couple, so that's where we are right now.

Melody seems to have no problem getting her head in the game. She's all business, I can tell by the straight line of her jaw and the way her eyes are set ahead. As we sit in the car, waiting for the splash of purple across the horizon to fade to black, we look around the cemetery for any sign of movement. All clear for the moment, so we continue to watch and wait. When darkness falls completely, we sneak outside and grab the shovel out of the trunk.

"I'll keep watch," she says as we slip through the cemetery gate. "If I hear or see someone coming, we'll both run to the car."

I nod and keep walking toward Edgar North's grave. The

air isn't quite as cold as it's been, so that helps. It's the sort of chill that feels more like fall than winter. I guess since we're in between seasons, with winter just a few weeks away, it could have gone either way. One of Melody's concerns was that it would rain or even snow when we were trying to find the map. I told her I would work through the rain or snow, but inside I was praying for the weather to cooperate. At least something has to go right for us.

We reach Edgar North's grave with little difficulty. It's dark, but I can see that baseball-hat guy covered over the hole Melody and I made earlier. Great. I check for the most direct route back to the car should I have to make a run for it, then do a quick once-over to make sure nobody is around. Melody kisses my cheek and tiptoes away until she disappears into the thin woods that line the graveyard. Without wasting a second, I drive the shovel into the ground just below the circle indicator. With any luck, I won't have to go down that far.

I scoop and toss dirt, doing it as quietly as I can. It's difficult. The shovel makes a loud scraping noise whenever the metal hits the earth, and once or twice I hear Melody shush me from her hidden location in the trees. A few cars pass by on the main road, but because Edgar North's grave is so far in the back, it's unlikely that anyone will see me. I keep going — scoop and toss, heave and dig.

I'm only a few feet down when something strange catches my eye.

For a second, I think maybe it's a reflection. Maybe a car's backlights striking an old piece of jewelry or metal in the ground, or some traffic light far away changed to red. But then I realize that whatever it is, it's not just red. It's glowing.

"Melody!"

I toss the shovel aside and drop to my knees, shifting dirt around to unearth the source of the glowing red light. Melody runs to my side as I grab hold of the item and tug it from the ground.

182

"Oh my God," Melody says. "What is it?"

I was just wondering the same thing. It's obviously not a map, not even a piece of paper. It's a red orb, radiating magical light, pulsing in my palm. It's so bright that I can see, tinged in red, every little detail of Melody's face, the greenish flecks in her eyes, and the tiny beauty mark on the top of her cheek. Edgar North's gravestone is illuminated red, as though engulfed in a sunset.

"It's not a map," I say, running my fingers over the smooth orb. "We're supposed to be looking for a map."

"It's what we're looking for," Melody says. "I mean, you just found a glowing red ball in the place we're supposed to be looking and you're questioning if it's the right thing?"

She's got a point.

"That's what the circle meant," she says and points to the circle indicator on the gravestone. "It's probably there to tell us we've got the right place *and* the right thing—something circular."

I hand the orb over to her, pick up the shovel, and move a little more dirt around just to be sure, then scoop dirt over the hole to fill it in. It's not like we don't know where to look if the orb isn't the map. I'll just have to dig up the grave again.

Melody inspects the orb, turning it over in her hands. "This is really something," she says. "How do you think it glows? Some kind of old magic?"

"Maybe," I reply. "Or maybe it just glows for people involved in—"

A distant crunch of leaves breaks me off. Melody shoots her gaze to the woods, not the thin woods close to us but the deeper ones a little off in the distance.

"An animal?" she whispers.

My body chills in unison with the thick scent of blood in the air.

I should have known.

"They're here," I whisper. "They found us."

Melody grabs my elbow. I wish she hadn't. I don't want

183

them to know I sense them.

"Hold onto the orb," I whisper. "We're going to run straight to the car. Don't look back."

Melody nods. I link my fingers with hers—and we take off.

We're fast. So fast, the gravestones blur by us in streaks of tan. The orb glows red in Melody's hand, leading the way. The shovel bangs and clangs against the ground. Finally, we reach the gate and run through, full throttle to the car.

We fling the car doors open and hop in. Melody sticks the keys in the ignition as I toss the shovel into the backseat. I lift the orb from her fingers and the car jolts ahead, cutting off a passing car and skidding them sideways into the far curb. I glance behind us as Melody drives away and catch the silhouettes of two figures jumping into their own car to make chase. Alexander and Lomidus.

I curse—a bad curse—but Melody ignores it. Her eyes are fixed ahead, and I'm uncomfortably reminded of my mother when she does the same car escape with me. A woman possessed. A woman who does not fool around with the safety of the person she loves.

"Can they cut or stab us from here?" Melody asks.

"No," I say. "I don't know. I think they have to be closer."

Anytime I've been in a violent slicing fight with Alexander or Lomidus, we've always been fairly close to each other. But that doesn't mean they can't focus and cut from the car behind us. Honestly, I don't know what they can do.

"How did they find us?" she says.

"I think they knew where we were since we left Connecticut or somewhere around that time," I reply. "Not by following us. They have some other way to find me."

She nods. "I can't lose them at this speed," she says, glancing into the rearview mirror. "But if we get pulled over for speeding...."

She peeled away from the cemetery in a hurry, but now, as we merge with regular traffic, she slows her pace. Cops could be anywhere, and somehow, I don't think they'll believe we're being chased by two guys who can slice us to shreds using only their minds.

"It's like telekinesis, right?" Melody says. "You have to really focus to use it."

I turn to look behind us. They're still following in what appears to be a dark, newer car, maybe a Toyota or something foreign. "What?" I say to Melody. "Teleki...what?"

"What you do is like telekinesis. Moving objects with your mind. Only you need to visualize the dagger and then use it *invisibly* to cut or slice. I would think you would need to focus to do that. You know, be really close."

She's still worried about them cutting her, and I don't blame her, but I don't have the time or energy right now to figure out and explain all the details of my ability. "Don't worry," I say, even though she really should worry. There's no way to block them. You can't fight against a weapon that's pretty much invisible. "I won't let them hurt you, okay?"

She nods and stops at a red light. I keep my eyes fixed on the car behind us, waiting for Alexander or Lomidus to exit their car and attack. From where I'm sitting, I can just see their faces and hair, Lomidus driving and Alexander sitting in the passenger's seat, eyes meeting mine. His stare is cold fury.

"They want the orb," I say. "It's the map. I don't know *how* it can be a map, but it's the map and they want it."

"I know," she replies. The light turns green, and she exhales and presses the gas. "We have to really sit down and inspect the thing, but it's obviously the map."

We drive through the town, getting lost, not going anywhere near the motel. I wonder if Melody is thinking the same thing I'm thinking.

"Just our toothbrushes," she says, reading my mind. "We've got everything in our carry-bags except our toothbrushes, and I think you left the bag of Doritos on the table."

Here's the one stroke of good luck — I did not pay the

forty dollars to stay at the Rowboat Inn tonight. I went down to the front desk three times, and every time, the red-bearded guy who runs the place wasn't there. I think we probably could have stayed the night for free and he wouldn't have noticed. He seems to have forgotten I was in the motel, or expected me to leave earlier.

"You have Benji Bear?" I ask.

"Of course I have Benji Bear." She takes a quick right turn, throwing me over. "And the dagger and the goblet are both in our carry-bags. Those are the only things we really need. We don't need to go back."

So we make the decision not to go back to the motel. Now, we just have to figure out how we're going to lose Alexander and Lomidus while maintaining a normal speed limit. I'm just about to discuss this when my cell vibrates in the pocket of my jeans.

"Wonderful time for my mother to call," I say, pulling my cell from my pocket.

"Maybe it's my dad looking for me," Melody says and shoots me worried eyes. "He's been having trouble with me being gone so long."

Her father has been texting her and calling more than is necessary. She hasn't been away from him for this long before, and I think he misses her. I only hope my mother isn't calling to tell us we need to get home sooner.

But when I check my phone, I see the call is from *Huntley, A.* It's not like I have my cousin in my contacts, but my phone has ID.

"It's Alexander," I say in shock. "What do I do?"

"Answer it," she says. "Find out what he wants."

I know what he wants, and he's not going to get it. Not if I can help it.

I put the phone to my ear but don't say hello or anything that resembles politeness or courtesy.

"Shaw?" Alexander says. "I can see that you're listening."

"What do you want?" I ask.

186

"We're going to make this nice and easy for you," he says. "All you have to do is give us the map. We've already seen that you have it. Just give it to us and nobody gets hurt tonight."

I tap my foot against the floor of the car. Remind myself to keep it together. Don't get angry.

"How about you and your friend Lomidus answer a few questions for me," I say. "Then I'll think about giving you the map."

Melody shifts her eyes at me, then turns left onto a main road lined with gas stations and little stores and restaurants. I shift my eyes back at her to let her know I have no intention of giving them the map; I'm just fishing for information.

"Go ahead," Alexander says.

"How did you find me?"

Alexander sifts an amused breath of air through the phone. "The dagger is my line," he says. "It's like a magnet. Sometimes it takes me a little while, but I'm always drawn to it and drawn to wherever you happened to be."

Great. As long as I have the dagger in my possession, Alexander can find me. I suspected it was something like that. We're connected by the metal, connected by blood. That's why I always *smell* blood or metal when he's near me. There's really no escape, because I'm not putting my dagger anywhere out of my sight.

"Listen to me, Shaw," Alexander says. "You know nothing about the Ritual and nothing about the incantation. You have no experience with this, so just give us the map. It's of no use to you."

"We can figure it out."

"Stupid," Alexander says back. "And getting a girl involved in this was stupid, too."

Melody stops at a red light. I'm not sure if she can hear Alexander from where she's sitting in the driver's seat, but she glances into the rearview mirror, shooting the car behind us a look that could kill.

"I have another question," I say. "Why did you kill Fraser?"

"He had something we wanted," Alexander replies. "And he was old and useless. Nobody will miss him."

I'll miss him. My mother will miss him, too. True, I only knew Fraser a day, but I did like him and looked forward to my next meeting with him. That meeting never came, thanks to Alexander and Lomidus. I'm sick of them taking people away from me.

"So you have the pentacle and the wand," I say as Melody pulls through the green light. "And I have the dagger and the goblet." I let out a fake little laugh, evil and mocking. "Oh, and I have the map, too."

Alexander doesn't reply. I contemplate hanging up, but I know they'll just continue following us, and I want to end this now. I'm done running.

"All right, Shaw," he says finally. "We'll make one last offer. You hand over the map, or Lomidus kills the girl."

I knew they were going to get to that particular threat eventually.

"You can't," I reply. "I'm with her. I won't let you." I'm not scared of the threat. I'm careful to keep my tone even, unafraid.

"She has to go back to Rockpoint," he says, confirming that he knows where we live. "And once she gets there, Lomidus will open her throat and let her leak out like a faucet. Do you understand that? Are you picturing that?"

My veins burn, not just burn like fire but burn like ice, and that might be worse, but I'm careful to control my anger. I have no choice. I have to keep Melody calm, especially while she's driving. I don't think she heard the specifics of the threat. I *hope* she didn't. They killed my father and Fraser, so I know they're not playing around. And yes, eventually, Melody has to go back to her father. Alexander and Lomidus used her at the perfect time. I have the map, they want it, and now they have a way to get it.

"The dagger and the goblet," Alexander continues. "We'll need them, too."

This just keeps getting worse.

"And I'll have nothing more to do with this after that, right?" I ask. "You'll take me out of the Ritual of the Four for good?"

A brief pause, and then, "We have a deal."

"All right," I say, relenting—but only sort of. I'm still hoping we can figure out a plan. "Tell me what you want me to do."

So we make a deal to meet at the fairgrounds in Fairchester, where we fought at the autumn carnival. There's a field and a parking lot, so I tell them to keep their distance while we park, and we'll only exit the car if they promise to stay away from us. Then, we'll leave them the orb, the dagger, and the goblet in the field, and they can go get them once we're safely away. I don't want them anywhere near Melody. I tell them that if they get anywhere close, I will destroy the map and cut every part of them I can.

When I hang up, Melody looks over at me like she can't believe what I just did. I think she figured out that they used her as a threat, because why else would I just hand the orb and my beloved dagger over to them?

"What are we going to do?" I ask her.

"Well," she says through a heavy sigh, "we could read the map and beat them to it. The problem is, we don't actually *have* a map." She glances at the glowing red orb in my hand. She slows down, buying us time and bringing us to a safer speed limit. "Try to figure out what you can while I drive, okay?"

I turn the orb over and over. I hold it up to my eyes. There are no letters, no markings, no symbols, nothing. It's just a glowing red orb—unique, obviously magical in some way—but still just a glowing red orb.

"Maybe it's not a map in the sense of X marks the spot," I say. "Maybe it's another way of saying something, like…. The

Red Ball Cemetery."

Melody shakes her head. "If it were that easy, Alexander and Lomidus would just use that information and wouldn't need the orb."

True, they've already seen the orb. They probably saw everything that happened in the cemetery, which is why I wish Melody hadn't kissed my cheek. That's how they know she's more than a friend or partner in crime to me, if they didn't know that already.

"We're screwed," I say. "We have no choice but to give them the stuff."

My chest tightens as I think about parting with my dagger. To hell with the map. They're going to change around the Ritual, and I've bargained with them to leave me out of it, which I'm sure they were going to do anyhow. All I've wanted from the beginning was to get out of it, even though I really don't want Lomidus having all that power. But giving them my dagger — my *father's* dagger — that's like a fresh stab to the gut.

Melody drifts off in thought. She turns the wheel and drives us into a residential neighborhood. Alexander and Lomidus follow behind. My head is spinning, trying to think of a plan while Melody does the same. Finally, she swings around on a dead-end circle, gripping the steering wheel hard. She closes her eyes for a second, nods her head like she just made a silent decision about something, and pulls us back down the road.

"We can switch it out," she whispers. "We can make them think we're leaving the orb and leave something else in its place."

"How?" I say. "They already know it's glowing. It's not like we can fake that."

"Yes, we can." Her shoulders drop, and she sighs again, pulling her cell from her pocket. "I have an app on here that's like a flashlight. I use it sometimes while I'm reading or doing homework in bed. It makes the screen glow in different colors, flashing lights, holiday themes, and it has the option of turning the entire screen red."

"But we'd have to leave your...." I don't need to finish the thought.

Melody's eyes turn glassy, as though she's losing her best friend.

"It's the only way," she whispers.

Chapter Twenty

We work up a plan as we drive. We'll hold up the orb to show Alexander and Lomidus we're seriously leaving it for them, then leave Melody's phone in its place, covered in my white T-shirt so the red light glows through. Then we'll leave the dagger and the goblet in the gift boxes my mother gave us but the dagger and goblet won't be inside. We'll wait for Alexander and Lomidus to get far into the field, then run to the car and drive off as fast as Fraser's car will go, shoot onto the highway, and get as far away from Fairchester as we can.

Alexander will eventually find me, of course, because the dagger is like a magnet. But it might take him some time, and maybe by then we can work out the map. It's a long shot and things could go wrong, but it's the only plan we have.

I direct Melody toward Fairchester fairgrounds, and when she gets on the main road, she hands her cell over to me.

"Okay," she says, eyes locked ahead. "You'll need to do a few things." She glances at her phone and lets out a tiny squeak, but then she pulls herself together and sets her jaw tight. "I need you to block my father's numbers so he can't call my phone—his work, his cell, and our home phone. Then, you need to go into my journal app and send the entire contents of my journal to my e-mail, then delete the app. My journal password is *pingpongchamp*, one word."

"Ping-Pong champ?"

"I've been the ping-pong champion at Leavitt Falls Summer Day Camp for the past four summers," she says.

"Huh," I say, blocking her father's contacts from her phone. "I'll take 'Things You Didn't Know About Your Girlfriend' for two-hundred, Alex."

"Girlfriend?" she says, shooting me confused eyes.

Here's the deal. Alexander and Lomidus are in the car right behind us. We're meeting them at a dark location in about five minutes, where we'll play a trick on them to keep them from the map and the dagger and goblet. They'll be majorly pissed about that. So yeah. Melody is my girlfriend right now. I don't want either of us to die not knowing that.

"We kissed today," I remind her. "What did you think we were to each other?"

"But you said...." She eyes me, still perplexed.

"I know what I said, it's just that we don't know what's going to happen with Alexander and Lomidus. If either one of us should —"

"Forget it," she snaps. "I don't want to be your girlfriend."

Like it isn't enough right now that we're being followed by two guys who want to kill us. Why does Melody have to make everything so difficult? Hasn't she wanted us together since the beginning? I give her the same confused look she just gave me. She shakes her head, her eyes glued on the road.

"Anytime you've been interested in me, it was because I was dressed sexy or you were guilty that you hurt me," she says. "Now you're afraid we'll end up dead, so it's like you're just granting me one final wish or something. That's not how I want to end up together."

I don't even know how to respond to that. Only part of it is true. Okay, it's *all* true, but that doesn't mean I don't want to be with her.

"Let's not talk about this now," I say. "Let's just focus on what we're doing. Just forget I even called you my girlfriend."

She opens her mouth to reply, but then closes it and turns back to the road.

After sending Melody's journal over to her e-mail and deleting the app, I take a second to glance over her other apps and make sure there's nothing else in her phone that she'd want me to delete, should Alexander or Lomidus inspect it. I actually suspect they'll chuck the thing in anger, but who knows? I look over all her games, hoping that if she gets a new phone, she can transfer all her apps and keep her progress. She's top level or close to top level in almost every game she plays.

"We still have my phone," I remind her, even though my phone sucks and we both know it.

"Yeah," she says in a low voice. "I guess."

"I'll buy you a new one."

She doesn't reply.

When we pull into the fairgrounds, the field and the parking lot are both empty. The field stretches out into the darkness like a rolled-out blanket until it disappears through the horizon. My mind flashes back to the autumn carnival, all the carnival lights and the sweet scents and colorful balloons. It's weird that the place is so vacant and dark, when in my memory, it's lit up and bursting with life.

There are a few tall lampposts in the parking lot, illuminating the area in white fluorescence. I tell Melody to pull as far away from the lighting as possible. She drives to the rear of the lot, closer to the field, which is perfect. She stops the car and opens the flashlight app on her phone, but doesn't set the color yet.

"Alexander and Lomidus are about three car lengths away from us," she says, glancing out the back window. "I assume Alexander is the one who looks like you?"

"Alexander is eighteen, and Lomidus is much older than us, at least forties or fifties," I tell her, not knowing if she can really see him from where we are. "And three car lengths is a little too close." I take a breath and step out of the car before

195

Melody can stop me. "Pull back!" I yell and gesture them away from Fraser's car.

Lomidus reverses until they're so far away I can barely make out their faces. Then I hold up the orb and catch the movement of Alexander nodding when he spots the red glow. When I slide back into the car, Melody has already gathered my white T-shirt and the two empty boxes my mother gave us just before we got on the train to Connecticut.

"You really shouldn't have done that," she says, worried.

"It's not like I haven't faced these guys before," I return. "Plus, we need them as far from us as possible if this is going to work."

We go over the plan one more time, then exit the car. Melody holds the car keys and the boxes; I have the T-shirt, the orb, and her phone. As we step over the curb and into the field, I keep my eye on Alexander and Lomidus, making sure they're not jumping out of their car. We keep walking into the darkness, away from the shining lampposts to where I suppose the carousel would have been when the grounds were set up for the autumn carnival. When I turn back, there's no movement in the field. We're so far off I have to squint to make out the two cars in the parking lot.

"You ready?" Melody says, kneeling onto the grass.

I nod. One last time, I hold up the orb so they can see I'm not playing a trick. Then I block the orb with my body while flipping to the red screen on Melody's phone and tucking the orb into the deep pocket inside my leather jacket. I slide my white T-shirt over the phone while Melody sets up the two boxes.

"Rest the phone up against the boxes," she whispers. "That will make it easier to see the red shining through."

When we step back from our work, it looks good. From a distance, it will look like two items behind a glowing red light: the dagger, the goblet, and the map. I move aside to show them what we've left. They exit the car, two distant silhouettes moving closer to the edge of the field.

"Ready?" Melody says, grabbing my hand.

"Let's do it."

Madly, we run to the car, passing Alexander and Lomidus who don't even try for us, they speed directly to the map in the middle of the field. Not looking back, we jump into the car and Melody skids off, hopping the curb at the back of the lot and catching the main road. She follows my directions as I scream them: "Right!" and then "Left!" until finally, we're on the highway. When I look behind us, nobody has followed.

"Get off at the first exit you see," I tell her.

"What?" she yells.

"They'll think we stayed on the highway," I explain. "Just get off the exit and take as many random turns as you can."

She slides into the fast lane while I keep my eyes sharp for state cops. Then she merges back into the right lane and gets off an exit, into a town that looks similar to Fairchester. She stops at the stop sign at the bottom of the exit, glances into the rearview mirror, then speeds ahead. She takes a random left, then a right, then another right until we're at the end of some wooded neighborhood with tall, majestic houses. She parks between two of the houses, right up against the curb, like we live in one of the homes or we're visiting. She kills the lights.

We don't breathe for about five minutes. Then, when I'm confident Alexander and Lomidus haven't caught up to us, I slide the map from my jacket and stare down at it, like maybe it somehow morphed into a true map while we were running from Alexander and Lomidus.

"Give me the thing," Melody says. She reaches out and grabs the orb, runs her fingers over it, then shakes it. She holds it to her ear. She flips it. Then she nods. "Well," she says finally, "I think I know what to do." She hands it back to me. "First of all, the burial site and the incantation won't be far from here. Back when they buried all of this, they didn't exactly have easy ways of getting around like we do now, especially with a dead body."

"Okay," I say. "So did you read the map?"

"Not yet," she replies. "The map is inside the orb. You need to break it open."

"What?" Before she can reply, my phone rings, and I pull it from my pocket. It says the call is from Melody, and it takes me a second to realize that it's not actually Melody calling me.

"Don't answer it," Melody says, staring down at my ID. "If they don't hear traffic in the background, they'll know we're not on the highway."

"Good point," I say and ignore Alexander's call. "So, you're saying we need to break the orb?"

"*You* do," she replies. "Just like you sliced the apple in half. You'll need to focus and crack the orb right down the middle."

I'm not sure if it's possible for me to do that. An apple is one thing, but the orb is a thick ball of glass. "Can't we just use the shovel and smash the thing?"

Melody shakes her head. "You want everyone in the neighborhood to come out here and see a glowing orb, broken into a million pieces in the middle of the road?"

With a huff, I place the orb down on the dash. I close my eyes and try to concentrate on my dagger, but the focus just isn't there. There's still some leftover adrenalin from our run from Alexander and Lomidus, so I try to tap into that and can manage some intense visuals. Gold dagger. Shining jewels. Sharp tip. But I can't project.

"Try to get me mad," I say.

"No," she says back. "You have to do it without getting mad."

Seriously? "Now is not the time for a life lesson," I snap.

She changes gears, and instead of making me mad—which I do admit she does very well lately—she smiles. Kind of flirts with me with her eyes. Soft and green, her eyes send me soaring, and I imagine kissing her on the bed at the

Rowboat Inn. I remember Fraser saying something about the emotions I draw on when I use my dagger. He listed passion, but back then, I knew nothing of passion. Hadn't experienced it. Now I have, with Melody. True love, true passion. It would be impossible for that to work as well as anger, but I try it anyway, focus on the memory of Melody in bed, scents and touches.

With a loud crack like a huge hatching egg, the orb splits into two pieces. One half stays on the dash, the other half falls toward the floor of the car, until Melody reaches out and snatches it. The orb stops glowing. The color dies. The orb is no longer glowing and red, it's now just two ordinary pieces of cloudy glass. The center of the orb is hollow, and curled inside the half of the orb in Melody's hand is a rolled-up piece of paper.

"The map," she says, triumphantly fisting the air.

"You're not going to ask how I cracked open the orb?"

She smiles. "I already know how you did it."

"Of course you do," I say and slide closer to read the map.

She unrolls the map. It's dark and shadowy, so I can't see what's written, but I can tell it's a series of steps or locations. Hopefully, it's not another clue she'll need to decipher. We just don't have time for figuring out clues.

"Okay," she says and scratches her head. "There are four steps listed here, and we've done two of them, so it's kind of redundant." She reads it over, again and again, then finally puts it in my hand. "I think we can do this."

The map is an old piece of brown paper or parchment, with a cross shape dividing the map into four separate squares. In the top left square, there's a picture of Edgar North's grave—a mound of dirt and a tombstone with North, E written in dark brown ink. We've been there, we've done that. Next, in the upper right square, there's a drawing of the red glowing orb, with long, inky lines depicting its radiating light. We've done that, too. In the bottom left square, there's a picture of what looks like a spiderweb. It's roundish with curved lines moving out from the center. There are trees around the web, tall and pointy. Beneath the spiderweb are the words *SW Lake*. In the bottom right square, there's a triangle, flanked by two larger triangles. In the center triangle are the letters *A.I.R.*

"Doesn't look too bad," I say. "A.I.R has to be Abraham Rane, right? Middle name begins with *I*?"

"Probably," she replies. "But why add the *I* now?"

I shrug. All I know is that our end goal is Abraham Rane's gravesite, and the last clue to that destination is a figure that looks like a triangular gravestone with letters inside that are close to his initials.

"SW Lake," she says, thinking. "Google Spiderweb Lake. I'll bet it's not too far from here."

My pay-as-you-go crappy flip phone gets the web, but my mother has to pay big bucks for every minute I'm on there. I sigh, knowing that if I make it back to Rockpoint, I'm probably going to catch hell for days to come. Then I remember that Melody has to explain to her father why she needs a new phone, and how she "lost" hers when he knows damn well it never leaves her side. I don't feel so bad about my predicament.

"We don't exactly have a lot of time here," Melody says.

I flip open my phone and Google "Spiderweb Lake."

"Okay," I say, clicking on the first hit. Then I read to her, *"Starlore Lake, originally called Spiderweb Lake for its unique shape and its habit of collecting families of spiders, is located in Starlore, Massachusetts. Starlore Lake is a popular vacation spot, known for camping, fishing, canoeing, and —"*

"How far are we?" she asks.

"Looks like Starlore is about three towns over," I reply, checking the map. "I'll guess about fifteen or twenty minutes."

She taps the steering wheel. "Let's wait ten more minutes," she says. "Just to make sure Alexander and

200

Lomidus are far, far away."

"Okay," I tell her and sit back. My stomach emits an audible groan of hunger, so I reach for Melody's carry-bag and pull out a chocolate chip granola bar. Melody gives me that look she always gives me when I eat at inappropriate times.

"Do you think your mother will ever tell my dad the truth about you?" she says, relaxing back in the seat. "I mean, about *both* of you guys?"

"Not sure," I say, chewing on granola. "It depends on how serious they get. I can't imagine it can go on too long the way it is, with him not knowing her real name or my real name."

"I almost slipped once," she admits. "I almost called you 'Shaw' when we were talking about you over breakfast."

"Mmm," I say back. I sit up and stuff the rest of the granola bar in my mouth. "Let's say we get to the lake, and we find Abraham's grave and dig it up," I say. "What do we do then? I mean, we've beat them to it, but without the wand and the pentacle—"

"That's another reason we need these ten minutes," she says. "We need a plan." She grabs the map off the dash and holds it in her hands, staring down. "They'll follow," she says. "Eventually, they'll find us and that's what we want. We need them to find us."

"Then we just kindly ask for the wand and the pentacle so we can reverse the Ritual?"

"I have a few plans," she says. "It all depends on the layout of the lake and the gravesite."

I slouch in the seat, still hungry, and try to figure out what kind of plans she's working up. I trust her, but sometimes she expects too much of me. "I'm not going to kill anyone," I say. "Not if there's a way around it."

Her gaze shoots over to me. "I'm hoping it won't come down to anyone getting killed." She shifts in the seat, and her eyes turn away. "But you might need to pull something from

201

your resources that you're unfamiliar with."

"Fire," I say.

"Fire," she confirms.

Great. She expects me to perform dazzling feats of skill and magic. I knew it was going to be something like that.

"I'm sure they're travelling with the wand, and we already know they have the pentacle," she says. "Let's say we get them in a certain location and separate them from the wand and the pentacle, then you can somehow enclose them in a ring of fire. They won't be able to get out, and *bam!* – we have the incantation and the four items in the Ritual of the Four."

"There's only one problem with that," I say. "I have no idea how to use the dagger to summon the power of fire."

Melody rolls up the map. She places it back in the orb, then carefully aligns the two pieces and puts the orb into her carry-bag. "Everything with you is about what can't be done, and why you hate this and that, and how you can't stand this cool gift left for you in your bloodline. What would your father have thought about that mentality?"

I really hate her sometimes.

She goes through her carry-bag, pretending to look through things or sort her belongings. It's just an act to give me time to think out what she said, so I turn from her and stare out the car window. She wants to know what my father would have thought about my pissy attitude about my ability. She wants me to think about that. Yeah, my father would have thought I should embrace the ability. He wouldn't have wanted me to reverse the Ritual. He would have wanted me to avenge his death by fighting this out with Alexander and Lomidus — fighting it out to the bloody end.

In the beginning, just before Rockpoint, I was pissed about having to run all the time and about not having a girlfriend and not having any friends. Maybe I was missing what I was really pissed about. Alexander and Lomidus killed my father, and I was angry about that, but I never let it go so far down into my bones that it rattled me enough to do something about it. And, damn it, I *could* have done something about it. Melody has been right about it all this time. What I have is a gift that I share with my father—a powerful gift that Alexander doesn't use properly and Lomidus could only hope to have in the quantities I have it.

"I've always looked at the gift the wrong way because I've struggled and sacrificed for it," I say to Melody, turning away from the window.

"That's true about any gift," she replies. "Especially the great gifts." She gives me a gentle smile. "I have faith in you. If I didn't, I wouldn't have gone on this trip."

She has faith in me. I let that ring in my ears for a minute, because I desperately needed to hear that right now. Then I lean over and kiss her. I think she just popped a mint into her mouth, because she tastes like peppermint. When I pull away, her eyes are still closed. I run the back of my finger down her cheek, and she exhales.

"Just for the record," I say, "there are other times I've wanted to be with you. Not just when you wore something sexy or I felt guilty about cutting you." She opens her eyes, fixes them on me. Sometimes I forget how lucky I am that this girl is not only interested in me romantically, but is also my best friend. "When we get back to Rockpoint, we're going to order five pizzas," I say, "all with different toppings. And we're going to watch *Star Wars* all day and read comics all night, and then kiss on my couch."

She giggles. "I look forward to most of that."

She shifts the car into drive and pulls away from the curb. Her eyes narrow, going into full-on kick-ass princess mode, navigating out of the rich neighborhood and back to the highway. While she drives, I reach into the backseat, find my duffel bag, and pull out my dagger. I hold it in my palm, then flip it over, inspecting the jewels and the gold, getting in tune with the power. I glance over at Melody, fire and emotion in her eyes as she takes us to our destination and formulates plans in her mind. My mother was right to give Melody the goblet. She was right to think that I would fall in love with Melody and that would change all my plans — because I think I just made an important decision about the Ritual of the Four.

Part III
The Ritual of
the Four

Chapter Twenty-One

The banks of Starlore Lake stretch further than the eye can see. The setting is park-like and wooded with a few cottages toward the rear banks of the lake, maybe summer homes or just housing for a warm weather sleepaway camp. The entrance to the lake is a short dirt road, edged in towering pines. A few brown signs along the dirt road give tourists the lake's backstory, even if right now the car is passing too quickly for me to read those stories in full. Something about spiderwebs. Something about mirrors. Something about mountains.

"How are we supposed to find the gravesite?" I ask. "This place is huge."

Melody pulls into a small parking lot. The car's headlights slice across the surface of the lake, joining with the moonlight so the lake looks like a big bowl of blue and silver liquid. Though I can't make out the full spiderweb shape, the early winter breeze on the water creates ripples that radiate outward from the center — a perfect spiderweb effect.

"We need to look at the map again," she says. "We must have missed something." She kills the headlights, reaches into the back for her carry-bag, and pulls out the orb. She splits it open and slips out the map, then unrolls the parchment and smooths it on her lap. "Three down," she says as her eyes move over the map. "We've been to the grave of Edgar North, then we found the glowing red orb with the map inside, now we're at the lake." Her shoulders drop. "We should be seeing the triangular gravestone of Abraham I. Rane somewhere."

It could be anywhere. Literally anywhere around the lake. The circumference is ridiculous. We could walk all night and not inspect the entire area, and that doesn't even include the woods or the mountains on the horizon beyond the edges of the lake.

Melody holds her hand like she's getting ready to karate-chop something, then rests it down on the vertical line in the center of the map. Then she shifts and holds her hand horizontally, placing it down on that line. "A cross," she says. "Why divide the map into four sections and why put Edgar North's grave and the orb on there when we would have obviously been to those two places to find the map to Abraham's grave?"

"Not sure," I reply, looking over her shoulder. In the silver light of the half moon, I can make out the outline of the map, all the drawings and letters. "It's possible these summer cottages were built over the gravesite."

Melody glances up. "I don't think so," she says, eyeing the cottages. "The gravesite wouldn't be so close to the water. It has to be in an area that's wooded or off the beaten path." She turns back to the map. "Remember what Fraser told us about the clues being difficult but not indecipherable? I think we're either reading too much into the clues or not enough."

"I don't think they *gave* us enough," I say, frustrated. "I mean, I know this is supposed to be difficult to figure out so not just anyone can do it, but so far we've had to find an old grave and dig up all that dirt, only to find this red, glowing thing. Now, we're sitting here by a huge lake that isn't even called what it used to be—"

"Wait!" Melody says and pulls the map closer to her eyes. "The map is in four parts: Edgar North's grave, the glowing red orb, Spiderweb Lake, and Abraham's hidden gravesite, A.I.R."

"And?"

"The Ritual of the Four," she says like I'm missing the most obvious thing in the world. "Earth, fire, water, and air." She points to the squares on the map, each one. "Edgar North's grave was earth, the red orb was fire, the lake is water...and Abraham's grave, that must be air! It even *says* AIR!"

I almost laugh. "You can't put a grave up in the air," I say. "But good guess."

"No, the gravesite will be near a symbol of air. Like the orb wasn't really fire, it was just *like* fire. Red and glowing, right?" She rolls up the map. "We're looking for something that's a symbol of air, and something that would have stood the test of time."

While she places the map back into the orb, I try to make myself useful and Google symbols of elemental air. My hits are plentiful but vague—feathers, smoke, birds, incense, wind, fans, spirits, a triangle with a line across the top.... "This triangle is similar to what Abraham's grave is supposed to look like," I say, showing her the symbol for elemental air that's on my screen. "But that doesn't help us locate the triangle."

"Maybe not from the ground." Her eyes gaze ahead, into the horizon. "But there are mountains on the other side of the lake, and I have a feeling we're supposed to be up high. Up in the air, so to speak."

"Great," I say. "Mountain climbing at midnight."

She rolls her eyes and begins to gather our things. We decide to take my dagger, her goblet, the shovel, a bottle of water, two granola bars, and the orb with the map rolled inside. We'll have to leave our carry-bags behind and just lug the stuff around in the plastic bag from the drugstore. The shovel will be the most cumbersome, hanging over my back.

When we close the car doors and Melody locks up, her shoulders fall, and she bites her lower lip.

"We've got everything we need," I say.

"It's just...Benji Bear." She stares across at me from her

side of the car. "I don't want to leave him out here. I mean, what if the car gets towed or someone breaks in or Alexander—"

"I'll buy you a new bear then."

"He wouldn't be the same." Her eyes shine green and teary in the moonlight. "Benji Bear will always remind me of the best weekend of my life."

"Best weekend?" Again, trying not to laugh. "Are we doing the same thing here?" I walk around the car and wrap her up in my arms. I don't know when I'll get the chance to do this again. If Alexander and Lomidus catch up with us before we're ready for them and things don't go well…. "Benji Bear will be fine in the car," I whisper in her ear. "I promise, okay?"

"I just have a feeling I'm going to need him."

"He'll be fine in the car," I say again. "He'll be fine."

She nods, and I realize that I just dodged a bullet, because I can promise her Benji Bear will be fine, but she didn't ask me to promise that *we'll* be fine.

"Ready?" she says and grasps my hand.

I take a deep breath. "Let's hike."

It's cold. I hadn't anticipated that. It's the end of November, so yeah, I knew it wasn't going to be sizzling, but I didn't think it would be freeze-up-your-lungs cold. Melody has a jacket on, but she's not layered like I am. I've got a shirt, a sweat jacket, and my leather jacket on the top half of my body, and jeans, socks, and sneakers below. It sucks that I can't stick my bare hands into my pockets because I have to carry the damn shovel. My icy fingers are curled around the shovel handle, my fingertips numb already.

And then it gets worse. As we weave through the canoe launch area of the lake, keeping away from the banks, the sky darkens and a few flakes of snow drift past my vision. I keep going, hoping it's just a passing flurry, but then it gets heavier. Melody doesn't even acknowledge the snow, but I'm sure we're both thinking the same thing: this is the last thing we need. It's going to make mountain climbing slippery and difficult, not to mention the visibility issues when we're trying to read the map and locate Abraham's hidden gravesite.

"Did you know that no two snowflakes are ever the same?" Melody says as we enter the woods around the side banks.

"Actually, I think I knew that one," I reply. The shovel bangs against a tree trunk, and I whisper a curse. "And don't start listing random facts about snowflakes. That just makes it worse."

She sighs and moves forward, shoving aside bare white branches, keeping her gaze fixed on the far banks of the lake. The silhouettes of two small, rocky mountains in the distance, the backdrop for falling snow, makes me think of fun winter things like skiing or snowboarding. Not that I've really done either of those things. I'd like to someday, though. Maybe with Melody, all bundled up, not in just a jacket like she is now. I can't imagine she'll make it a few more hours in this weather without something warmer.

I haven't told her yet that I changed my decision about the Ritual of the Four, mainly because it's not something that's easily digestible, even for me. I've decided that I'm going to keep my ability — no, my *gift* — and give Melody the power of the goblet. The power of the wand and the power of the pentacle will stay in the original bloodlines, who have all, unfortunately, died out over the years. Of course, all of this hinges on what happens over the next twelve hours or so. If by some miracle Melody and I find the gravesite, dig up the grave of Abraham Rane, unearth the incantation, and happen to trick Alexander out of the wand and the pentacle, then I'll tell Melody my decision and make that decision a reality.

I think about all of this as we trudge on. The snow intensifies, sticking to tree branches and silently falling over the lake. Snow always seems to bring on this strange, muffled quiet, like the world has on earmuffs. Even Melody's footsteps through the woods are cushioned and mute. To keep her distracted from the cold and snow, I talk about school and homework, things that don't matter right now but keep our sanity intact. After a while, her responses are short and breathy, so I stop talking.

Sooner than expected, the mountains loom before us. From the parking lot, they didn't seem so grand, and up close, they're still not all that impressive. I'm not even sure they qualify as mountains, more like dark, rocky hills that happen to join up and roll through the horizon. The rocks are straight up, jagged, and attracting snow. Not huge mountains, definitely passable, but with the snow and no clear destination, it's not going to be a jolly little hike.

"Any chance Abraham's grave is right down here?" I say, pointing to the foot of the mountain.

"We have to be up high," Melody says. The moonlight faded with the snowstorm, so with no illumination, I can't see much of Melody's face or expression. I can sense more than see that she's pale and blueish, shivering. "I guess we should just start climbing."

Normally, I don't argue with her. She always knows best, and I will openly admit that she's smarter than I am with a lot of things, decoding clues being one of them. But it seems too random to just climb a mountain and hope to come across an old grave with a triangular marker.

"Wait," I say, holding her back. "Let's take one more look at the map, okay?"

She huffs, like she can't believe I've lost faith in her. Then I hear the plastic bag shift and crinkle as she rummages through and pulls out the orb. By the light of my phone, we look over the last square on the map — Abraham's gravesite.

"I get that it's earth, fire, water, and air," I tell her as snow falls over the map. "And I think you're right about that and right that we have to be up high. It's just that we have to find a specific location. There has to be something we're missing. We can't just walk around the mountains all night."

212

"The mountains aren't that big," she replies. "We can manage, probably." She fades off in thought, gazing over the mountains. "Let's say the grave has to be in the ground, obviously," she says. "But we're looking from up high, in the air. That would lead us to someplace that's like an overlook. Someplace with a crevice or gap."

"Actually," I say, "when we drove in, I saw some signs about the mountains. I couldn't really read them, but I do remember one of them mentioned mirror mountains. Like, two of the same." We both look up at the mountains at the same time. Melody's eyes shift back and forth, from one mountain to the next. The mountains aren't mirrors of each other. One of them is slightly bigger than the other one. But still, there are two definite, separate mountains—with a gap between them.

"Time and erosion," she whispers. "Maybe they were once mirrors, but now they're just two mounds of eroding rock, one larger than the other. That explains the two larger triangles drawn around the gravesite." She points down at the map again, at the triangles flanking Abraham's gravesite. "Identical mountains." She rolls up the map. "We need to climb one of the mountains, and then look down into the gap between them. We should be able to see the gravesite from there."

I take the map from her and open it up again, looking it over one last time, trying to judge by the location of the three triangles where, approximately, Abraham's gravesite would be located. It seems from the map that it would be smack in the middle of the mountains, in between. My first instinct is that we should just completely forget the mountain climb and concentrate on the gap between the Mirror Mountains, but Melody is pretty sure we have to look down on the grave from the air. I trust her on this.

"Let's do it," I say, rolling up the map. "And take my jacket, okay?"

"No!" she replies. "You'll freeze!"

213

It's too late. I've already started taking off my jacket. "I have a sweat jacket on plus a shirt," I say. "I'm okay for now."

Grudgingly, Melody puts my leather jacket on over her own jacket. It's about a hundred sizes too big for her, and I laugh until the light from my phone goes dim and we start moving forward again, up the base of the closest mountain, the smaller one. As suspected, the rocks are slippery. I have to keep my hands around Melody's waist while she edges upward, which means that I have to place the shovel down on the ground at regular intervals. This is going to take a while.

We're almost halfway up, Melody just ahead of me, when I lose my footing. My sneaker slips down the rock, and my right ankle twists and pops. I clamp my teeth together and shout out in pain inside my head—I don't want Melody to think there's something wrong. I place my gaze back up at the dark sky, snow floating into my eyes, and carry on. The air smells like pine trees and earth, and that scent would be soothing and welcoming if not for the cold sting in my nose, the sharp pain in my ankle, and the numbness in my fingers. Still, we're nearly there, closer than I ever thought we'd get when we started this journey.

At the top of the mountain, Melody grabs hold of a jutting rock and pulls herself up and over. She stands tall against the breeze, sticks her hands on her hips in triumph, and sucks in a deep breath. I hop up beside her and catch my breath, wondering how she could possibly be in better shape than I am when all she does is play video games all day. Maybe she's not so out of breath because I was lifting her most of the time.

"We did it," she says. "We're almost there."

"Easy for you to say," I reply. "You don't have to dig up a grave, and then possibly fight with two guys who want to slice us up dead."

"Speaking of them," she says, looking out and over the

214

woods. "I have a feeling they'll catch up to us soon. And if they don't, you'll need to call them and let them know where they can find us. All of this is for nothing if we don't get the wand and the pentacle."

"Tell me something I don't know." I drop down on the rocks and snow, then open up the plastic bag and remove the bottle of water. Melody senses my crankiness and takes a few steps away. I keep my eye on her as she drifts closer to the edge of the mountain. My stomach does not like it when she gets that close to falling. "Watch it," I call. "It's a long way down."

"Shaw," she says, moving farther away from me still. "I just realized that it might be impossible to see anything that far down when it's so dark out."

She's telling me this now? "So we have to climb back down and wait until morning to do this again?"

"Or we could wait out the snowstorm," she replies. "It's already slowing down, and hopefully the moon will come out again." She comes up behind me and sits down. "Maybe my eyes will adjust, and I'll be able to see something down there."

As we sit in wait, the snow changes from thick flakes to powdery white specks. We stay stationary for a while, Melody pushed up beside me for warmth, both of us waiting for the light of the moon to break through the night clouds. We talk about her father and how she's starting to miss him, and I even admit that I'm missing my mother. It seems so long ago that we were in Rockpoint.

A splash of silver moonlight drenches the mountains, and the last bits of snow float through the air, shining like tiny pieces of tinfoil. We stand and hike over to the middle of the mountain, which isn't too far off, then step to the edge and look down. A sea of black. No triangular gravestone, but even in the day it might be difficult to spot. Melody keeps moving back and forth, shuffling through the fallen snow on the edge, which makes me nervous. Finally, she stops and squints.

"Maybe the gravestone isn't a triangle," she says. "Look at the position of the rocks down there."

When I look down, I can't see a thing except maybe a few of the larger rock formations and tangled trees and bushes in the gap. But Melody points to each rock, and I notice that they make a shape—a perfect, three-pointed triangle. We couldn't have seen the shape from down in the gap. We needed to be up high.

"You think the grave is right in the center?" I ask.

"Has to be," she replies. "Mark the location. Drop something down there, right in the center of the triangle."

With all my might, I hurl the shovel. It was bothering me to carry the thing anyhow. It flies through the air, a shadowy, lengthy shape, and then slams down to the earth below. It's so far down I only hear a pitiful little echo.

"Let's go," Melody says. "And try to keep track of where it landed."

Back down the mountain. And I'm already out of steam.

Chapter Twenty-Two

It's after midnight, well into the darkest hours of the night. Melody and I touch down at the base of the mountain, then hike through the gap between the Mirror Mountains, trying to find the shovel I threw down. Walking through the woods at night, even if they're sparse woods, is no easy feat. Sometimes I hear animals shuffling by in the distance, maybe deer or raccoons. Sometimes the cold gets the better of me, and I wonder if I'll ever feel my hands again. Sometimes I worry that Melody won't be able to manage the trek. But mostly, I wonder if Alexander and Lomidus will find us before we're ready. I don't smell blood in the air, but I somehow sense that Alexander is close.

Even though we're pretty sure the shovel is right in the center of the two mountains, it takes longer to find than expected. We're tired and slow and cold. I'm hanging on to the memory of my father and know he would have wanted me to do just what I'm doing now, finding the incantation, keeping my gift, and taking Alexander and Lomidus out of the equation. And as I think about taking Lomidus out of the equation, I question something.

"If I recite the words to the incantation," I say to Melody, careful to word it so she doesn't know what I'm truly planning, "then it will change or end what's existing now, but Lomidus was never in the bloodline. He learned how to cut on his own somehow. Would that mean Lomidus would still

217

have the power?"

"Yes," Melody replies as she ducks under a sagging pine tree bough. "But remember we're also keeping him from gaining the power of all four elements. He's really after that."

"True," I reply. Something still seems off about Lomidus's involvement in this. Who is he? How did he learn to cut? How did he trick Alexander into turning against me and my family? Why does he want the power of all four items in the Ritual of the Four? How did he even find out about the Ritual of the Four?

"I think I see the rock formation up ahead," Melody says.

She has said this five times already, but it always turns out to be a bunch of rocks with no shovel in between. This time, though, when I lift my phone and try to shine the light onto the ground, I see the edge of something pointy and metal — the shovel.

"I know you're going to argue with me about this," she says, "but I want to start digging. You can rest for a while, okay?"

I'm not going for a "boys are stronger than girls" debate here, but Melody isn't exactly the type to exert truckloads of physical energy. She's most comfortable playing games and figuring things out, studying for school, or sitting in front of the computer. Not that I do much physical activity either, but I still think I'm the best one for the job of grave excavation.

"It'll warm me up to do some exercise," she says.

I wish we had two shovels, because I see her point. Even though we've been walking around the woods, doing something like digging will get our blood pumping a wee bit faster and a wee bit warmer. I nod to her and sit down on one of the rocks, the one that makes the top point in the aerial triangle shape, then I pull out a granola bar.

Melody starts right in the center of the triangle. The *dead* center. Yeah, there's extra room to spare, and she could be a little off, but we have no choice than to just start someplace. She scrapes some of the snow aside, then plunges the tip of the shovel right into the earth. If it was a few weeks later and into December, the ground may have been frozen, and digging might be more difficult or even impossible. As it is, she's struggling, and I can't help but tap my foot against the rock, wanting to switch places with her.

As Melody digs and tosses dirt aside, I try to see the lake but realize that we're so far in between the mountains that the lake probably hasn't been visible for quite a while. I can't even hear the water brushing against the banks, just the silence of the woods at night, penetrated by the sound of metal scraping earth. I can't explain it, but as I watch Melody, I get the sense that she should be digging just a foot over. I tell her this and she changes direction, not even questioning me.

When my phone reads two-thirty, Melody and I switch places. She curls up on the rock exactly where I was and closes her eyes. I wish I could say she made some progress with digging up the grave, but it still looks like I have a way to go. It's difficult not to think about what lies beneath. A body? A coffin? I'm hoping it's like Edgar North's grave, and we won't have to go as far down as a body, but I do remember Fraser saying the incantation was buried *with* Abraham. That makes me pretty sure that sometime tonight, I'll be seeing a skeleton.

For a while, I draw from inner strength and pull up dirt. Melody is asleep—I can tell by her silence and her deep breaths. As I dig, I try to think about happier things, like my time with Melody in the hotels. It was only two nights with her beside me in a bed, but it feels like I'll never be able to go back to sleeping alone. All craziness aside, I got a taste of playing house with her. I know that she sings in the shower and gets nightmares at night and brushes her teeth with warm water instead of cold. I know that she will never yell at me for messing up a room, because she's already used to living with a guy and cleaning up after him without complaining. I know that falling in love with her was the easiest thing, but admitting to it was the hardest. I still haven't really told her that I'm in love with her.

Sooner than expected, the tip of my shovel smacks into something hard. Something wooden and rotting. My body reflexively cringes, and I take two steps back, my ankle still throbbing in pain from twisting it on the mountain.

"Shaw?" Melody says, waking. "How are you—"

"I hit," I say. "I found the coffin."

Melody gasps and leaps from the rock. "Are you sure?"

"Yeah," I reply as she speeds to the edge of the hole and looks down. "Can you believe it? I honestly didn't think we'd make it this far."

She gives me a sleepy smile. "Honestly, neither did I."

We both laugh, then get back to the serious matter of dirt removal. We carve into the earth, around the coffin, exposing the wood edges. The coffin isn't like the nice, shiny ones you see on TV funerals. It's basically an old wooden box, with long, rusty nails sticking out from the top. And when I say it's rotting I mean it looks as though it's been under water for hundreds of years. The edges are frayed and look like driftwood.

"Take my phone," I say to Melody. I need the light, but I'm starting to worry that my battery will die. "I'll just have to go on memory and hope I scoop away all the dirt."

"I'll just stand over here," she says, taking my phone.

"You don't want to see Abraham."

"No." She shakes her head. "I have enough problems with nightmares and dead things."

I'm not all that enthusiastic about seeing a real skeleton either. But I try to think of this as something that needs to be done. Get all technical and scientific about it. Underneath our skin, we're all bones. This is how I'll look in a few hundred years. And besides, without the light from my phone, the middle of the woods is ridiculously dark. Maybe I won't have to see a damn thing.

After I scrape away all the dirt, I descend further into the hole. Get the breathless, trapped sensation of being buried alive. I relax my shoulders, relax my muscles, and suck in a few deep breaths. Just a skeleton. Just what's underneath my own skin. Technical. Scientific.

With the tip of the shovel, I bang away at the wood, watch the old nails shift and yield to the pressure. The top of the coffin moves over an inch, so I toss the shovel behind me and use my fingers to edge the coffin open, hoping I'm at the right end. Maybe the incantation is so close to the top that I won't have to see Abraham.

"Shaw?" Melody calls. "You okay?"

I try to answer her, but I'm spent. My voice is strained, and my vocal cords are frozen. By the light of the moon, I shift the wood all the way over, then shut my eyes against what I'm about to see. White light falls over my closed eyelids as Melody shines my phone down into the opening. She gasps. I ease my eyes open—and find myself face to face with Abraham Rane.

His skull is ivory-yellow. His eye sockets are barren. His nose is a triangular wedge of empty black. Jutting up from the wood is a scroll of brown paper, thick as a paper bag, and I tug it from inside the coffin, shift the wood back into place, and climb out of the hole.

"I have...the incantation," I say, gasping in waves of cold air.

Melody squeaks out a cry.

"Let me check it," she whispers finally. "So you can cover him back up."

Melody has to pry my fingers off the incantation to remove it from my grasp. She reads it over while I stand in shock of what I've done, and then nods to give me the okay.

As fast as I can, I cover Abraham. It's such an automatic, instinctual action that I don't even have time to feel the scream in my muscles or the shivers in my brain. What did I just do? I dug up a grave and took something. There are so many broken morals associated with grave robbing that I can't even count them all, yet I did it. I'll have some kind of afterlife hell to pay for the deed, I'm sure.

When Abraham is covered up, I pat down the dirt and drop to the ground. Everything falls over me at once, like a million pounds of stone. Suffocating.

"You okay?" Melody says and sits down beside me.

"Just wondering…was it all worth it," I whisper. "Now we have to wait for Alexander and Lomidus before we can do anything, and it just seems like…suicide."

"This whole trip was suicide," she responds. Typical Melody, giving crappy pep talks. "I mean, we knew where it was going to end up." She hands me my phone. "Text them," she says. "Tell them where to find us. It's the last step."

Earlier, I sensed that Alexander was close, and I think he's even closer now. If I had time, I would just wait here for him to narrow in on my exact location. But I don't have time. I need to get Melody back to her father in a few hours, and I need to put all of this behind me for good.

With a numb thumb, I send a text to Melody's phone:

"Starlore Lake. Come and find me."

Chapter Twenty-Three

While I rest from my dig a safe distance away from Abraham's gravesite, Melody sits on a rock and looks over the incantation. She's using my phone like a flashlight, so I can see the expression on her face as she reads. I can tell from her squinty eyes that the incantation is serious business. When she had to decode the first clue, she was persistent but still having a little fun with it. With the map, she was giving herself a challenge. But the incantation is totally throwing her off her game—and it's supposed to be the easiest part. We just have to read some words, and how hard could that be?

"So, what's the plan?" I say.

Melody sighs and rolls up the incantation. "Maybe changed a bit," she says. "I mean, you're going to have to change the wording to end the Ritual. I don't see any kind of reversal."

Oh good. She's worried because she thinks I want to reverse the Ritual of the Four. I don't want that anymore.

"I guess you'll have to say something opposite," she says. "Like instead of 'invoke your power,' you'll have to say something like 'take away your power'."

"The spell says 'invoke your power'?"

"Among other things." She gazes out into the distance, then turns back to me. "You're sure you don't want to read it?"

"Not until it's time," I reply. "I just have a feeling it'll be stronger that way."

"You're probably right." She hops off the rock and sits down next to me on the patch of cold but snow-free dirt I found beneath a pine tree. "Listen," she says. "I don't know if you're going to be able to do this." She holds up the incantation but doesn't unroll it. "The original incantation is...sealed in blood. I mean, it's an old document and it's pretty faded—I can't even believe it's in as good a shape as it's in—but I'm pretty sure the brown spots beneath each item in the Ritual are fingerprints of blood. In order to reverse it...you might need to cut yourself."

I glance at the white plastic bag containing my dagger. It shouldn't be a problem to cut myself. The dagger is sharp enough at the point to do the job. But Melody doesn't know that she'll be involved. I hate to think that I might have to cut her with my mind or my dagger, even if those two are kind of the same source.

"Your blood is already entwined with the dagger and the element of fire," she says. "It's your ancestor's blood on the incantation, written down as 'Intention: Morrison Huntley'."

"Morrison is a family name," I tell her, thinking of my grandfather's name and my middle name. "So if my family name is already on the incantation, why would I need to cut myself? My blood is already on there."

"To reverse the Ritual," she says. "Or possibly because the incantations are separate and look as though they're to be spoken by each party. Like, Abraham Rane probably just wrote the incantation and presided over the spell, maybe sealed it. But it looks as though each person spoke his or her incantation, recited their intention and their name, and then sealed it in a blood fingerprint. All the other families are dead. Do you understand what I'm saying?"

"That in order to reverse it, each person would have to be here and reverse their own spell, but that doesn't matter," I say. "All I'm interested in is my own."

Melody shrugs. I think she's trying to tell me that I might

not be able to reverse just one part of the Ritual. So yeah, I guess when the time comes I'll have to figure out what I'm going to do about the family lines that are no longer living. I don't want to change the part of the Ritual that involves the wand and the pentacle; my plan was to just keep that the same. But if I can't do that, I'm not really sure what I'm going to do.

"How long do you think before Alexander and Lomidus find us?" Melody says. She's remarkably calm, like she's asking me about a homework assignment or something.

"Soon," I reply. "You're not nervous?"

"A little," she says. "But we have a good plan for when they get here."

We don't have a good plan. We barely have *any* plan. She thinks I'll be able to trap them in some great magical ring of fire, and that's just not going to happen. She says she has faith in me, and while I appreciate her confidence and feel more powerful than I've ever been, I still hear a voice in the back of my mind telling me the icky truth—I'm just a sixteen-year-old geeky kid who happens to have a dark gift.

Melody moves closer to me. "Before they get here, I just wanted to tell you…you know, if things don't work out as planned, that this weekend was incredible."

I wrap my arm around her shoulder. "So when we get back, you'll be my girlfriend? Or is that still out of the question?"

"I've wanted to be your girlfriend since the first day I saw you in the school office," she says and leans into me. "The problem was, you didn't want to be my boyfriend. You wanted Ariana."

Ariana. My longing for her seems so long ago. The younger Shaw. The stupider Shaw. I remember starting Rockpoint High and wanting to be anyone *but* Shaw Huntley. As Shaw Huntley, I was marked for death, and I hated my ability. I tried everything to change all that or make myself different somehow, tried the messed-up loner routine, tried dating the "it" girl at school, but that didn't work out for me. I guess I ended up being exactly who I was. I fooled nobody, but I especially didn't fool Melody. Or myself.

"You know there's a big difference between wanting a girl and needing a girl," I say. "I wanted Ariana, but you…I need you."

"So you don't *want* me?"

That came out wrong.

"Melody—"

She laughs and kisses me. If I'm going out of this world tonight, this is the way I want to go out—with Melody's lips on mine. There are a million things I want to say to her before Alexander gets here, before all of this ends however it's going to end. But I let the kiss tell her how I feel. She's good at decoding, so hopefully…*wait.* I've backed out of telling her how I truly feel for days now. I told myself I would do it, and even though I've led her to believe I was in love with her, I never really said it. And that's a pretty cowardly thing to do.

We stop kissing, and I grab her hands. I see the mark from where I cut her thumb, and I can feel, *intensely* feel, the very moment when I saw her blood, saw what I'd done to her. Why she wants a guy like me I will never understand. But I do know why she came along with me this weekend and why she helped me along on this suicide mission.

"I have to tell you something important." I squeeze her hands. She looks at me in question, rolling up her eyes. "I love you."

"You what?" she says.

"I love you," I repeat. "I'm in love with you. I just wanted you to know that."

I move to kiss her again, but she rests her hand on my chest. "You're sure?" she says. "You're not just saying that because we're about to face…."

"I've been sure for days," I reply. "Maybe even weeks." I smile. She smiles back. "And I'm going to prove it to you. I'm going to prove it soon."

"How will you—"

She breaks off as a twig snaps in the distance and echoes around the mountains like a gunshot. It was much too loud of a snap to be from a passing animal. Too heavy to be from a fallen tree branch.

We have company.

Chapter Twenty-Four

Footsteps through the woods, no mistaking it. Melody grabs my upper arm.

"Give me the incantation," I whisper.

She puts the rolled-up scroll in my hand. I stuff it inside my sweat jacket.

As we stay huddled at the base of the pine tree, the beam from a flashlight bounces around tree trunks and slices through hanging branches in the near distance. The footsteps halt, and two silhouettes stand still. I'm sure they've spotted us.

"Here we go," I say to Melody. "Make sure you stay back, okay?"

"You'll be okay," she says, her voice shaky. "You'll do fine."

It was a quick pep talk, but at least it didn't suck like her usual pep talks. I nod to her and she stands and takes a few steps back, away from the pine tree. Alexander and Lomidus are heading toward me, faster and faster, even though it's obvious that I'm stationary and waiting for my foes.

"Interesting maneuver," Alexander says, approaching. He's bundled up in a dark ski cap and a puffy winter coat. "Any particular reason you sent us your location?"

"Just wanted to make it nice and even, cousin," I reply.

"He's lying," Lomidus says. He stops in front of me, the deep scars in his face silver and hideous in the moonlight.

"Of course I'm lying," I say and stand up to face them. "You just have a few things that I need."

Lomidus lets out a sinister laugh. "You have the incantation?"

"Maybe," I reply. "So here's the deal." I step closer to them, hoping this makes it seem as though I'm not afraid and I'm the one running the show. My fight voice has improved, I will give myself that, and every fleck of confidence I can give myself right now is crucial for success. "I'm going to end the Ritual," I say, lying. "Reverse the entire thing so that it no longer exists. All you have to do is give me the wand and the pentacle. Then we're all on even ground and can walk away from each other."

As expected, Lomidus looks at me like the cold has addled my brain. "No deal," he says back. "Just give us the incantation and nobody gets hurt." His eyes shift to where Melody stands, partially hidden behind the pine. My mind flashes back to the girl in Fairchester with the brown feathery hair and how Lomidus sliced up her cheek. I'm not going to let him cut Melody like that.

"If Melody gets so much as a scratch on her, I'll burn the incantation," I say. My veins feel like rivers of fire, but I control my anger. I have to.

"All right," Alexander says. "Let's just get everything out in the open here. We're all trying to do the same thing, but missing two important items that the other one has."

Yeah, but I'm a step further than they are. I have the incantation.

"So we have to make some kind of bargain," Alexander continues. "Let's go back to the original plan, Shaw, before you pulled the phone trick."

"Don't want that anymore," I say. "I don't want this guy involved." I shift my head toward Lomidus. "He's not involved in the Ritual of the Four and never was."

Lomidus strikes unexpectedly. He whips his finger through the air and makes a downward slash, a physical movement I've never had to make and Alexander has never had to make. Melody gasps as I grab my wrist. My skin burns from the scratch, but it was just a warning. It's not too deep.

"You think I'm not involved in the Ritual of the Four?" Lomidus bellows.

Now I'm pissed. "You have zero natural ability," I taunt. "Whatever you're doing is just learned and not even all that impressive."

His face reddens. He throws another slice my way, and this one is bad. I feel the skin split down my face, from the bottom of my eyeball down to my lip. Melody screams out my name. Alexander winces and turns away.

Blood runs down my cheek, and I squint away the pain. In the past, I would have lost control and Lomidus would be injured beyond recognition. But now, I just wipe the blood away with the back of my hand, keeping my mental dagger aimed and ready for when I truly need it. I'm sick of this back and forth slicing game that Lomidus and I play.

"You were born with the gift my great-great-grandfather left for you and the others," Lomidus says. "Which means that what you do is not all that impressive either, and that I am more involved in the Ritual than you have ever been."

What is he talking about? His great-great-grandfather?

"Where is he?" Lomidus says, stepping up to me. "Where's his grave?"

"Abraham?"

Lomidus doesn't answer. He just starts moving around the woods, stomping through the snow and dirt, weaving around trees, looking for the gravesite. Melody and I had migrated away from it earlier, just because it was creeping us out to be so close, but we're still near enough for Lomidus to find it. I turn to Alexander, hoping he'll clear this up for me.

"His full name is Lomidus Rane, if you must know," Alexander says. "Abraham Rane was his great-great-grandfather." He watches Lomidus in the distance, as though worried he'll get in trouble for spilling this information. "He

231

believes that all the items in the Ritual of the Four rightfully belong to him."

"And you agree?" Melody says, moving closer to us.

I put my hand out for her to stay away, but she keeps walking.

"Yes," Alexander replies. "The four items belong to him. They're rightfully his and so is the incantation. His ancestor wrote it."

"Abraham obviously wrote that for his coven," I say, trying not to focus on the searing pain down my cheek. "If he wanted the power for himself, he would have included himself in the incantation."

"Lomidus doesn't believe that to be true."

"That's what he told you," Melody says. "He brainwashed you to believe anything he says."

Alexander gives me a look like "who the hell is this girl?" For a second, just for a tiny speck of time, he looks like he used to when we were kids. Completely harmless. Maybe even a little shy or naive. But I can't let myself forget who Alexander is now. He's become a ruthless killer, whether that was Lomidus's doing or not.

Melody presses her hand to my cheek. "That might need stitches," she says. She tends to the wound, gently wiping blood away with her thumb. "It's deep."

"It must be the cold," I reply. "I can barely feel it." I'm lying, of course. My cheek feels like it's coated in a rush of hot lava. "Let's just focus for now, okay?"

She nods, still concerned as she dabs her fingers over the cut, then turns back to Alexander. "How did he learn it?" she asks him in a low voice. "How did he learn how to cut people up like this?"

"Dark occult stuff, mostly black magic," Alexander replies and shifts his eyes toward Lomidus again. "A combination of telekinetic power and elemental magic. It's really not too much different from how the Ritual originally began."

In the absence of footsteps, I turn. Lomidus has stopped in front of Abraham's grave and is bent down over the pillow of dirt that conceals his great-great-grandfather. I can't really see what he's doing, but I'm sure he knows by now that I was decent enough to cover up the grave after I desecrated it. That should mean something to him if he has any kind of family values.

"No more games," Alexander says. "Give us the incantation. Lomidus is not playing around. He'll kill you and the girl in a second."

"You shouldn't have gotten involved with him," I say. "You've killed two people now, and—"

"I haven't killed anyone, Shaw," Alexander says. "You forget that your dad was my uncle, too. Lomidus killed your father and he killed Fraser. Both of them. That's why I'm trying to tell you that he's much more powerful than you think he is, and he's not playing around. Just give him what he wants. Trust me on this." His lifts his eyebrows, as though urging me to see reason.

All this time, I believed Lomidus didn't have the power to kill my father and Fraser. I thought for sure Alexander killed them. Now, I realize that maybe I did underestimate Lomidus. I know the guy is unpleasant, and I know he's after something he believes is rightfully his, but he's willing to kill for it, and that's the mark of insanity. Alexander was pulled into this. Brainwashed, as Melody said. That doesn't mean I forgive him for slicing up my neck when we met up at the autumn carnival or for any of the other times he has cut me.

"You're not innocent in this," I say.

"I never said I was," he returns. "But let's not forget that you nearly killed me back in October. You're not innocent either."

I'd almost forgotten that I launched my dagger into his chest that night. That was in self-defense, though. He can't try to tell me I purposely attempted murder.

In the distance, Lomidus moves away from the gravesite,

still looking behind his shoulder as he walks.

"Give me the incantation," Lomidus says, coming at me with his hand extended.

"I don't have it," I reply, lying.

"You dug it up. Give it to me."

"It's buried somewhere." I move in front of Melody, sensing he's going to attack. "And if you hurt Melody, you'll never know where I buried it. I won't tell you." I turn my head in every direction, pretending the incantation could be buried anywhere in the woods. "So just leave the wand and the pentacle and let me do what I came here to do."

Before I can process what he's doing, Lomidus shoves me aside and hooks Melody around the neck. He presses her to his chest. I lurch forward, ready to wound this guy with my bare hands.

"Let go of her!"

"Find it!" he demands Alexander.

Alexander starts wandering the area around us, searching for the incantation that's stuffed inside my sweat jacket. Melody locks eyes with me. I don't see fear, not like I thought I would. I see a plea. She wants me to do something. God, Melody. Why such faith in me?

While Alexander stomps around looking for recently dug-up earth and Lomidus continues to hold Melody in a lock around her neck, I close my eyes. I see my dagger, shimmering and gold in the forefront of my mind, ready. My weapon. If I wanted to, I could use the same force and might I used back in October when I hurled the thing into Alexander's chest. I could send Lomidus back into the rocky wall of the mountain behind him and leave him there for dead.

Or I could summon fire, like Fraser told me I could do, even though I have no idea how to do that. It's not even the right time to do it, because so far I haven't seen the wand or the pentacle and don't know if Lomidus or Alexander even have them at all. They must, because they came here thinking they would get the incantation from me, but I need a visual first. Proof. Then I can attempt to do the impossible.

"Look faster!" Lomidus says.

"I don't see anything!" Alexander says back. His voice is a little shaky. I almost feel sorry for him. "I think maybe he's bluffing," he says to Lomidus, looking at me to gauge my reaction to his insinuation.

Lomidus turns his eyes to me. He tugs Melody closer to his chest, nearly strangling her. She lets out a quick breath and sucks it back in. "I'm going to be really clear here," he says to me. "Give me the incantation, or I'll kill her."

Before I can reply, he pulls Melody backward through the trees.

"Melody!" I yell, running at Lomidus.

"Back!" he says, and I halt, knowing he's seriously going to cut her up if I make another move. "I'll give you five minutes," he says, jerking his head for Alexander to come with him. "If you don't call out to me that you're leaving me the incantation and the dagger and the goblet…the girl comes back to you in chunks and pieces."

Before I can react or try to stop him, Lomidus pulls Melody away from me and into the darkness. She kicks out and screams until the screams become muffled and she disappears from my sight. My blood runs cold. I think about texting my mother, using our code word "lightsaber," but that's no help to me now. My mother is too far away.

I'm alone.

Chapter Twenty-Five

Maybe I should have tried harder to save Melody, but instincts told me to stay back, that Lomidus was furious and would have cut her throat and threw her to the ground if I'd tried to rescue her from his grip. I could have cut him—my dagger was aimed and ready—but it would have been like two people with guns pointed at each other. A draw. Maybe I would have won and maybe I wouldn't have. Now we're in hostage negotiations. It wasn't supposed to happen like this.

I strain my ears to detect any sound in the woods, but it's unnervingly quiet. Melody is no longer screaming. There are no footsteps or moving tree branches through the woods. My breath rises in fast, smoky puffs. I'm trying to produce some kind of plan here, maybe something intelligent and tricky like Melody would suggest, but nothing comes to me. Fake an incantation? I have nothing to write on. Tell them to come back and then slice them both to pulp? That's murder, and I'm not going for that, though if Melody ends up hurt in any way, I might rethink my principles.

With the thought that Melody is brave and can probably hold out for another minute or two, I walk to the pine tree where we stashed the plastic bag. I kneel on the ground and open the bag, pull out my dagger, then Melody's goblet. Gold plating and blood-red gems glisten against silver moonlight. I place the dagger and goblet on a rock, kneel before them, and close my eyes, thinking so hard that it hurts. No great plan

237

comes to me. No latent power surfaces. Not even with the source of my gift right in front of me. I feel like a waste of my ancestor's blood and intentions. I can't figure out a way to save my dagger, Melody's goblet, or the incantation. I can't figure out a way to renew the Ritual of the Four. I can't even figure out a way to save Melody without resorting to death and violence.

Melody so far away from me now is like being without my right arm. Most of the time we've been together this weekend, or anytime since we met, really, she's been the one who figured things out and decoded all the clues. She's the plan-maker and the one who can think so fast in moments of terror that it makes my mind whirl in admiration. She's not here right now, but she has faith in me — I need to do this on my own. *Think, Shaw!*

All the things I need to do rush through my mind like splashing waves, tumbling around each other but somehow not coming together. I need the wand. I need the pentacle. I need to get rid of Alexander and Lomidus so I can recite the incantation to the Ritual of the Four. I've come this far, and I've done all the work — me and Melody, not Alexander and Lomidus — so it's my gig now. This is my time, and I need to play my own game of strategy and trickery.

I think about the source of my power: my dagger. I think about the element *fire*. The dagger is a symbol of fire — that's what Fraser said to me. I let my mind work on all of that, until the separate splashing waves come together in a tidal wave of realizations, thoughts, and plans. I wade through, pulling out the bad ideas and keeping the good, until something forms. Not the grandest of plans, but a place to start. And I hope to God that it works.

"Bring her back!" I yell through the woods. "Here's the dagger and the goblet! You can have the incantation!" My bare hands slap down on the rock, just below the dagger and the goblet. Then I pull the rolled-up incantation from my sweat jacket and toss that down.

In a flash, Alexander appears from the darkness. He notes the three items on the rock, and then turns and disappears back into the woods. Faithful servant. Dutiful pigeon.

When Lomidus comes back, he's no longer strangling Melody but gripping her shoulder. He shoves her to me, then nods to Alexander.

"You can leave now," Lomidus says to me. "I have what I needed from you."

"Don't want to kill me anymore?" I ask.

"Don't push me," he says back. "I've hated the idea of you for just long enough to be tempted."

"Same here," I reply.

Melody is still bundled up in my leather jacket, but her face is pale, exposed to cold and fright for far too long this night. We exchange a despaired glance, her at the drying wound on my face, me at the pink lines across her neck — the remnants of when Lomidus nearly strangled her.

"You okay?" I ask, lacing my fingers with hers.

"Peachy," she replies.

We turn to depart, leaving everything behind.

"What are you doing?" she whispers. "We're leaving?"

"They've won," I say loudly as we walk away. "So be it."

"What do you mean?" Melody says. "Shaw, you're not going to—"

"Wait for it," I whisper.

We walk through the woods, then fake footsteps fading away before we sneak behind a tree trunk and crouch down. Through the moonlight, I can see Lomidus setting up for the Ritual, unrolling the incantation, and positioning my dagger and Melody's goblet at the base of a square-shaped rock. Alexander pulls the wand from the inside of his coat. We're too far off to see precisely, but even from this distance I can tell the wand is awesome, just as Fraser described — a length of crystal quartz with a snaking gold band around the base and a blue diamond set in the center.

"So what's your plan?" Melody asks.

"This is it," I say. "We're doing it."

"Give them all the stuff?" she says. "That's your plan?"

Playfully, I whack her shoulder. "I thought you said you had faith in me."

"I did," she says. "I mean, I do."

Lomidus holds up my dagger, inspecting it.

"He's going to list his own name on all four," Melody says. "We need to do something."

"Shh," I say, moving forward.

Okay, do or die time. But first I need a distraction, a way to throw them off their game. As Lomidus rests the gold-plated pentacle against the rock, a small, barren tree snaps behind him and crashes to the ground. I don't have enough force to cut through a thick tree trunk, but the smaller tree works just fine. Lomidus jumps back, knocking the wand over and creating a domino effect as it hits the goblet and the dagger.

Then another small tree comes down, shaking old dirt off its branches and into Lomidus's eyes. I can't help but laugh as he tries to figure out what's going on.

"Shaw," Melody whispers. "Are you doing that?"

"Needed kindling," I reply.

When my tidal wave of thoughts and plans came together, something important Fraser told me stood out the most: *"The power of the dagger lies not only in the visual, but also the symbolic."* Visually, I've used the dagger as a weapon and projected it from me to wound and slice. But thinking of it as a *symbol* of fire....

The spark ignites from somewhere inside my mind, like a growing, fiery ball of thought, and projects onto the fallen tree. With a puff of smoke and a dance of flame, the branches catch fire. Lomidus has figured out what's going on and starts looking around for me. Alexander shakes his head, and I can swear I see a hint of realization, like he saw this coming. I'm still not sure if Alexander can summon fire too, but so far, I've seen nothing like it from him.

"What is it?" Lomidus says to Alexander. "How is he doing this?"

Alexander shrugs, kind of grins.

"He's cute," Melody says, watching Alexander.

I shoot her a look.

"Sorry," she says. "He looks just like you."

I have no time to grapple with jealousy issues, so I'll deal with Melody's infatuation with my evil cousin later. Now I have another concern—I've just set the woods on fire.

Lomidus senses the urgency and grabs the incantation, moving it from harm's way as the fiery branches spark and sputter around him. I hadn't thought about accidentally burning the incantation, but Lomidus will of course protect the thing with his life. He eyes the Ritual of the Four items at the base of the square rock, and I realize he's about to scoop them up and make a run for it. Melody must realize this too, because she grabs my arm and squeezes like my plan is in jeopardy.

I concentrate on my dagger again, not seeing the sharp edges, but the flame the dagger represents, the danger and the fury. Another spark ignites from my fiery ball of thought, setting a fallen branch on fire just beside Lomidus. I move the dagger circular in my mind, tracing the shape around Lomidus's frame until he roars in rage. Melody gasps, and Alexander moves away from the circle of flames I've just conjured. Lomidus is trapped in the middle.

"You did it!" Melody says.

Yeah, I've succeeded in making a ring of fire around Lomidus. What I didn't anticipate was that he'd have all four items of the Ritual of the Four with him *inside* of that circle. Alexander screams my name, and I guess it's pointless to pretend I'm not here and doing all of this.

"Stay here," I say to Melody, knowing she's probably not going to listen. She never does. "I need you safely away from the fire."

"Someone is going to see that smoke and call the fire

department," she says, pointing.

Streams of gray smoke drift toward the sky. It's late, the middle of the night or maybe even close to dawn, so hopefully most of the people in the town are asleep. Still, Melody is right. The fire department might come here, and once again, I'm smack in the center of the scene of the crime.

As Lomidus roams around inside the circle, trying to find a break in the flames to escape, I dash forward, keeping my concentration on the ring of fire. Alexander spots me and lifts his hand to hold me back. I'm still not sure whose side Alexander is on, but whatever he's doing, I ignore him and keep running. Then I realize it's not me he's trying to hold back from danger.

From behind me, Melody wails in pain. It's the most godawful sound I've ever heard in my entire life. I turn around just in time to see her grab her throat with both hands and fall to the ground. As I run to her, my concentration slips, and I can physically feel the cooler change in the atmosphere as my ring of fire dissolves. But that's not my concern right now.

Melody's throat is smeared in blood.

Chapter Twenty-Six

I'm not sure if Melody is in shock, but something isn't right. She's flat on her back, her eyes glazed over and pinned to the sky. Her limbs are shaking like mad. Alexander is at my side, bent over Melody just as I am, inspecting the gash on her neck. He seems to have taken a liking to her, somehow, in the short time he's been in her presence. Or maybe he just has a soft spot for girls. Whatever. I need the help right now.

"We have to put pressure on the cut," he says, ripping off his ski cap.

He hands me the cap, and I press it to Melody's neck. I can't tell how deep the wound is, but I do know that she's losing blood. And that's all it takes for me to swing in the opposite direction, from keeping the peace to plunging into a full-out war.

"You'll take care of her?" I say.

"I've got her," Alexander says back.

There is no other choice right now but to trust him.

I press my hand to Melody's shoulder, squeeze, then spin back to Lomidus, knowing that he's ready to flee the woods with the Ritual items and the incantation. That's not happening.

"Valiant effort," he says to me, gathering the items. "Your mistake was bringing the girl."

"Leave the items," I say. "I'm not playing around

243

anymore."

He laughs into the night. "One more cut and she's dead," he says. "I know the exact amount of pressure I need. I know the exact amount of cuts. So I would advise you not to take one step closer."

Again, we're at a draw. I could cut him good, and he knows that, but if I do, he'll kill Melody. He may have already come close.

"You have nothing left to play with," he says. "In case you haven't noticed. The girl is wounded, and I have the incantation and all four items I need."

I glance back at Melody, still lying on the ground. Then I tell myself, before I do something stupid, that there is no power worth killing for or dying for. I could use my dagger for flame or for slicing, but Lomidus will kill Melody if I do. Deep in my stomach, the reality hits. I have lost.

"I suggest leaving soon," Lomidus says, waving his hand around the smoldering branches. "Thanks to your little fire show, the police will be here any minute." He holds the rolled-up incantation in his hand, trying to stuff the wand inside his shirt with his other hand. He casts a nasty look at Alexander, obviously pissed that Alexander switched sides and can't help him carry the items out of the woods. "He was dispensable," he says to himself. "I would kill him for betrayal, but I don't really care. I have what I need."

Alexander tilts his head to listen as he keeps his ski cap pressed to Melody's neck. He obviously heard Lomidus, but he doesn't seem to care. Maybe this is all an act, a fancy trick or a trap. I have no way of knowing what side Alexander is on. All I know is he's keeping Melody alive, so I have to trust him right now.

"It's what you wanted," Lomidus says to me. "You're out of the Ritual forever."

Maybe it is what I wanted. I mean, even if I did change the Ritual, Lomidus would still have his power. He was never in the bloodline and had the power from other magical sources. He's right, I did want out from the very beginning of my quest. Once he speaks the incantation and names himself as the power on all four items, I'm out, and so is Alexander. I may never see Lomidus again. He can just go wreak havoc wherever he wants.

"Shaw?" Melody whispers.

I run to her side and kneel down.

"You okay?" I ask.

"Benji Bear," she gasps. "Can I have him?"

"You're okay," I say and brush back the little wisps of hair on her forehead.

"No I'm not," she replies. "But that's okay. I'm not afraid to die."

"You're not going to die."

She chuckles, then coughs. "It's okay," she whispers. "I knew I might die when I went along with you this weekend." She lifts her hand to my face and touches the slice on my cheek with cold fingers. "My dad had me all this time...it's okay if my mom has me now."

"No," I say, shaking my head. "Melody, you're fine."

Lomidus rushes by us, fleeing the woods. Alexander shoots me a confused look.

"You can't let him go," Alexander says to me. "He's going to take away our power."

"And whose fault is that?" I ask, holding Melody's hand.

Alexander lowers his head. "I'm sorry," he says. "Sorry that people were killed and sorry Lomidus got the incantation and our wand and dagger."

"Sorry doesn't heal my girlfriend," I reply. "Sorry doesn't bring back my father or Fraser."

"I know." He shakes his head in mourning. "But there's still time. I know exactly where Lomidus is going. I know where he was originally going to perform the Ritual of the Four."

Melody closes her eyes. My heart stops beating in my chest.

"Melody?" I say. "Stay with me!"

"She's okay," Alexander says. "Just let her rest for a second."

"And you know this how?"

"Because I'm an EMT," he replies. "Just shut up and listen to me, Shaw. We don't have much time."

How does someone sworn to save lives get mixed up with someone like Lomidus? I'm still not sure why Alexander did what he did, but again, I don't have much of a choice here. I have to trust him and do what he says. Melody's life might depend on it.

"Do you know that graveyard where you found the red glowing ball that contained the map?" Alexander asks. "The one where Edgar North was buried?"

I nod.

"That's where Lomidus will perform the Ritual," he says. "If we hurry, we can stop him."

"What if I don't believe you?"

"Then I'll steal your car and go after him myself," he replies. "But I would prefer help from my cousin."

"Go," Melody whispers. Her eyes are still closed. She sniffs in some air, and her body shivers. "I'll be okay."

"I'm not leaving you here," I say. "Not in a million years."

"We'll carry her back to the car," Alexander says. "Do you have some food in there? Water?"

I nod again.

"Good," he says. "Let's go."

Without waiting for my reply, he bends over and scoops up Melody, cradling her like a child. I watch helplessly as he moves onward, motioning for me to follow. It doesn't exactly do wonders for my manhood to watch another guy carry my wounded girlfriend. But we march on through the woods, around Starlore Lake, back to the car.

"I'll drive," Alexander says, resting Melody down on the backseat of the car. "Stay back here with her, keep the cap pressed to her neck, and when she's a little stronger, give her food and water."

"Benji Bear," she whispers.

Quickly, I pull Benji Bear out of her carry-bag. She holds him to her chest.

Alexander narrows his eyes, and for the first time since we were kids, I see a true smile grow at the corners of his lips. I'd forgotten what my cousin looked like as a normal, caring human being.

"Cute," he says, looking down at Melody.

I try not to remember, as he hops into the driver's seat and starts the car, that Melody thought the same thing about him.

Chapter Twenty-Seven

As the car rolls on, I hold Melody's hand in the backseat. She still has Benji Bear to her chest, but her hold is loose and he keeps falling over. I'm trying to keep Alexander's ski cap pressed to her neck, but the car bouncing along does not help. I'm having trouble holding it steady.

"It's not as easy to cut into veins and arteries as you think," Alexander says from the driver's seat. "She's got a deep cut there, but I think she'll be okay if the bleeding stops soon."

"Are you sure?" I ask, hoping this will ease Melody's mind a little. Even though she told me she was okay with dying, I'm sure she's frightened. *I'm* frightened. Who wouldn't be?

"You have no idea what kind of force he used to kill Fraser," Alexander returns. "Using what we have, it's not easy to kill, so I don't think he really wanted to kill her. If he did, he would have cut her with much more force, and more times."

Inwardly, I thank Alexander for not telling me the same thing happened when Lomidus killed my father. I'll just pretend that my father went quickly and painlessly. It's a coping technique that works well for me. Denial is sometimes the best remedy.

"Can you summon fire?" I ask Alexander to change the subject.

"No," he replies. "But my father did tell me once that it was possible."

"And Lomidus?"

"It wasn't important enough for him to learn, I guess," he responds. "Or maybe he just never figured out the secret method of summoning that you seem to know."

I don't trust Alexander enough yet to share my secret for summoning fire. I'm sure he knows this because he doesn't ask me to share. I'll just let him stay in awe of what I can do. It may be the one thing I have over him, because God knows that even though we look similar, he's older and stockier, and yeah, probably better looking.

"Give her some food," Alexander says. "She's weak and she'll need some iron in her."

There's not much left in our food supply, but I do find a bag of almonds, and I'm pretty sure those have protein and some iron. I get her to a sitting position so she doesn't choke, then help her eat. Her skin is still ice and she's trembling, but I think the bleeding has stopped. The collar of my leather jacket is saturated in blood, but I don't want to take the jacket off her. She needs the warmth.

"How long have you two been dating?" Alexander asks, eyeing me in the rearview mirror.

"I don't know," I reply, feeding Melody some almonds. "A few hours or maybe a few weeks."

Melody lets out a faint chuckle. Our relationship has been rocky and weird, and I guess looking back, I can see why she finds it humorous. We could use some humor right now anyhow.

"I knew when Lomidus took me into the woods that Alexander was on our side," she says in a strained voice. "I could see it in his eyes."

"No talking," I say. "Just eat and relax."

I don't want to ruin her faith in Alexander by spilling to her what I'm thinking, that Alexander might still be in Lomidus's command, driving us to our deaths instead of driving us to a possible last-hour victory. Still, there was no way of knowing where the night was going to lead, so how could Alexander and Lomidus have thought up a plan like that in advance? There are too many variables, so again, I just have to trust Alexander.

"He's probably doing the Ritual already," I say to Alexander. "We're probably too late."

Alexander shakes his head. "He's slow and methodical," he replies. "You saw him back at the mountain, taking his time, savoring every moment." He gives the car gas. "We'll make it."

We speed along until we hit Fairchester. Alexander seems to remember his way to the cemetery, and when we reach the gate, he slows the car and parks just behind Lomidus. It's a blind darkness out there in the cemetery, so I can't tell if Lomidus is still in his car or is already somewhere out by the gravestones.

"What's your plan?" I ask Alexander.

"I want my wand back," he says simply. "So I guess we have to take him down somehow."

"I see he makes plans the same way you do," Melody mumbles. "Which is basically no plan at all."

"Shh," I tell her. "You stay here."

As I rest my hand on the car door handle, Melody sits up. Alexander steps out of the driver's side, quietly closes the door, and walks around to us.

"Back," I tell Melody. "Stay down and stay —"

"I'm going," she says.

We argue in hushed tones until Alexander steps in between us. "She can come," he says to halt the argument.

"She's injured," I explain. "Plus, I really don't want Lomidus to try to finish her off."

He ignores me and reaches down for Melody. "I'll carry you," he says. "Can you wrap your legs around me?"

"No, she can't wrap her legs around you," I say and push him out of the way.

251

"So we're just going to fight all night about this while Lomidus reads the incantation and takes away our power?" he says.

I ball up my hands, making tight fists, and then let out a breath to calm myself. I reach down for Melody. If she's going to wrap her legs around some guy, that guy is going to be me. I hoist her from the car and tuck her legs around my back, my arm muscles flexing and aching as I try to balance her and keep her upright.

"I didn't know we were at this point in our relationship," she says in my ear.

"Ha ha," I tell her. "Just relax, okay?"

"I'm fine," she says as I struggle to keep her around me. "You can let me down. I can walk."

I exchange a glance with Alexander. He nods, and I wonder how we ended up on the same side, making decisions together. Slowly, I slide Melody to the ground. She's unsteady on her feet, wobbles, and closes her eyes as Alexander's arm shoots out to catch her if she falls.

"I'm okay," she says, holding out her arms to steady herself. "Let's just go before it's too late."

Taking small, careful steps, we creep toward the gate of the cemetery. Alexander has a flashlight, but it's not turned on. He has it out and ready in his hand, whipping it around like it's on, using it like a pointer.

"Why here?" I ask. "I mean, why is he doing it specifically here?"

"This cemetery is particularly magical," Alexander replies. "Which is why it was chosen as a place to bury the orb. We figured this out a little too late, of course. But once Lomidus saw what grave you had dug up, he knew."

"Edgar North?" Melody says.

"He was an outsider," Alexander says as we walk through the gate. "Kind of like Lomidus. He knew about the Ritual but was never a part of it. He made a nasty bit of ruckus in his time."

That's all I really need to know. Edgar North was just like Lomidus, trying to inch his way into something that did not directly involve him. Maybe Abraham Rane's family felt sorry for Edgar North and buried the orb along with him to make him a forever part of the Ritual of the Four. Maybe they just liked that his last name might throw a would-be map-finder off track. Maybe Edgar North made *too* much ruckus and got his way in the end, sealing himself within the secret pact of the Ritual. Whatever. That's history, and I'm more concerned with the here and now.

"Oh," Alexander says, stopping. He pulls something small and rectangular out of his coat pocket and hands it to Melody. "I forgot to give you back your phone."

Melody jerks away. "Did Lomidus touch it?"

"No," Alexander replies, smiling. "Only me."

Melody smiles back, taking her phone from his hand as I scratch my head and tap my foot. It drives me insane just to see their hands touching. Now I know what Melody went through when I was hung up on Ariana.

"I wrote you a message on there," Alexander tells her as she examines her phone. "It's in your Notes."

Melody cocks her head, then winces in pain and holds her hand to her neck.

"Read it when you can," he says.

We move forward again, just behind Alexander and his pointing, turned-off flashlight. He guides us past the gate, inside the dark depths of the graveyard. I can't see a thing and wonder how many graves I'm trampling over, how many gravestones I've just missed slamming into. Finally, up ahead, I see what looks like a flickering light, maybe from a candle.

"He's by Edgar North's grave," Melody says. Her voice sounds faint again.

"You okay?" I ask and wrap my arm around her shoulder.

"It just...hurts," she replies. "The cut is stinging. I'll be okay, though."

"The cold air is probably not helping," Alexander says. "Just take it easy, and try not to move your neck around too much."

"I could have told her that," I say.

Alexander huffs and keeps moving toward the flickering light.

"I don't understand," Melody says in my ear. "Are we trying to stop Lomidus for ethical reasons, or is Alexander trying to keep his power? Does he know you're going to end the Ritual for good?"

I'm actually not sure what Alexander thinks, or maybe he's pieced together my intentions based on some things I've said. I still want to keep this information from Melody, because I don't want her to get her hopes up if we're too late to stop Lomidus. And if we're *not* too late to stop Lomidus, I want to see the look on Melody's face when she realizes I'm giving her the power of the goblet. It may be the only truly great thing I can ever do for her.

"I don't know what the plan is," I whisper to Melody. "I think we're just going with the flow here."

Alexander stops about twenty feet away from the flickering light around Edgar North's grave. The graveyard is pretty barren as far as trees, except for the surrounding woods, but there are a few smaller birch trees and skinny pines scattered here and there. Alexander slips behind a tree trunk and we follow, crouching down.

"You feel it?" he says to me. "The pull of the dagger?"

I hadn't. Not until he mentioned it. Now it feels like my best friend is drowning in a sucking whirlpool somewhere close to me, and I'm being pulled in for a rescue.

"This is how I always found you," Alexander whispers. "This pull in my blood. I think it was stronger for me because you had the actual physical dagger."

I nod. I'm not sure if he can see me. A strange instinct kicks in, and just for a moment, I feel connected with

Alexander. Family. *Trusted* family. God, I hope my instincts are right.

"Let's just storm him," he says. "I'll take the wand, you take the dagger."

"What about the incantation?" Melody says. "Fraser's pentacle? My goblet?"

Alexander thinks on this. "You stay here," he says to her. "You'll be our secret weapon. Once we get our wand and dagger, he'll chase us. Then you run in and gather the rest of the things. Wait for our cue."

"And if you two get hurt?"

"It's two against one now," Alexander replies. "Shaw and I, we got him."

"I'll call for you when it's safe to run in for the goblet and pentacle," I tell Melody.

With that, Alexander stands and moves away from the tree. I kiss Melody's cheek, squeeze her hand, and follow Alexander. We move in like a SWAT team, with crouching, gentle steps. A twig breaks and Alexander halts. Simultaneously, we suck in a breath of air, then creep forward again, in sync.

When we get closer, the scene before me unravels in varying shades of black and orange, glitters of gold. Lomidus has set a black pillar candle just in front of Edgar North's gravestone. He's sitting just beside the grave, closer to the woods, his body circled by the four objects in the Ritual of the Four. He seems to be absorbing the items, his eyes closed and his lips slightly parted as though drinking in the scene around him.

"I know you're here," he says without opening his eyes.

Alexander turns to me. "Get it," he mouths.

I mentally recite our plan. *I take the dagger, Alexander takes the wand.* As I ready to spring into action, my cousin and I lock eyes. Once upon a time, his eerie battle eyes were against me. They hunted me down, sliced me, and wounded me. Now, the eyes are pleading, demanding this—*get our stuff, our team of two Huntley men, and keep what is rightfully ours.*

I dive for my dagger, hit the ground and curl my fingers around the handle. Easy. Too easy. Clambering to my feet, I hold my dagger out—it *is* a weapon, I always forget—but Alexander hasn't moved an inch. He didn't go for his wand. What the hell?

"Please tell me you didn't play me," I say.

He laughs. "Too easy, cousin," he says, shaking his head.

Chapter Twenty-Eight

With glazed triumph in his eyes, Alexander joins Lomidus, who has lifted himself from the ground. The two stand side-by-side, against me, both of them circled by the pentacle, the wand, and the goblet. Lomidus has the incantation opened up in his hand. My stomach twists and pitches. Why did Alexander drive me here just to turn on me? Why did he even bother saving Melody's life? I trusted him, and that was my mistake, but for the life of me, I can't understand how it ended up the way it is now.

"Once again, you are in my way," Lomidus says to me.

"Without this, you have nothing." I wave my dagger in front of his eyes. "You need all four items."

"So you'll give it to me," Lomidus replies.

"Like hell," I say.

I've learned control over the last few weeks. Melody has taught me how to control my gift, how to project my rage onto things other than human beings. But none of that registers in my mind right now. All I see is blazing red before me, pulsing rage and betrayal. These two guys not only tricked me, but also cut up my girlfriend and killed Fraser. They killed my *father*.

Lomidus is not ready for the blow. His body jolts as my mental dagger slices across his forehead, carving a thick, bloody line into his skin as though he were just struck by a flying disc of jagged metal. Blood oozes down his nose, seeps into his deep scars, and lingers at his lip. He cups his forehead with one hand, still holding the incantation with the other. Alexander rushes at me, and I thrust my dagger, my physical weapon, through his coat. He screams and falls to the ground, holding his upper arm.

"That was for my father," I say to them. "And this is for Melody and Fraser."

I step over Alexander, bend down, and scoop up Melody's goblet and Fraser's pentacle. Balancing all three items—I don't care right now about the wand and the incantation—I try to make a run for it, back to Melody, but Alexander grabs me around my ankles, and I crash to the ground. I had no time to brace for my fall, went straight down, so my face is pressed against the old dirt and soggy leaves of Edgar North's gravesite. I inhale soil and cough, make some feeble attempt to gather all three items again, but can only reach Melody's goblet. I've just palmed the thing when the pain hits.

It feels like a needle being dragged down the back of my thigh. A *hot* needle. I try not to scream but something worse comes out, like the yelp of a wounded animal. My face contorts in pain, and I can't see anything in front of me. Just the darkness behind my closed eyes.

Something hard slams into my side, and my body nearly lifts into the air from the force. Despite the searing pain in my side and down my thigh, a flashback bolts through my mind of Sal and his gang beating me behind the school at the Halloween dance. I couldn't project my dagger to defend myself that night. I was already too far gone, too weak. I can't let that happen now. I have to stay strong.

With all my might, I pull myself to standing. Lomidus, always one step ahead of me, has all the items back in his possession. His bloodstained face shines in the flooding candlelight, and I almost can't stand to look at him. Alexander is still on the ground, writhing. I must have cut him pretty deep with my dagger. It's never been used for physical damage before. At least not by me.

"I guess you'll just leave him and run," I say to Lomidus and point down at Alexander. "That's what you always do when he's hurt."

"It seems that you and your cousin don't know where your loyalties lie," he replies. "You're with him, you're against him. He's with you, he's against you."

"He's the one who turned on me," I reply. "Not just tonight…a long time ago."

Alexander looks up at me. His eyes are still set in that eerie, warlike glaze. I can't make sense of the change. Maybe Melody softened him, if only for a little while, and that's why he helped us earlier. Maybe he's afraid of Lomidus and only remembered how much when he faced battling him. Or maybe he just planned to betray me from the moment he pretended to turn to my side.

"We can leave together now," Alexander says to Lomidus. "We have what we need."

Warm blood from my injured thigh soaks through the back of my jeans. It's only a matter of time before I end up like Alexander, on the ground, faint, and in excruciating pain.

"Help me up," Alexander says to Lomidus. "I'm too weak to stand."

Lomidus turns to him. He looks down on his wounded ally, his eyes blank and uncaring. He wipes fresh blood from his cheek, then fades away in thought.

"You can't just leave me here," Alexander says.

"You were faithful," Lomidus replies, eyeing Alexander's wounded arm. "But now I must cut ties with the Huntley boys." He takes a deep bow. "Good evening to you both."

"Lomidus!" Alexander screams.

Lomidus steps away for good, cradling the four items in the Ritual of the Four. The incantation, smeared with his blood, dangles from his clenched fingers. We can't run after him this time. Alexander isn't on my side, and I don't know if Melody can drive, not to mention I have no idea where

259

Lomidus will go to continue the Ritual. I'm about to attack one last time just to see if I can take him down on my own, even in this condition, when Alexander roars out in pain and frustration.

"You said we would always help each other!" he shouts, his voice hoarse and angry. "That night Shaw hit me in the chest, you said you wouldn't let me die!"

"You won't die!" Lomidus says, turning back. "You stupid, ignorant kid! You just have a flesh wound on your arm!"

"Then take me with you!"

The pleas explode from Alexander to Lomidus, and I watch and listen, revolted. It's pathetic, Alexander pleading for Lomidus to help him and to take him along. In the short time I was with Alexander in the woods and in the car, he didn't seem so needy and dependent on another human being. I actually thought he was in control of the situation, maybe even a little brave.

As the gash in his forehead bleeds into his eyes like dripping paint, Lomidus relents and bends over Alexander. "I'll pull you up," he says, "only because you've helped me for so long, but after that, you're on your—"

Before I can register what's happening, Alexander slams Lomidus, sending him tumbling backward. The goblet and dagger fly into the air, catch the candlelight, and then crash to the earth. Alexander grabs my dagger, fisting it as he uses his free hand to tug the incantation out from between Lomidus's fingers.

"Shaw!" he says as Lomidus tries to fight back, punching at the air. "Take it!"

I'm anticipating another trick, like I'll step forward and Alexander will kill me with my own dagger. What the hell is going on? Whose side is Alexander on?

"Give me my dagger," I say, stepping forward.

"Help me, Shaw!" Alexander says as Lomidus gets to his feet.

260

"I'm not playing this game," I tell him. "The dagger is mine. I want it."

"Take the damn thing." He throws my dagger at me. I clap my hands as it soars past and trap the handle.

Lomidus reaches for the incantation that is now tight in Alexander's hand, and the two scuffle, falling back to the ground. Alexander screams my name, and I grasp my dagger, deciding what I should do. Probably just let the two of them kill each other. I have my dagger, and not only does that mean Lomidus can't finish the Ritual, but also that my family heirloom is back in my hands. I can leave now knowing everything is tied up nicely.

"Shaw!" Alexander says.

"I'm leaving!"

"You can't leave me here with him!" Alexander says, wrestling Lomidus. "He's going to kill me!"

"Better you than me."

And that's when Melody, unsteady on her feet, face white as fresh milk, rushes out from behind the tree trunk.

Chapter Twenty-Nine

"You need to distract Lomidus!" Melody says, holding onto my shoulder. "You need to summon fire. He'll kill Alexander if you don't do something!"

When I glance over my shoulder at Alexander, still on the ground fighting off Lomidus, his face is lined with blood. Honestly, I don't know if Lomidus attacked physically with his fingernails or something, or with his mental weapon. Alexander is inching away, crawling backward along the ground, still trying to keep the incantation away from Lomidus.

"We're leaving," I say, grasping Melody's arm. "You need the hospital. I might need the hospital. It's over."

"Shaw, he's your cousin," she pleads. "Save him."

He's not my cousin. He's just some guy who helped murder my father and then turned on me when I thought he was on my side. I was telling him the truth—I am not playing this game. Alexander is a traitor, and he betrayed me. He betrayed Melody and now he's trying to pretend he's the hero, fighting Lomidus for the incantation, maybe even fighting Lomidus to the death.

But then, even in the middle of this insane candlelit graveyard battle, I remember something about *Star Wars*. In *Return of the Jedi*, Han Solo saves Lando Calrissian, even though Lando betrayed him in *Empire Strikes Back*. Damn it.

Visualizing my dagger as a symbol for the power of fire, I

summon a burst of flames to the base of Edgar North's gravestone, this time using my swinging arm to conjure the blast. The ball of fire is so close to Lomidus's boot that he nearly catches on fire and rolls to the right to get away. Alexander's eyes reflect the flames, and for a second his eyes flash in triumph—but the triumph is short-lived. Lomidus, breathless and obviously hanging onto the last string of his power, attacks.

I'm not sure where Lomidus cut Alexander, all I know is that Alexander's eyes widen in alarm and agony, then snap closed. His body twitches, then stops, motionless, as Melody shrieks and runs to him. Lomidus reaches for the incantation in Alexander's loosening grip, but I dash over, wedge myself between, and rip the incantation away from Lomidus.

"You killed him!" Melody shouts at Lomidus, her hand pressed to Alexander's chest. "You crazy, crazy—" She's incomprehensible after that, throwing herself over Alexander as though she's known him forever.

Alexander turned on me, and I don't consider him my cousin anymore, but God, I didn't want him to die. I hope Melody is wrong. Lomidus has killed too many people now, and as this sinks in, my thoughts, my morals, burn and dissolve into ashes until I'm left with nothing but revenge.

Lomidus stretches his hand out, going for the incantation, and I decide I've had enough. I need this night to end—and I need it to end right now. With all my might, I stick my dagger into Lomidus's chest. I cannot say with any certainty if I used my mind dagger or my physical dagger. All I know is that a gold blade penetrates the center of Lomidus's dark coat, deep and forceful. And I know, just by instinct, that he's wounded beyond repair. He claws at his chest, heaving, and then dashes away through the graveyard.

His distant shadow staggers, unbalanced and leaning, until he crashes to the ground. I think that's it, he's dead and gone, but then he clambers to his feet and continues his escape to the cemetery gate. In the distance, a car engine starts up, and through the light cast from a few far-off streetlights, I watch Lomidus's car speed away and then veer off the road. I hear a crash but can't tell how far off the crash is or even what Lomidus hit.

"Do you think he's...." Melody starts.

I glance back at the street. "He probably lost too much blood, passed out, and crashed his car. Yeah, probably dead."

"The cops will come any minute," Melody says, tears streaming. "What do we do? We can't leave Alexander here."

Now that I look down at my cousin's graying face, I feel the sting and grief of death. He was too young. He was stupid to get involved. I had a feeling it was going to end like this.

"He shouldn't have done what he did to us," I say. "But I didn't want him to die."

Melody sniffles. She pulls her phone from her pocket, opens her Notes, and holds the phone up to my eyes. There, glowing against the dying fire at the base of Edgar North's grave, is the message Alexander left for her:

"I'm on your side but will pretend I'm with Lomidus. It will work."

I drop to my knees. "He was on our side all along?"

Melody nods. "He must have written this when we were in the car, coming here."

God, God, God, how did this happen? Why didn't he tell me his plan? *Because there wasn't enough time. Because he didn't want Lomidus to overhear. Because he wanted my surprise to be genuine.*

Melody sobs and inches her finger down Alexander's bloody cheek.

"He looks so much like you," she whispers.

"But better-looking," I say.

She smiles sadly. "I'm still partial to you."

Weakly, I smile back at her. I still don't know what she sees in me.

"We should get out of here before that neighbor comes out," she says and points to the house that edges the graveyard. "And I'm sure that crash woke someone up and they're calling the police."

"What time is it?"

"Almost four-thirty," she says. "Probably only an hour or so until sunrise."

"Okay." I look down at Alexander. A few things happen, one being a particularly vivid image of the crying faces of my Aunt Ginny and Uncle Carlton. My mother and I haven't spoken to them in years since the big split in my family because Alexander took another side, but that doesn't mean I want them to have to deal with Alexander being...gone.

"Can you carry him to the car?" Melody says, rubbing her cheek.

"God, Melody, he's bigger than me." I exhale. "Maybe we can drag—"

"Wait a second," Melody says and cocks her head. She places her hand on Alexander's chest. "I think he just...God, Shaw. I think he just breathed!"

"I thought you said he was...."

"He wasn't moving!" she says.

I thought she checked his vitals or knew he was gone from whatever wound Lomidus inflicted. But now that I think about it, I didn't really see a physical wound, except for the tear in his coat from my dagger. And that wound might not even have been as horrible as Alexander made it out to be.

"Do you think he's...."

"We have to get him to the car!" Melody says. "He might still be—"

"I'm okay," Alexander gasps. "Guys...don't bury me alive."

"Alexander!" Melody screams and throws herself over him again.

With Melody draped over him, he smiles up at me and gives me a sarcastic wink. I smirk back. He's back to life so now I can say it: God, I hate this dude.

"She's cute," he says.

"Ladies' man," I say. "Great."

I reach down and offer him my hand. Color oozes back into his cheeks as he accepts my hand, pulling himself to a sitting position.

"What happened?" Melody asks.

"I was on your side," he replies. "You read my message, right?"

"Yes, but that's not what I meant," she replies. "What did Lomidus do to you?"

"Oh." He puts his hand to his head. "Knocked me out, somehow. Took my breath."

Melody pours out her sympathy, rubbing his temple, but she's not in the best shape, either. We're all in rough shape.

"We need to get to the car before the cops get here," I say. "Is anyone okay to drive?"

"I can," Alexander says and wobbles to standing. "At least to someplace safer." He glances around him at the four items and the incantation. "You going to do it?" he asks me.

"We should probably get some medical attention."

"We'll be fine," he says. He takes off his coat and hands it to me. "Wrap this around your leg until the bleeding stops. Melody is already looking healthier."

"So, we're really going to end the Ritual?" Melody asks. "I mean, now that Lomidus is probably...."

"He is?" Alexander asks. "How do you know that? Where did he go?"

I point down the street. "Dead," I say. "Dagger to the chest. Car off the road and into probably a tree or pole."

"Excellent," Alexander says and claps my shoulder. "So I assume you'll want to involve her?" he says, lifting his chin to indicate Melody. "She has the goblet, right?"

Melody shifts her eyes to me. Way to let the cat out of the bag, Alexander.

"I wanted to give the power of the dagger over to you fully," Alexander continues. "Never wanted that one. Maybe you could change me over to the wand?"

"Find me a secluded place," I say and start picking up the four Ritual items. "Hopefully before dawn, we can change the original Ritual of the Four."

Chapter Thirty

We decide on the fairgrounds in Fairchester — home of the autumn carnival — to attempt the Ritual of the Four. I'm a little worried about Alexander behind the wheel because he keeps nodding off and jerking back. Melody is quiet beside me. Before we left the cemetery, running to the car with the little bit of steam we had left (we had to step on it when blue and red lights flashed in the distance), I didn't say anything to Melody about the Ritual. She's Melody, so I'm sure she knows what I'm planning and what I've *been* planning. It's easy for me to ignore her, because we're all so exhausted that conversation is impossible. I just don't want to have to say my plans aloud. I wanted it to be a surprise gift, even though Alexander kind of ruined that.

As we get closer to the fairgrounds, Melody trembles beside me in the backseat. Her teeth are audibly chattering. I move over and drape my arm around her, rubbing her shoulder to generate some heat. She mentioned, just as we got back into Fraser's car, that she's never been so cold in all her life. I'm not sure if that's from the air temperature, the wounds we've sustained, or a combination. All of us have probably felt better and have definitely looked better. Even Alexander, "King of Good Looks Town," has so many scratches and bloody lines you can barely make out his facial features.

Two streets from the fairgrounds, Melody falls asleep on

269

my shoulder. I catch Alexander's eyes in the rearview mirror.

"Let her," he says. "Just for a few minutes."

"You said we need to do this before dawn," I reply in a low voice so I don't wake her.

He nods. "I know that. It's just that the Ritual is draining, and she's already spent."

"How do you know the Ritual is draining?"

"Lomidus explained it to me," he replies.

We stare at each other through the rearview until I turn away. There will never be a truce between Alexander and me. There will never be a time I don't remember how he attacked me when he was with Lomidus.

"Still don't trust me?" he asks.

"Would you if you were me?"

"Nope," he replies.

He's quiet after that and turns the car onto the road that leads to the fairgrounds. The day has not dawned yet, the sky is still varying shades of deep gray and true black. The half-moon is up and shining, and I remember how it illuminated my way at the lake until the clouds rolled in and snow fell over the mountains. The moon's presence, back in the mix of the night, is soothing.

"Why did you?" I ask Alexander.

"Excuse?" he says.

"I mean, unless you have a good reason for turning on my family. Like, Lomidus threatened Aunt Ginny's life or something. I can't think of any other reason why you would—"

"Shaw," he says simply. "Sometimes people do stupid things because they're young and confused and think someone knows better than they do. Some of the strongest minds in history have succumbed to people less persuasive than Lomidus." He sighs. "All I can say is I'm sorry. I thought I made it up to you by what I did in the cemetery."

"In the end, I was the one who killed him."

"You couldn't have done it if I hadn't taken him down."

270

He turns into the parking lot of the fairgrounds. "Weird for me to run away from those emergency vehicles. Usually, I'm inside of them." He parks the car close to the field. "Probably should have stuck around to make sure they pulled his lifeless body out of that car."

"Probably," I reply. "But I have a feeling I ended him. It was a kill stab…I'm nearly positive."

"If you're capable of a kill stab," he returns. "I never was."

Mind rewind. All the times Alexander and I fought, none ended with a kill stab from either side. I remember thinking if Alexander had been going for a fatal stab, he messed it up royally. Still, I can't say with any certainty that I used my mental dagger and not my physical dagger. There was blood on my dagger, but there was blood on everything. If Alexander is right and I'm not capable of a mental kill stab…it doesn't matter. Lomidus crashed his car. He's dead.

"Got the incantation?" he asks.

"Yeah," I reply, then palm Melody's cheek and stroke her skin.

She awakes with a start. Maybe from a nightmare.

"Is it time?" she whispers.

"Yes," I say back. "It's time."

She nods. We gather our things and make our way through the fairgrounds, trying to find the best location to perform the Ritual. We have to do this quickly, so we pretty much ignore the coldness and just plow across the frosty grounds. Alexander said the Ritual has to be performed at night or it won't work. Something about the cloak of darkness, the power of nighttime, and the moon. We're amateurs at best and know little about magic, so it's probably a good idea to follow what we know of the rules.

We end up in a secluded section of the grounds, where during the autumn carnival, if memory serves, some of the more obscure food booths were nestled in the trees. Booths like Joe's Famous Frog Legs, and beside it, a booth of those tiny pellets of ice cream that nobody ever seems to buy. I think there was a lady selling bags of apple chips back here, too, but I'm really not sure. When I smelled the blood in the air that always announced Lomidus and Alexander's presence, I jetted for the Ferris wheel, so most of my autumn carnival memories are just blurs of neon lights.

Alexander sets up quietly. It's obvious that his training is from Lomidus. He takes his time, savors the moment. After he rests the wand on the ground, making sure it's perfectly straight, he continues to make a circle of Ritual items with the goblet and the pentacle. I place my dagger down on the snow-speckled grass, completing the circle. I stay close.

Melody unrolls the incantation, then moves it out of my vision. "You said you didn't want to see the words until it was time," she whispers to me.

"It's time," I say.

"Okay." She hands the incantation over. "Are you sure you want to do this?"

I glance at Alexander. "Alexander will take the wand," I announce. "I'll keep the dagger, and Melody...you're the goblet."

She nods, and even though she's trying to be serious, she's biting her lip to hold back her excitement.

"What about the pentacle?" Alexander says.

"That was Fraser's."

Alexander bends down to adjust the pentacle. "His line is gone," he says. "And since I'm taking the wand, you'll have to word it so the dagger stays only in Shaw Huntley's family line, not the entire Huntley line." He stands up. "Somebody has to take the pentacle. It won't work unless one of us speaks our intent on that item."

"He's right," Melody says. "If you look at the incantation, you'll see that each person said their specific intent and spoke their own incantation. I told you that before."

With a sigh, I raise my phone up so the light shines on the incantation, then skim the words. Yeah, they're right. Each item in the Ritual has one specific owner, one person who spoke intention for its power. With nobody left in Fraser's family line—

"Take it," Melody says to me. "Take the power of the pentacle."

"No," I say quickly.

"Fraser would have wanted that," Alexander adds.

When I first went into this, I wanted to end the Ritual. Then I decided to keep it going for my father and for Melody. Now, not only am I keeping my gift of slicing things up and summoning fire, but also gaining a new power—great strength.

"Okay," I say, relenting as I let out a breath of held air. "What do we need to do next?"

Alexander shrugs. "I saw Lomidus work rituals, and we don't really have the things he had when he did them. He used black cloaks, candles…you saw what he had going on in the cemetery. We're just going to have to summon our collective power, concentrate, and give it a go."

"Give it a go," I repeat. "Sounds incredibly technical."

Melody laughs. Even though the laugh is faint and shaky, it's still good to hear.

"Before dawn, Shaw," Alexander says, looking to the horizon. "If we have any chance at all of pulling this off, it has to be done right now, before the sun comes up."

Instinctively, I grab Melody's hand. She reaches out and grasps Alexander's. We stand in a semicircle, close to the four items, and I bend down for my dagger. I hold it up to the moon, and something inside of me changes. It's almost as though I'm recharged, or I have double the power I had, like the dagger somehow senses that I alone hold the power now. It's not split up or diffused among the remaining Huntley men. It's all mine.

Thrusting the dagger into the air, I read the top line of the incantation:

"Element of fire, I honor you and invoke your power — courage,

fire, and destruction, lace into my being and my blood. I raise the dagger, I raise the flame."

"Your intention," Alexander reminds me.

"Intention: Shaw Morrison Huntley," I say. "And my future Huntley bloodline."

What happens next takes me by surprise. In the center of the ring of Ritual items, a fire grows as though spit up from the ground. Melody jumps back, away from the flames, but I grab her hand and keep her close, still in our held-hands semicircle. The fire blazes toward the sky, screaming out sparks and ashes, illuminating our faces in a pulsing orange glow. Alexander stands mesmerized, until the flames suck back into the earth. He turns to me, and I know what he's thinking, what he's going to do next.

And it doesn't work.

"Gone," he says. "I can't cut anymore. Not even a little."

I nod, then hand over the incantation. "You're next."

Alexander takes the old paper from me, eyes wild and eerie like they are in battle. It reminds me too much of the old Alexander, so I turn away as he raises his wand to the sky. Out of my side vision, I see a white beam form, cast from his raised wand filtering moonlight. I have no choice but to watch full-on, in awe.

"Element of air," Alexander recites, "I honor you and invoke your power – mind, air, and flight, lace into my being and my blood. I raise the wand, I raise the wind." He blows out air. "Intention: Alexander Emmett Huntley and my future bloodline."

A gust of wind blows over us, emanating from inside the circle. The wind is so strong that it nearly rips my hand from Melody's. Her braid blows back, and I can see the gash in her neck, raw and maroon. Alexander steps forward, right into the full force of the wind, and closes his eyes. His body levitates a few feet into the air, and Melody gasps. We watch, transfixed on Alexander's floating body, until the wind stops. Alexander lands back on the ground, his wand glowing white and blue.

The horizon skips to light purple.

"Melody, go!" I say. "Do it fast!"

Melody is in the center of our semicircle, so she has to detach herself from Alexander's hand to hold up the goblet. To keep our flow of energy, Alexander places his palm on Melody's back. My teeth clench.

Clutching the goblet around the base, Melody holds it to the sky. The goblet flashes gold in the waning moonlight, and I don't remember ever seeing anything so illuminated and alight. Alexander holds the incantation up for her to read.

"*Element of water,*" she says in a loud, strong voice, "*I honor you and invoke your power—emotion, water, and intuition, lace into my being and my blood. I raise the goblet, I raise the tides.*" She squares her shoulders. "*Intention: Melody Renee Tufts and my descendants.*"

I look to the horizon, half-expecting a roaring flood of water to roll toward us. But Melody's eyes shift to the center of the circle. There, a glowing blue stream of light, waving and shimmering, grows out of the earth, just like the fire but not quite as violent. The light seems to locate Melody like it has its own eye and bends toward her before rushing into her chest. She falls to her knees, weeping, as the blue light dissolves.

"*Melody!*" I scream.

"No time!" Alexander says. "Keep it going, Shaw!"

Melody continues to sob, but lifts her hand and gives me a weak thumbs up. Holding her around the shoulder, I bend down and scoop up Fraser's pentacle. I envision his face, recite a few mental words to him like good-bye and rest in peace, and then stretch my neck over Melody to read the words on the incantation Alexander is holding:

"*Element of earth, I honor you and invoke your power—growth, earth, and strength, lace into my being and my blood. I raise the pentacle, I raise the power.*" I hold the pentacle to the sky, where the purple of daybreak kisses its edges. "*Intention: Shaw Morrison Huntley and my future bloodline.*"

275

The ground beneath us shakes and quakes. My body flings forward, and I fall flat to the ground, grasping at bits of frozen grass as though that's enough to keep me from falling off the face of the earth. And then I feel different. My muscles harden…it's not like they're physically growing but they feel heavy and padded. It's a peculiar sensation, but I think I might like it.

When the earth finally stops vibrating, I'm able to pull myself to a sitting position. Dawn has brightened the surroundings, exposing dead trees and a vast field. Alexander stares out into the horizon, his eyes calm and neutral. Melody is crying beside me, so I wrap her up and rock her.

"It's okay," I say. "It's going to be okay."

She presses against me. "I just feel…it felt like every sad thing in the world fell on top of me," she gasps. "Just like that. All the sad things."

"It's okay," I say again.

Every time I think she's going to stop crying, she falls back into sobs. Some are soft, rattling sobs, some are so loud they boom through my chest and echo through the trees. Alexander turns away from the sky and sits down beside Melody. He rubs her back, and even though he's just trying to help, I still feel like decking him for touching her at all.

"We have to sign it," Alexander says. "The incantation."

I'd almost forgotten about that. Weakly, we pass around the incantation and dot it with our blood prints. There is no need for cutting; we're all already bloodied up enough.

"Here's what we're going to do," Alexander says, rolling up the incantation. "I'll drive us back to my house and bandage everyone up. Then I'll take you guys to the train station."

All I can manage is a slight nod. I'll have to call my mother later and tell her to come pick us up at the train station in New York. At least we'll make it back in time, although I really don't know how we'll explain our wounds to Melody's father.

"You have to be strong," Alexander tells Melody. "You have to pull it together."

Melody doesn't reply. She just keeps sobbing. Alexander and I lock eyes. Yeah, maybe it was a bad idea to give Melody the power of the goblet. I thought I was doing a good thing for her. Now I realize what I've known all along, that this ability, or this *gift* rather, comes at a cost. It always has.

"You just have to get in tune with it," Alexander tells her, rubbing her back. "With all the new emotions you'll be feeling."

It takes a while to fully calm her, and by the time we gather our things and head back to the car, the horizon has swallowed the half moon. A weak winter sun casts a silver-purple light over the grass, and nothing feels the same. I get the feeling I've only just begun to absorb what has happened to me over Thanksgiving weekend.

"Who keeps the incantation?" Alexander says as we near the car. "I mean, at some point we should probably write our names over the existing names on there, right? Under intentions?"

I open the car door, rummage through Melody's carry-bag, and find a pen. Then, I take the incantation from Alexander and scribble our names down on the Ritual of the Four, over the existing names of Morrison Huntley, Thomas Solan, Lizzie Marrin, and Fergus Terra.

"There," I say. "Changed."

Alexander nods. "Excellent," he says.

"Excellent," I echo.

And then I summon fire to the corner of the Ritual, and the entire incantation goes up in flames. Alexander reaches out to save it, but it's too late. The thing is black and charred.

"Forever changed," I say. "No one will ever be able to take the power away from us."

Melody lifts her hand to my cheek. I'm expecting the "Wrath of Melody" for what I just did, but she only smiles.

"A quiet hum," she whispers. "You're...content."

"I'm guessing you can feel my emotions."

"Not just feel them," she says and kisses the center of my forehead. "I can hear them, too."

Part IV
Unexpected Goodbye

Chapter Thirty-One

Sunday night, just after six o'clock, Melody and I arrive back in Rockpoint. Alexander did a good job of bandaging us up. All we have to show for our weekend quest are two gauzy white strips, one on Melody's throat, and one on the back of my thigh. My face is messed up. I hadn't realized how bad it was until I looked in Alexander's bathroom mirror. He said the slice needed stitches, that it's going to leave a nasty scar, and I should probably get myself to the ER. I made the decision to have Alexander clean it out so it didn't get infected, and just take my chances.

"Your father is waiting at my apartment," my mother says to Melody, turning the car onto Uptown Road. "Just so you're prepared for that."

We've already told my mother the entire story of the weekend, which took most of the car ride back to Rockpoint, but we still don't know what we're going to tell Melody's father.

"He'll see our cuts, obviously," I say to my mom, hoping she'll know what to do.

"Shaw and I were dancing, and we lost our balance and fell into a glass coffee table," Melody says.

"What?" my mother says back.

"That's what I'm going to tell my father about our cuts."

My mother spins the steering wheel and turns the car into the apartment complex. "No," she says. "I think it's about

281

time we told him the truth. Him and I spent the entire weekend together, and we've become...very close."

"Gross," I interject.

She flashes me reprimanding mom-eyes from the rearview. I've kind of missed her pissed-off expressions. "Anyhow," she continues, "I think it's best that we tell him the truth about all of us. It's going to happen sooner or later. Like I said, he and I have become close. I don't want any secrets between us."

She parks the car and Melody sighs, then reaches for her carry-bag. We haven't said much about Melody's new ability. Or as she would say, her new *gift*. I haven't said much about my new gift, either. My muscles still feel oddly padded, but there's no visual difference. Alexander has the gift of flying, but he didn't attempt to do that at his house. He just bandaged us up, pretty professionally I might add, and drove us to the train station. I'm not sure what he's going to do with Fraser's car. He said the last thing he wanted was to go back and leave it in Fraser's driveway, knowing Fraser's body was still inside the cabin. Or maybe my mother took care of that already, I don't know. At this point, I don't want to know anything at all. I just want to sleep.

"You have Benji Bear?" I ask Melody as we step out of the car.

"I wouldn't have gone home without him," she replies.

"Benji Bear?" my mother asks, closing her car door.

"Long story," I say and smile.

Inside my apartment, Melody's father is sitting on our living room couch but jumps up when he sees Melody. He runs to her, immediately spotting the gauze on her neck.

"Hi, Dad," she says and hugs him around the waist as though nothing is wrong.

He glances at me, takes in my face. His eyes flash, making some connections, probably envisioning a million scenes of violence.

"What the hell?" he says. He tosses up his hands, losing

all composure. "What happened?"

"Dad," Melody says. But before she can get the words out, she chokes on a sob, and that's the end.

"What's the matter?" Stephen says, alarmed. "What the hell is going on? Was there an accident?"

"They're okay, Stephen," my mother says and caresses his arm. "Everyone is okay."

Wow. I have to move away here. My mother speaks to Stephen in quiet tones she never used with my dad, touches him in soft ways she never touched my dad. Melody and I are not the only ones who had a severe change in relationship this weekend.

"Why don't you walk Melody home and say your good-byes for the night," my mother tells me. "I'll talk to Stephen."

Melody is blubbering and inconsolable, but I manage to get her to the door. Stephen storms at us as though he doesn't want me to take Melody away when he's finally got her home, but I just close the door behind me, leaving him with my mother. She's the best person to deal with this situation, talk him down, and explain what's going on.

"I've never seen him so mad," Melody says, wiping her tears as we walk. "And it wasn't just that we were hurt, it was that nobody told him."

"My mother knows how to deal with problems," I assure. "She's very good at that."

We stop at Melody's front door. She drops her carry-bag down on the ground, and I wrap my arms around her until I can physically feel her calm down. I guess they've turned the fountain in the center of the complex off for the winter, because I've just noticed a strange silence. I've also just noticed that unit seven circled their front door with a string of glowing white Christmas lights. How quickly this place transformed in just a few days, from warm weather heaven to winter wonderland.

"I can't believe I won't be sleeping with you tonight," Melody says. "I've gotten used to it."

I let out a laugh. Then this weird panic bubbles inside of my stomach, this monster that's been growing inside of me since we left the cemetery, but I've tried to ignore. The bubble grows stronger and more painful until I can't bear it anymore.

"Am I going to burn in hell?" I say.

"For killing Lomidus?"

I nod. She got that so fast.

"You didn't kill him, the car accident did," she says. She rests her palm against my cheek, over my cut. I mold myself to her, and instantly my cut is soothed. It almost feels like she completely…no, she couldn't have. It would be impossible.

"Alexander said we should keep checking newspapers and stuff," I say. "For any word on what happened to Lomidus."

"I'll find the local news for Fairchester," Melody says. "Now that I have my phone back. I think I stuffed it inside my carry-bag or someplace, so I'll check later." She glances down at her bag, and shrugs. "Thanks," she says, looking up at me. "For what you did for me. I really wanted to be a part of the Ritual."

It didn't work out exactly as I'd planned. I didn't expect she'd cry constantly after being given the power of the goblet. What I really did was change her into a human emotion detector, and too much human emotion is enough to really break someone.

"Thank you, too," I tell her. "I couldn't have done what I did this weekend without you."

That's our cue to kiss. Plus, I have a feeling my mom will be a while with Stephen, and Melody and I deserve this quiet moment with nothing over our heads. With both arms, I lift her into the air and wrap her around me, backing her against the wall of her apartment. It's as easy as lifting a kitten. Why the hell couldn't I have had this power when Melody needed to be carried from the woods?

"Still trying to top that first kiss," I tell her.

"Our first kiss *was* pretty hot, wasn't it?"

We laugh, and then we kiss. For a while.

I've just put her back on the ground when a door slams in the near distance. Stephen plows down the apartment complex walkway, heading for us. When he passes unit seven, the glowing white Christmas lights illuminate the redness of his face and a few bulging blue veins in his forehead. I move away from Melody.

"Dad," Melody says as he approaches. "Please don't be mad."

"Inside," he says to her. He turns to me. "I don't want you anywhere around her," he says. "You understand that?"

"I...." All I can do is mouth wordlessly at him. I expected he'd be mad when he found out who I really was, but the guy is normally laid-back, easygoing. I never would have expected him to react this way.

"Do you understand that?" he says again.

Melody breaks down again. She holds her hands over her ears and cries to the point where the sound digs into my stomach. God. Even when you try to do the right thing, it turns out wrong.

"I'm going home now," I spit out finally.

Melody and I lock eyes, then her father ushers her away from me through the door of their apartment. The door slams closed. I walk back to my apartment in a cloud of confusion, and when I open the door and go inside, I find yet another crying female.

"I guess he didn't take it well," I say and drop down on the couch beside my mom.

She sniffles, squeezing a scrunched-up tissue. She shakes her head.

"He'll calm down, right?" I say. "I mean, the dangerous part of this is over."

"I don't know," my mother replies. She stands from the couch and dabs at her eyes with the tissue. "You should unpack and then get some sleep. You have school in the morning."

With that she turns from me, leaves the living room, and disappears down the hall.

****

Melody was not on the bus. I waited at the bus stop, even though I had the suspicion that her father wasn't going to let her ride the bus with me today. Now I'm at school, walking in alone, the lights in the school hallway white and burning, giving me a headache to start my day. People keep looking at my cut-up face and making an expression like, *"Ow, that looks like it hurts, dude."* I'm happy to finally get to my locker so at least I can turn away from everyone. I'm just taking out my Spanish notebook when someone slides into my side view.

"What happened to you?" Ariana asks. She looks different. I can't really explain exactly what the difference is, maybe an all-around softness. Makeup not as bright. Clothes not as tight.

"Fell into a glass coffee table over the weekend," I say, going with Melody's made-up story.

"Holy shit," Ariana says. "Did she too?"

"Who?"

When I follow Ariana's gaze, I see Melody walking toward us, a fresh new bandage across her neck as though she went to the hospital.

"Yeah," I reply. "She fell too."

Melody lifts herself on tiptoes and kisses my cheek. She gives me a "we need to talk" look.

"Sal and I broke up over the weekend," Ariana tells me, ignoring Melody.

I can't help but laugh over that one.

"No," she says, stomping her foot. "For real this time. For good."

"Better off without him," I tell her. "So, congratulations."

"Yeah," she says and nods in agreement. "He just...I couldn't take the constant fighting with him anymore, you know? Plus, what he did to you at the Halloween dance."

I never paid Sal back for that near-death beating. He got

away with it, full and clear. Sometimes that happens, but I would bet my dagger that karma catches up to him in the end, whether I have a hand in it or not. Things will be unpleasant between the two of us for the remainder of my time at Rockpoint High—from now until graduation—and that's fine. We will probably either dodge each other or continue to fight it out. But I do think maybe Ariana, for as much as I hated what she did to me because of her weird thing with Sal, might finally be coming around. Too little, too late, though. I'm with Melody now.

"I need to talk with my boyfriend," Melody says to Ariana. "So if you wouldn't mind leaving...."

"Whatever," she says. She clicks her tongue, then storms away.

Melody shakes her head. "She just won't give up on you, will she?"

"It's like I told you before, all the girls want me."

That makes her smile. And here I thought that smile was gone forever.

"So?" I say.

"He's beyond angry," she says as I close my locker. "That your mother lied to him about her name and who she really was, that your name isn't really Chase, that we lied to him about the weekend, and if he'd known what I was doing, he never would have let me go...it's a mess. I don't think he's ever going to forgive you guys."

"But he'll calm down enough to let me see you, right?"

She shrugs, and we continue walking to her locker. "I'm grounded for a full year for driving without a license," she says. "And if you hadn't burned the incantation, I think he probably would have used it to take it all away from me, too. The power. He doesn't believe in any of that stuff. He's like a Dursley when it comes to magic."

"Great," I say.

She sighs, and we embrace in front of her locker. Her body trembles in my arms.

"Sorry," she says. "I just felt that you were…unhappy."

"You think?" I say, moving away. "I mean, you didn't exactly need the ability to read emotions to know that." I rub my forehead. Still have a headache. "Sorry," I say.

The bell rings.

"See you at break," she says. "Make sure you're there. I don't know how much time we'll get to spend together outside of school. Maybe none."

I wait a few seconds as she pulls books from her locker, and then I head to homeroom. For some reason, I'm just as shaky as I was at the fairgrounds, when the entire world quivered beneath me.

****

When I get home from school, something doesn't feel right. I don't even walk all the way into the apartment, just stand in the front doorway. The place seems too clean. Too vacant.

My mother walks out from the hall, into the living room. She normally takes Mondays off from work, so I'm not surprised to see her home. I *am* surprised to see her dressed in sweats, her hair pulled back in a messy ponytail as though she's been doing some major cleaning.

"Going jogging?" I say.

She points to the couch. I drop my book bag on the floor.

"What's the matter?" I say and sit down on the couch.

She sucks in a breath of air, blows it out, and then sits down beside me.

"I've been packing up," she says. "We're moving back to New England."

Chapter Thirty-Two

It takes me a few seconds to absorb what my mother just told me. Moving? Is this a joke? Something breaks inside me, but I try to keep it all together because I'm not the kind of person to cry. When my father died, I shed some tears, but they were death tears—mandatory for the moment. I never let myself feel the deep-down emotion of true loss, never let the true emotion travel from my heart to my eyes. It was much easier to let the crush of sadness dissolve into anger, then course through my veins. Then at least I could take some kind of manly action.

"We're not moving," I say, fighting away the burn in my eyes. "I've just spent the weekend from hell making sure we didn't have to move. I want to stay in Rockpoint and settle in. I want to stay with Melody."

"I know," she says gently. "And I get that, I really do. But now that all of this is over, we can live a normal life again. I want to be close to our family in New England so we can start a relationship with them again. I've always liked it better home in Connecticut. Plus...there's nothing for me here now."

"Ha," I say as her eyes travel to the window facing Stephen's apartment. "You're honestly going to sit here and tell me you fell in love with that guy in the short time we've been in Rockpoint?"

She turns back to me. "It happened to you, didn't it?"

"We're teenagers," I remind her.

"Adults fall in love too, Shaw."

Thankfully, I've learned to control my gift, or else I'm sure I would have cut her by now, by accident. I'm *that* pissed. And now that I have great strength, too, I'm not sure what's going to happen if I ever lose control.

"I'm not going," I say and stand. "I have a girlfriend here. I like the school, and I like the apartment complex."

"Your points are taken," she says. "But in the end, I'm still the one who manages this family, and I've decided it's best to move on now." She stands and faces me. Her eyes soften. "You've given Melody a gift she'll have for the rest of her life, something rare and powerful. Let's leave on that note, and if you still want to come back here when you're eighteen, that's your choice."

"This is going to kill her," I say. "Do you realize that none of this would have been possible without her? Do you have any idea what kind of sacrifices she made and what kind of things she did to make sure I would be safe and could stay with her here in Rockpoint? Does that mean anything to you?"

"Of course it does," she replies. "But I have to do what's right for us."

"What's right for us is staying here!" I say. "I'm sick to death of you running away from things all the time and dragging me along with you!"

The fight goes on for a while, until I lose steam and head for my room, slamming the door behind me. I drop down on the bed and rake my fingers through my hair. I shouldn't have come home. If I'd known what awaited me here, I would have just taken Melody's hand and ran, ran far away, the two of us, not stopping. Ever.

****

At six o'clock, I sit in the dark of my room, waiting for a text from Melody. Her previous text said she would let me know as soon as her father ran out to pick up dinner, so I could sneak over there to talk. Time will be short—and I haven't told her yet that I'm leaving. If I have to break her heart, I'm not doing it over a text message.

Finally, my phone lights up with her text, and I grab my leather jacket and hop out the door, not acknowledging my mother. I make my way down the path to Melody's unit, and she sticks her head out her front door, looks both ways, and tugs me inside.

"This sucks," she says. "That we can't go talk out on the bench anymore."

"Yeah," I reply. I don't have much time. I take both of her hands in mine.

"You said you had something to tell me?" she says, reading my eyes and probably my emotions. "Something important?"

I didn't think telling her would be easy, but I didn't anticipate not even being able to get the words out. It takes three tries, but I finally produce something that resembles speech.

"She wants to go," I say, kind of incomprehensible. "Back to Connecticut."

Melody steps back, zapped. She closes her eyes.

"Say something," I tell her.

When she opens her eyes, the tears are there, sure as I knew they would be. She shakes her head like I've just told her a lie, and I pull her close. In case I haven't said this before, she's not only my girlfriend, she's my best friend. It's like leaving behind an entire life. And that doesn't even include everything she did for me this past weekend, how she was the brainpower of the operation. My guardian angel, through and through.

"I'll come back," I tell her. "As soon as I graduate, I'll get a job in Rockpoint, maybe at the garden center or something. We'll keep in touch until then, text every night, okay?"

She sniffles into my shoulder.

"Hey," I say. "No crying. It's not really good-bye. It's just...."

We stand in her doorway, hugging, until I get jittery that her dad is going to come home with a bag of fast food, throw it down to the carpet, and kick my ass.

"I have to go," I tell her. "I don't know if I'll be in school tomorrow."

She reaches out to me as I open the door. I grab her hand.

"Shaw?" she says and squeezes my hand.

"Don't," I tell her. "Let's not make this good-bye."

"Just listen," she says. "If something should happen and we drift apart, will you promise me something?"

"That's not going to happen," I say.

"Shh," she says. "Just promise me that when a girl like Ariana takes your heart away from me, that you'll know, deep down, that she'll never love you more than I do. No one will ever love you more than I do. You know that, right?"

I swallow, trying to hold back, but it doesn't work.

My last vision of Melody is blurred in tears.

Chapter Thirty-Three

As I said in the beginning, my mother and I are professional packers. We know how to do it fast, how to get away from a place in a hurry. Usually, we're running from the bad guys, but the bad guys are gone. One presumably dead, the other changed back to human form. Now, my mother and I are running from love and loss. And that, I've just found out, is a lot more painful than running from hate.

By the time we tie up everything, it's late evening. We're on the road at dark, heading for the border of New York into Connecticut. We'll stay with my mother's parents for a while, until we can get settled somewhere in the area. We also have the matter of Fraser's funeral. Last I heard, the police had his death open for investigation. That was the best my mother could do, being so far away. But Alexander did phone in an anonymous tip linking Fraser to Lomidus. Hopefully, that will help the investigation.

The closer we get to Connecticut, the more I want to just jump out of the car and run down the highway, back to Melody. A million memories play in my head—the Halloween dance, the nights in the hotels, Benji Bear, even the night at The Black Crow when Melody pulled me to safety behind the dumpster. I stare out the window and let the memories of Rockpoint knock me around for a while, until my mother pulls off the highway and into a Wendy's parking lot.

"My favorite," I say.

"I know that."

She's been extra nice since she announced she was ruining my life.

"Cheeseburger?" she says.

"Bacon cheeseburger," I say. "And have I mentioned that I hate you?"

"Got it," she says. "Fries, too?"

I sigh and slouch in the seat as we go over the full order. She grabs her purse and starts to open the car door when her cell rings. She pulls it from her purse and just stares down at it.

"What?" I say.

"It's Stephen."

I sit up in the seat. "Is something wrong with Melody?"

"How would I know?" she says. "I haven't answered it yet."

She doesn't look like she's going to answer it. I have to physically push her hand to snap her out of her trance.

Finally, she holds the phone to her ear. "Hello?" she whispers. "Stephen?" She fumbles with her purse and takes some cash from her wallet, then tosses the bills at me. "Go," she says, holding her hand over the phone.

I contemplate staying, but I guess I have to respect her privacy. Slowly, I walk into Wendy's, order at the counter, and pay the short-haired girl who can't stop staring at my sliced cheek. What the hell could be going on with Stephen? Why call my mother when he basically told us he never wanted to see us again?

When I get back to the car, I have to stand outside for a few minutes while she finishes up. She's crying, I can tell. I realize I'm supposed to respect Stephen because he's older, but it really pisses me off when people make my mother cry. Stephen was never my favorite person in the world anyhow. Something tells me that if we'd stayed in Rockpoint, he and I would have had some major issues.

Resting against the hood of the Jetta, I stick my hand into

the Wendy's bag and pull out a few fries. My cell goes off in my pocket—a text from Melody. It just says that she's going to sleep now, so I guess she has no idea that her father is talking to my mother. That just makes things more confusing.

I text back: "*Almost in CT.*" Then another: "*Miss u.*"

"*Miss u more,*" she texts. "*But good news. Mrs. Wyles says new student orientation on Wed. and who knows what kind of magical powers he'll have?*"

"*LOL.*"

"*Love you.*"

I reply: "*love u 2 say gn to BB.*"

After I stick my phone back into my pocket, hating my mother more than I ever have in my entire life, she gestures me inside the car. I drop in, open my bag of Wendy's, and unwrap my burger.

"So?" I say, stuffing the burger into my mouth. "What did he want?"

She has pulled herself together. Somewhat. She's not crying, but her cheeks are streaked in tears. "He didn't know I was going to just pick up and leave like that," she replies.

"It's what you do," I say back. "When the going gets tough, Jenna takes off."

She ignores the smart-ass remark, but it feels good, so I smile to myself as I eat my burger. She ruined my life. I think I'm entitled to smart-ass comments forevermore.

"And he was upset about it," my mother continues. "Really upset."

I stop eating. "So what does that mean?"

"Nothing," she says. She stares up at the glowing Wendy's sign. "It's not like I can change what's done. I broke my lease on the apartment and—"

"Mom," I say and throw my half-eaten burger into the bag. "Are you telling me he wants you to come back?"

****

Ten minutes later, my mother backs out of the parking space at Wendy's. She gets us onto the highway while I dig

295

cold fries out of the Wendy's bag.

"I'm sorry," she says. "That I put you through this." She reaches over and smoothes my hair. "You were right. I always run away from things. I'm too old to keep doing that."

"You're not that old," I tell her. "What are you, like fifty?"

She laughs and gives me a reprimanding little smack against the head.

"Better watch that," I say. "Now I have super strength, remember? I picked Melody up like nothing the night we got back to Rockpoint, and when we packed, I had to get one of my comics from under my bed, and I just lifted the entire bed up in the air like it was a piece of cotton."

"From what I hear, Alexander is having fun with his new ability, too," she says, slipping into the fast lane.

"Melody's power is weird," I say. "She says that not only can she feel emotions, but she can also *hear* them, like humming. What does that mean?"

"I'm not entirely sure," my mother responds. "But if I had to guess, I would say that maybe these abilities merge with another special ability, something a person already has."

That makes sense to me. Melody is musical, it's in her blood.

"Any word on Lomidus?" my mother asks.

"None," I reply. "I've been checking the news in Fairchester, but there's nothing about him or the accident. I guess his death would be under obituaries but maybe not for a few days?"

"I'm not sure," my mother replies. Her eyebrows pull together. "But let me know if you read anything."

****

Ten thirty-six p.m.

Back in Rockpoint.

It feels like coming home. Unit seven, white Christmas lights. Turned-off fountain in the center of the apartment complex. The bench where Melody and I used to sit and talk and play games on her phone. Our old apartment that my mother is going to have to beg and plead to get back in our possession.

Stephen is waiting outside his apartment door, and my mother doesn't even look back at me, she just rushes over and falls into his arms. I have to force myself to take in the scene, my mother's happiness with a man who is not my father. Yeah, maybe I need to stop running away from things, too.

Stephen holds my mother up like she's a rag doll and throws his thumb back at the apartment door when I get closer to them.

"Melody is sleeping," he whispers. "You can just go right in."

"She doesn't know?" I ask.

He shakes his head as my mother nuzzles his shoulder. "She hasn't really spoken to me since you left," he says. "She's been devastated." He kisses my mother's forehead. "I have too."

Leaving them in their romantic scene, I head inside Melody's apartment. It's similar to my apartment except the kitchen is not behind the living room, it's more to the left. I head down the hall until I find a closed door. When I quietly turn the handle and step inside, I can just make out Melody's sleeping frame. Her hair is down, spread all around her like a wavy blanket. She's holding Benji Bear to her chest.

I tiptoe to the side of her bed, kneel, and rest my hand against her cheek. Her skin is warm, a little wet and sticky like maybe she cried herself to sleep.

Slowly, she opens her eyes and blinks twice as she focuses on my face.

She sits up, taking Benji Bear with her. "You're not real," she says.

"I'm real," I say back, smiling.

"Not a dream?" she whispers.

I shake my head and crawl into her bed beside her. I'm not really sure how to prove that I'm not a dream, but I once heard that if you pinch someone and they feel it, that means they're awake. Pinching her does not seem like the best idea, so I kiss her instead.

And I'm pretty sure she can feel it.

END

**Join our Newsletter & Receive Release Day
Announcements, News, and Special Sales!**

Before You Go...

Share your voice and help guide other readers to these wonderful books. Even if it's only a line or two your reviews help readers discover the author's books so they can continue creating stories that you'll love. Login to your favorite retailer and leave a review. Thank you.

About the Author

Carla Trueheart is a New England-based writer who holds certificates in poetry, romance writing, copyediting, forensic science writing, historical fiction writing, and writing for young adults. She has studied writing at Gotham Writers' Workshop and The Writers Studio, and is currently working toward completion of her BA in Creative Writing and English through Southern New Hampshire University. She has worked as submissions editor for various online publications, and her poetry and short stories have been featured in such online magazines as *The Litchfield Literary Review*. Recently she was awarded a Certificate of Distinction in Academic Writing, and she is a proud member of The National Society of Leadership and Success.

www.ingramcontent.com/pod-product-compliance
Lightning Source LLC
Chambersburg PA
CBHW020255200626
46816CB00001BA/311

* 9 7 8 1 6 2 9 8 9 3 4 7 1 *